The Sons of Masguard

Book One

The Mosque Hill

FORTUNE

Written and Illustrated by

VIVIENNE MATHEWS

COVER ART BY JEROME JACINTO

A MOLLIFIED MEDIA PUBLICATION

DEDICATION

To my husband. To my son.

To friends I no longer know. Whether or not you are in my life, you are still in my heart and my thoughts.

Booya and long live the GPT.

CONTENTS

ONE STORY ENDS

"Fate is a callous thing. An infinite, cyclic machine that moves and ever moves until all is swallowed or forgotten. We try to measure it, try to understand it, only to fail in fantastic fashion. Then we explain away our incompetence by pretending it is all part of some great mystery.

What a lark.

Give it long enough, and it will show you the truth. That our relationship with life in all its wonder is a one-sided love affair, where we press our faces to a clock and imagine it as a form of intimacy. That it is the minute hand, the hour and the second, stretching in every direction beneath our breath, crumbling mountains and turning tides. And that we are spectators, wondering at our own reflections and nothing beyond. What fools we must seem, standing with our noses to the glass while the hands revolve around us, over and over. Stubborn. Oblivious. Champions of willful ignorance, forever missing the point.

Are we truly so helpless to alter the course of time? I'd never thought to consider it. But as I sit here writing what is likely to be my final correspondence, I'm forced to wonder whether things might have been different if only I'd traded the mystery for clarity of vision while I still had the chance. If only I'd bothered myself to step away from the glass for even one, blighted moment.

We found it, my friend. We found it and it is NOT what it seems. It's bigger, and the truth of it terrifies me in ways I am willing to admit to none but you. The things I have learned... the things I have seen... They would baffle and amaze the greatest of our scholars. They would put my every discovery to shame.

They would paint fools of us all.

Truth be told, none of that matters anymore. I didn't see this for what it was until it was too late. There is only one way out for me now. Since I've neither a fox's intuition, nor an Ancient's soul, I can only guess at the ramifications of what I am about to do. And I know that wishing alters nothing.

Perhaps my course has already been set.

Perhaps the clock itself is untouchable, regardless of where I stand.

But if I cannot change it for myself, I must at least try to change it for you, my friend. For Secora, may her Banners ever wave. And, most of all, for my son.

My little Marshall.

Will he ever forgive me for this?

It is my dearest hope that I will one day be able to ask him in person.

But should Fate will differently, please tell him..."

Tell him...

Masguard's quill froze above the parchment. Tell him what? Garrulous and clever though he may have been, here at the end, the otter captain found he had nothing to say. Nothing that would matter. The boy on the other side of the world didn't want another speech regarding duty or the fate of the Secoran kingdom. He wanted his father.

And that was the one thing Masguard couldn't give him.

What a failure was he?

He had discovered more lands than any explorer before him, met every mythical creature in the book and many besides. He had brought kingdoms to their knees and lords to his service. He had pulled the most dreadful artifacts the world had ever seen from the very brink of Oblivion itself. And for what? To disappear into the annals of history as someone who might have mattered? What was the point of his success if it prevented him from offering even that small measure of solace to the only family he had left?

Dropping his quill, he pressed his palms to his eyes.

Masguard the Relic Hunter. Masguard the Bold. For all his titles and accolades, he was now a long-forgotten voice. A nondescript explorer with no account for wandering and no excuse for fame. Maybe it was a strange form of justice that had him turning at last into what he had always been, deep down. Masguard the ghost.

"The crew's ready whenever ye are, Cap'n."

Masguard looked up to see a grungy marmot standing in the door of his cabin. The quartermaster's habit of intruding unannounced had become a welcome discourtesy over the past few months. So few of his crewmembers had any remaining interest in conversation. There was too much they didn't wish to say aloud. Too much they didn't want to hear.

"And Ustim?"

"Silent as ever," the marmot shrugged.

"Thank you, Fender," Masguard lifted his quill and resumed toiling over the words on the parchment. "I'll be along shortly."

If Fender should have taken that as a cue to exit, he ignored it, coming instead to stand over his captain's desk and peer down at the paper with unabashed interest.

"Ain't exactly how this li'l adventure o' ours was 'sposed te turn out, eh?" He said, his voice gruff and quiet.

Masguard sighed, leaning back in his chair. His shoulders were slumped in something very like defeat. "I know. Believe me, I know. But if we turn back now…"

"Dumb things will happen, Cap'n. We got that," Fender finished for him. "Don't make it any easier."

"No, I don't suppose it does."

The two were silent for the longest time, staring in separate parts at a ship that was practically rotting beneath their feet. With only a skeleton crew remaining, the sound of the open sea overtook the vessel with little resistance. It creaked and moaned as the waves bullied it about, whimpering with all the strength of a fragile old woman. In a way, Masguard supposed, that's exactly what it was.

Don't give up on me just yet, old girl, he thought. *We've a few miles and one more task yet to complete.*

"There's still the matter o' the demon on deck." Fender bit his pipe, expressionless.

Masguard rolled his eyes. "Must you call him that?"

"Jus' saying, if I'm out te meet me doom, I'd rather not do it wi' him o'er me shoulder, yeah? Still gives me the willies, an' I ain't the only one what feels that way."

"Fine, fine. I'll talk to him. We have an outstanding matter to discuss anyway. Just let me finish up here and I'll meet you on deck with the… the…" Masguard furrowed his brow and rummaged through his desk. "Where is it?"

Fender was slow to respond and looked uncomfortable when he said, "Same place it's been since I walked in here, Cap'n. In your hand."

At that, Masguard felt a chill creep up his arm. He suppressed the urge to swallow and looked accusingly to the relic in his palm.

Of course.

The blasted thing would be the death of him yet.

Wincing inwardly, he whispered, "For what it's worth, Fender… I am sorry. For all of it."

Again, Fender shrugged, this time a little slower, a little more deliberately. "We're with ye, Cap'n. Always have been. Always will be."

Masguard could only nod in response as his Quartermaster left.

After putting the final touches on his letter, the otter captain tucked the relic into the pocket of his burgundy coat and turned his focus to a very different item; one seated prominently on his desk.

"Are you ready to finish what you started?" He smiled wryly as he hefted the stone carving in both hands and turned to leave his cabin. "Neither am I."

On deck, he made his way to the fore of the ship, avoiding eye contact with his crew wherever possible. When he arrived at the prow, he spent several long moments looking over the mist before addressing himself to the feathered mass atop the bowsprit.

"Lovely weather today," he said to the great bird without turning to face him. "I imagine one could almost see their own hand held before their face, if they concentrated quite enough."

The massive creature shifted beside him, causing the timbers beneath his talons to shiver in complaint. "I told you before, Wanderer. These mists are not of my doing. I cannot lift them, not even for you."

Stoic as any carving, immovable as any mountain, Ustim reminded Masguard of the monumental statues of Secora Tor. Cold stone and intimidating, representing the strength of a protected and enduring society, they lined the streets of the capitol city as a warning to all that the land beyond had survived far greater threats, and had prospered besides.

He made a nice feature on the ship.

It would be a shame to lose him.

"The fog is the least of my concerns, I'm afraid."

The great bird shook his grey-black feathers and turned on the bowsprit, sending a tremor across the whole of the ship. Tipping his head to levy an avian eye at the artifact in Masguard's hand, he nodded slightly in understanding.

"I see." He said simply in his accented tone.

Setting the stone artifact on the wide rail before him, Masguard seemed not to concern himself with the possibility that the thing might fall into the sea below. Holding Ustim's gaze, the lost explorer pulled his most cursed find from his pocket and held it in his palm, outstretched in offering toward Fender's demon.

"You've earned a final chance to do with this as you will. Consider it payment – or, repayment, as the case may be."

The great bird looked down at the thing with such longing that Masguard thought his heart might break.

At length, Ustim met his eyes. "No, Wanderer. I have lived free of its grasp for far too long. No longer can I delude myself into believing that it still belongs to me, or to anyone. I must let go, whether I want to or not. Someday, you will do the same."

Masguard was silent for a long moment, stunned. "But…"

"It is in your hands now. For that, I thank you. For that… I am sorry."

The captain scoffed before he could think better of it. In an effort to conceal his blunder, Masguard pulled the letter from his coat and a chain from around his neck. "That aside, there is one thing more I would ask of you before you leave my service. If you would do me the honor." He added the last part belatedly.

The creature echoed something that may have been a laugh, though it would have been difficult to say for sure.

"These items…." Masguard began hesitantly. "It is imperative that they reach Constance Prideaux in the capitol city."

"An errand?" The massive bird looked offended. "You cannot do this yourself?"

Masguard chose his tone, and his words, carefully. "No. I cannot do this. Because I'm not going back. Not yet." *And possibly not ever*, he would not say aloud. "Please." He continued at length, when Ustim made no move to comply. "It is more important to me than you can imagine. More important than *anything* I've asked you to do."

Maybe the creature saw the truth in his words. Maybe he was simply taking pity on a desperate father. Either way, Masguard was grateful when he relented and took the items in a massive claw.

"I do this," Ustim said, "And we are finished. My debt is cleared."

Masguard smiled humorlessly. His look was difficult to read when he agreed, "Ustim, you do this... and I promise... you'll never see me again."

Slowly, deliberately, the unknowable bird straightened his spine and stretched his feathers. His colossal tone softened as he glanced back over one shoulder, saying, "That... would be regrettable." With a forceful motion of his wings, Ustim shot from the bowsprit, leaving only a shadow and a farewell in his wake. "Hunt well, Wanderer."

"Yeah..." Masguard said to the space before him, where Ustim had been, knowing all too well that his words went unheard. "You too."

When he was sure of the silence that followed, Masguard lifted the artifact from the rail and threw it into the sea with all his might. There, it sunk like the stone that it was, drawing the mist into the sea behind it like the tail of an unnatural comet. Through sediment and current and years, the artifact would drift – at times dragging across the ocean floor as if by invisible hands. Eventually, it would come to rest in a little-known cove off the Bannered Shore, a world and a lifetime away from the explorer and his forgotten ship, never having heard Masguard's final words.

"Gate and Key and cursed destiny. May Fate carry you to the hands for which you were meant. I pray that you are found before it's too late."

Fender watched the scene unfold with regret and no small amount of distaste, echoing quietly, as if to himself, "Better to pray that it's never found at all."

☐

7

1
ALONG THE BANNERED SHORE
(TWENTY-FIVE YEARS LATER)

It was the salt.

The fishing from this stretch of beach was poor, at best. The low tide and lack of competition were pleasant enough, but those too could be found elsewhere. No, there was a reason the two hunters returned to this particular cove night after night to set their traps, and that reason was far from practical. Tattooed and fierce. Hardened, these two. Never daring to openly acknowledge the childish reminder of a home they'd been forced to leave too soon, when they were young and careless and didn't know any better. Saying it aloud would have been as silly as refusing to discard a blanket after waking. But here, in this unique joining of grassland and ocean deposits, the aroma played at a memory that left them feeling all of those things; an aroma unlike that of any place they had ever been – save one. Though they went about their work in silence, they both knew it was the intensity of the smell that brought them here. The smell of balsam... and salt.

By evening, the shore was lined with handcrafted crates of wood and cord, most of them empty, but they were used to that. When the smaller hunter hauled at the final towline and found resistance, her shoulders slumped in dismay. Grand as it may have been to assume the trap was overburdened with something marketable, she shuddered at the more likely scenario that one of the dolphin Regulators had gone snooping and gotten snagged for his efforts.

Imagine explaining that one to Her Majesty. *'Pardon me, milady, but I'm afraid I've drowned one of your officers with twine. Quite by accident, of course. So sorry.'*

For shame.

Maybe Fate had been kind and simply placed the trap on the edge of a riptide. That would explain the pull, and it would do so without the gruesome side effects.

She might have known better.

Fate was never kind.

"Something is wrong?" The other noted and came to her side.

"I can't be sure." She evaded, though she felt the lie as acutely as she would a pinprick. Something was wrong. She could sense it in her very bones.

Recognizing that he shouldn't press the issue, the larger joined her in heaving against the line with the full of his weight. At length, the crate emerged from the surf, though seemingly more by the will of the sea than by their efforts.

The trap was occupied, but not by any dolphin. It was a stone, one that was far too large to have entered the trap by any conventional means – one that glowed with an alluring light, as though it had devoured the dusk and now spat its remnants upon the shore. Waters that should have washed over the caged artifact instead held back, diverting their flow around the crate in an unnatural and tentative surge.

The hunters exchanged stony glances.

This thing – whatever it was – did not belong on their

9

beach.

As if to confirm their suspicions, the stone began to pulse. A quiet, rhythmic sound that the sea rose up to match. Unafraid, the delicate hunter nodded to her weathered companion and the two approached, watching the light from the object grow ever more intense until its heat was almost unbearable, but familiar in the strangest of ways.

Like salt.

Discarding any trace of sentiment, the large one drew a utility axe from the sheath on his leg and hacked through slat and twine until the stone fell to the shore with a wet thud.

It rolled once and stopped at their feet.

The two gazed upon the carvings of ocean, wind, fire, and air that made up a single face and an all-too clear expression of fury. Then the light of Fate exploded around them, completely consuming their corner of the shoreline, there in the fruitless cove.

When finally it receded, darkness had fallen.

And the mist had come.

≈

Marshall had spent his childhood in central Vernos, staring at this very spot, waiting. It seemed strange now to be approaching it from the other side, as a visitor rather than a lonely inhabitant of the small cottage at the end of the walkway. He almost didn't recognize the building through the fog. It had the same thatched roof and tattered shutters, but it seemed so removed from the welcoming home he remembered that he had to clear the condensation from the plaque on the gate before he could be certain. The letters did not lie – this was indeed the home of Abner Frum, the town's Elder, a librarian and historian whose expertise was so highly coveted by the Scholars Guild that they'd held campaign after campaign in an attempt to recruit him. Fun though it was to watch them stoop and squirm, they'd no hope of snagging the curmudgeonly old brute. He was too old for agendas, as he often said, and the Guilds had them each in spades.

It wasn't the only lesson Marshall had learned within these crumbling walls.

It wasn't the only one he'd had to test for himself, either.

With a smile of remembrance, the otter captain pressed through the gate, tucked his hat neatly beneath his arm, and rapped politely at the door. One minute became two, and two became serious reason to consider knocking yet again when a voice burst through the door with all the warmth of a northern wind.

"Who is it?!?"

Marshall winced, "Abner, it's me."

"What?!?"

"It's Marshall."

"Who?!?"

Marshall shot a pleading look to the sky. He supposed it was nice to know that some things never changed. "It's Captain Marshall, old man! Will you open the bloody door? You're the one who sent for me, remember?"

"Marshall?" His tone changed, seeming more surprised than irritated. There was a rustling and a clinking as of locks unlatched and papers brushed aside, then the door ripped open to reveal a stout gray creature in dusty clothing and mussed fur. The old badger squinted, adjusting the bifocals on his heavy face before recognition overcame his elderly sense of confusion and suspicion. Then his mouth parted in a semi-welcoming grin, "Marshall, my boy!"

"Hello, Abner." The otter couldn't help but smile, even through his frustration. "It's been far too long."

"Oh, pish-pot. What's a few years of complete and utter silence at my age, eh? Not as though I might've keeled over in your absence. I mean, just look at me. Spry

11

as a schoolboy, aren't I?" Cane in hand, he turned very slowly from the door, leaving it open for Marshall's entry as he ambled through the library and ranted over his shoulder. "Well? Don't just stand on my stoop like a doorstop. You're letting the mist in. It'll dampen the books. A letter would have been nice, though. Haven't they parchment and quill on those ships of yours?"

"Yes, Abner," said Marshall patiently. "As the flagship of the entire Secoran kingdom, the *Albatross* is indeed fully stocked. But, as you might have heard, the Armada has been on high alert for quite some time now. My hands have been rather full."

The Elder arched a condescending brow, proving that the subtle reminder of Marshall's success in the Queen's Navy had not gone unnoticed. It should have come as something of a compliment. Abner had been Marshall's primary tutor, after all.

"Oh, is that pesky Marauder at it again?" The old badger feigned sympathy. "That no-good, guildless wretch. I heard about the rash of recent break-ins here in the outer territories. A house just down the street, in fact, lost a family heirloom to the thefts a few nights ago. Some antique weapon or another. I've done my old badger best to keep the library buttoned down, but I'm afraid I'd have no defense against a thief with any real intent. Can you imagine me standing up to that brute?" His crabby tone concealed a note of genuine concern. "Perhaps if the Queen's Armada wasn't so busy protecting its resources, it could be bothered to safeguard its citizens as well?"

Marshall read truly into the old caretaker's sense of unease. Abner would feel much better if only his former pupil could lend his strength and sword to secure the borders of this quaint and forgotten village, for sentiment's sake, if nothing else.

"Is that your way of saying you've missed me, old friend?"

"Pshaw." Abner waved a hand, clearly annoyed, though

he said no more.

"I'll do all I can, while I'm here," the stoic captain conceded in an honest tone. "I won't abide even the smallest of infractions against the people of this kingdom, and I will not ignore their defense. You know that. But I'm afraid the alert has little to do with petty theft or home invasion."

"What then?" Abner demanded accusingly.

Marshall hesitated, as reluctant to concede ignorance as he was to admit the truth. "I don't know," he said at last. "Something has Her Majesty on edge."

"Political?"

"Maybe. But I think it's more than that." Marshall absently took stock of the library that was Abner's home. "Either way, I don't think McKinley can be blamed. Not this time."

Abner lifted his bushy brows. "No? I never thought I'd see the day…"

Marshall squared his shoulders but would not take the bait. McKinley the Marauder had been the bane of his existence for years, ever since making his debut splash off the coast of Port Sundry with the most explosive and profitable haul in pirate history. Four ships at once, as the story had it – and from a barely-manned frigate. There were fireworks and everything. He'd certainly gone down in the world since then. Still, the blackguard had built a successful career on staying two steps ahead of him at every turn.

And Abner gained no end of pleasure from reminding Marshall of that annoying little fact.

At every turn.

"A thief's a thief, once and always," the Elder said. "And profit is profit, regardless of the source."

"True enough, but these inland break-ins have been item specific with the culprit leaving all else untouched. Your thief has intent, whereas our pesky Marauder has proven time and again that he will consume everything in his path with a possible payload. If *he* were to target a neighborhood – *any* neighborhood – he'd leave nothing but the foundations in his wake."

"Not even the pitter-patter of evil footsteps?" Abner smiled sweetly.

"Scoff as you will, but it's not an outlandish exaggeration. His latest victims have been ships of the poorest merchants, well known to have nothing more than the wood that built them when the *Negvar* attacked."

"Then what did he hope to steal?"

"Apparently…" Marshall clasped his hands behind his back, "The wood that built them."

Abner made no move to hide his amusement.

"It was an act of desperation," Marshall continued, almost as admonishment. "The ships were hardly out of port at the time, well within reach of the dolphin Regulators."

Unabashed, the Elder needled, "And they couldn't catch him either?"

"It's the mist." Again, Marshall ignored the dig, glancing through the window to the harsh sky. "Seems to unnerve them. They've been moving closer and closer to the shore over the last year. The Marauder struck too quickly for them to react and, when he left, they would not pursue beyond the bay. He knew they were afraid and he used it to his advantage."

"Oh, of course," the Elder bit sarcastically beneath his breath. "The mist. Yes, must be."

"Are you saying you doubt their intentions?"

"Not at all. I'm simply agreeing with your oh-so-astute observation, Captain." Abner's seemingly playful note bled away as he spoke, his voice becoming a little harder with every uttered word, a little more cruel. "That's certainly the most logical explanation as to how McKinley has managed to elude the whole of the Queen's Armada, headed by one of the most learned creatures in the kingdom – Secora's beloved *prodigy*, no less. That's the only reason why, even at the lowest point in his game, that sub-intellectual pirate has successfully outwitted, outmaneuvered, and outplayed one of the most widely-renowned military figures in history, isn't that right? Such an important fixture you make on the big open sea. Why, if not for you, the Marauder wouldn't have a hope of leading anyone about by the maw, day after day. It's a good job you left here when you did, without a word. A good job indeed."

Marshall would take no more. In forceful strides, he crossed the room, coming to stand over the aging badger with a calm but demanding steel in his eyes, "Do you have something to say to me, old man?"

"Me? No." He glared back, matching the captain's well-earned aura of authority with sheer stubbornness. Untouchable as any antique, the Elder was too old to be swayed by anything, or anyone, and – unlike Marshall – he had no compelling reason to supplant his emotions for the sake of peace or propriety. "What could I possibly have to say to the son of Masguard? You clearly have everything under control. You certainly put that family fortune to fantastic use, out there in the world, paying dues, joining Guild after Guild. One would be sufficient for most folk, but not you. Scholars, Warriors, Artisans, Apothecaries, even the Nobles Circle. No expense spared, no accounting for time or taste, just hopping between every major focus of study with your fingers crossed. Hoping that none of them would find you out, but not going out of your way to make it difficult for them. You didn't even have the wherewithal to keep your head down. You had to excel at every bloody thing, didn't you?"

"I wanted an education, Abner."

"Which you could have gotten without drawing attention to yourself – I was educating you here!" The Elder yelled.

"Exactly!" Marshall yelled back. "Right here! No," he amended, storming to the window, where he placed his palms over the tiny scuffs at the bottom of the frame and lowered his voice to conclude, "Right *here*." Closing his eyes, the captain bowed his head ever so slightly and forced his usually-steady breath to calm itself. The gouges in the wood pricked unkindly at the memory of a child ignoring his studies, slipping away to pull himself up at the window, hoping to see his father – explorer, nobleman, friend to Knights and Queens alike – on return from his latest adventure. "You were an incredible teacher, Abner. The best. But the only lesson I could ever learn here, the only one that would stay with me over years of trying to forget it, was how to wait. And if I hadn't left, I'd still be right here. Waiting."

In the silence that followed, Marshall looked to the scroll on the wall; the one bearing testament to Masguard's long and notable career in relic-hunting. The *Dreyan Ashes* in 15802. The *Mark of Oblivion* in 15805. There was, of course, special calligraphy surrounding the note on the *Gryphon's Talon* from 15810. In small and sloppy handwriting, somewhere in the middle, a younger Marshall had scribbled a question mark near *Masguard's Unknown Relic*, the one his father swore to be purely fictional, despite the strange glint in his eye whenever the topic arose. All of it leading up to the final entry.

The one which held a date… and nothing more.

According to the story, Masguard had gone in search of an Ancient fortune, one rumored to be buried at the heart of the Mosque Hill. Whether or not he'd reached his goal was anybody's guess, since he hadn't returned to tell the tale.

Looking now over that blasted list, Marshall realized it had always been destined to turn out as it did. The famed explorer had lost so very much in his search for the unknowable. It seemed only fitting that he would lose himself in return.

Abner drew a curmudgeonly breath. When he replied, his tone had lost much of its slighted edge. "Were you hoping to find him, then? Is that why you joined those ridiculous communities? And the Navy?"

Leaning away from the window, Marshall squared his shoulders, the hint of a smile in his voice. "I was hoping to find my place. Somewhere where I could be more than just... Masguard's forgotten son. Another relic to add to the list. The Guilds were a mistake, each and every one, I'll admit." He turned to face Abner with no hint of regret or shame. "But the Navy is where I belong. I could feel it in my bones from the moment I set foot on a ship. I am sorry that it meant leaving you behind, but I had to make an individual of myself. And I have."

"Is that what you think I'm angry about?" Abner moved between the haphazard piles of books and shelves to smack Marshall in the chest with his cane. "I'm not angry because you grew up, you toad. Fate's sake, everyone does that – maybe not quite with your flair, but they manage. I'm angry because you put yourself at risk. He may have been a thrill-seeking nutter, but Masguard loved you. He wanted you here, where he knew you'd be safe. A secret, yes. But *safe*. Your father had some very powerful friends, as you know, but he also had powerful enemies. As a peacekeeper and a prominent friend to the throne, you're making enemies enough of your own. If you keep on like this, if you continue in your success, their numbers will only grow. And should your enemies ever cross paths with his..." The old badger raised his eyebrows and quirked his cane, turning away with a determined step. "Well, let's just hope that day never comes. I'm too old to live out this life with a broken heart, Marshall. Don't ever put me in that position."

The otter captain drew himself into a stoic shape, as if to hide the lump in his throat. Abner was the only family he'd known in far too long. It seemed only natural that the two would each be the source of the other's strife, however unwittingly. But to think that he had ever left the Elder waiting at this same window...

It was the one way in which he longed to be nothing

like his father.

"Well, come on." Abner interrupted his thoughts and gestured for him to follow. "I didn't call you here for a dress-down, did I?"

"Certainly you did, old friend. And quite right, too. But one would hope it wasn't the only reason." Marshall retorted in an even tone that made the Elder chuckle.

"Keep it up and I'll have you indexing the farming reports."

Marshall winced. "I'd prefer to avoid that."

"Wouldn't you, though? It always was the surest way to knock the cheek out of you. Out of your father, too, Fate bless his mischievous hide." Abner's grin was somewhere between fondness and cruelty. "This way."

Through dust and maps and a sea of scrolls, the two waded to the door at the end of a hall.

"It might seem hypocritical, after all I just said." Abner clinked through the keys on his belt. "But I called on you because I needed someone from the Scholars Guild, someone who's studied in the Archives."

Marshall courteously neglected to show any indignation. "You might have gone to them directly," he offered instead.

Abner scoffed, "They would have loved that, I've no doubt, but this isn't about maintaining a grudge. I couldn't tell anyone else because, well..." He paused before opening the door. "Maybe you should just see for yourself."

Ushering Marshall inside, Abner lit a lamp, but he needn't have bothered. The artifact on the table was emitting a glow on its own, more than enough to light the small room. Marshall looked to him in confusion when he locked the door behind them.

"Are you so worried about the thief, even with me here?"

"No, nothing like that." The Elder seemed hesitant to explain, for fear of looking foolish. "It... it was pulling the mist in through the front door."

Marshall shot him a searching look.

"Every crack in the mortar, every leaking window. Any avenue it could take to reach this thing." The badger jabbed his thumb at the carved stone. "It's as if the mist has a life of its own when it's around."

Curious.

Marshall recognized it immediately, of course. He had seen similar things in artist's renderings, read its descriptions in the Ancient texts. The Guilds each had their own take on the artifact. The one thing they agreed upon was that the stone carving existed in name and legend only. Yet here it was. A representation of the old gods put together as one to form a single face, as though meant to unify the elements of everything. It seemed a peaceful sentiment. But the countenance created was far from pleasant.

It was the face of anger.

Fate alive, Abner had found the Key.

"How did you come by this?" The stoic captain kept his amazement concealed.

"A pair of tribesmen pulled it from the sea just down the coast a year ago, roughly the same time that the mists started. Despite its obvious value, they gave it to a broker at no cost and he brought it here."

"Maybe they were frightened by all of this and simply wanted to be rid of it," he gestured to the glow and the eerie shadows it cast on the wall. "Who was the broker?"

Abner sniffed, replying a little too quickly, "Don't remember."

"Abner…"

"What?" he demanded with an indignant glare. "I'm old, I forget names. Do you want to see a bloomin' receipt?"

Marshall drew his mouth into an irritated line and stooped to inspect the Key, deciding to let the matter lie. Too likely, the broker's identity was as personal as it was irrelevant. Tipping the item on its side, the captain turned the stone toward the pointless lamp and traced his finger along the markings. They were insignias; the family crests of more than a dozen royal houses; the kings and queens of Secoran history.

All except the last one.

That one was his.

Marshall dropped the artifact in surprise.

"As you can see," Abner said. "I couldn't tell anyone else about this. I may not know what this is, or what any of it means, but I know enough to recognize your father's seal."

Gritting his teeth and rubbing at his jaw, the otter captain stepped away from the table, saying nothing, revealing less. Abner made no move to rush him. After a long and quiet moment of staring at the artifact from across the room, Marshall gestured to the statue's base.

"It's larger than it should be. There's a seam across the center of the stone connecting the original artifact to a newer substance." He approached once more and turned the item upright, a little more roughly than before.

"Those younger eyes must be very useful. I don't see any seam," Abner said.

Marshall waved a dismissive hand. "It's not a result of superior vision. Simply of knowing where to look."

Pulling the artifact from the table, he flipped it over in his hands. On the bottom was another symbol, a circle composed of two crescents, sun and moon. He had seen that before, too, hadn't he? But where?

Odd...

With his near-flawless memory, he could usually cite text and page number.

"Stand back," Marshall said to Abner, giving him little warning before laying the artifact cross-wise on the table and bringing down the hilt of his sword with blinding speed. The base shattered in a cloud of dust.

Abner gasped and sputtered in disbelief. He was still in

shock when Marshall brushed through the fragments and pulled a folded piece of parchment from the debris.

"It's quite alright, old friend. The artifact itself is still intact. I do apologize for damaging your table, though." He winced at the gouges beneath the ceramic shards as he opened the paper to read in silence.

Abner watched a slow sadness creep over his face. When pressed, his former student passed the note to him, but did not meet his eyes.

Pushing his glasses up on his nose, the elderly badger squinted and read aloud, "*Write your name upon the sand and it is washed away. The grains are towed into the sea, and here it Ever Stays.*" Abner's squint deepened. "This is Masguard's handwriting. It's a message, that much is clear, but what in blazes is it supposed to mean?"

Captain Marshall could only smile weakly in response. "Nothing we didn't already know. That my father is gone, and that his name died with him somewhere on the sea."

Abner's face fell in sympathy. "You should keep it anyway. Maybe it has other meanings as well. And, Fate's sake, take the stone too. Blasted thing scares the daylights out of me. Just promise to keep it locked up."

Abner wrapped the artifact in a blanket and handed parchment and stone alike to Marshall, who took them with a bow of his head.

"It was good to see you again, Abner," Marshall cleared his throat. "I've taken enough of your time, and I'm afraid there are things to which I need attend. So, with your permission, I think it's best that I take my leave."

"Oh, sure," the Elder shook his gray head. "Now you ask my permission. You couldn't have done that the first time? You might have saved me ten years of worry."

Marshall sighed, donning his hat and bowing slightly in strained respect. "Thank you for your hospitality. I'm sorry I couldn't be of more assistance with the artifact."

Abner caught his arm as he reached for the door. "You have nothing to be sorry for, Marshall. I mean that."

Looking down at Abner's aging hand, Marshall felt the lump forming in his throat yet again, but could say nothing.

"And, for what it's worth," The Elder met his eyes with sincerity, "Your father would be very, very proud of who you've become."

At length, the captain forced himself to nod gratefully by way of farewell, then he made his retreat along the memory-filled walkway, refusing against all impulse to look back on the front-facing window with the tiny scuffs along the frame.

Abner watched him disappear into the fog with a knowing light in his old eyes, one that mirrored the glow from the artifact in the strangest of ways.

"Don't give up yet, my boy. Not just yet."

≈

Captain Marshall stood on the beach of Vernos, solemn as the waves lapping at his boots. Flipping at the compass in his hand, he watched his ship idle in the distance. Behind him, the monolithic structures for which the Bannered Shore was named seemed to be joining him in this task. And who could blame them?

The *Albatross* was quite a sight, after all.

One hundred and ten guns spread across three decks. Stretching over two hundred feet from stem to stern. Even through the mist, the evening's crimson sky seemed impaled on the strength of her towering masts, and the proud figurehead – a gryphon, head tipped skyward in preparation for flight – emblazoned the prow with an ancient lore. Protecting. Benevolent. Of all the ships in Secora's fine fleet, she was the finest. She was the flagship. And she was his.

Not even the Bannered Shore could hold a candle to that.

"I never get used to the sight of these things up close."

Pulled from his reverie, the captain turned to see his first officer, Commander Gray Calum standing on the stone base of the nearest Banner. The ringtail cat's head was tipped back to allow him to stare up at the ironwood pole in awe and disbelief. From the top, a flag the size of a small ship waved back at him with gleeful disinterest, as though defying him to reach it.

"Makes you wonder who could have built them, or why," he indicated the impossible diameter and height of the structures. Hundreds of them lined these shores, for miles and miles. Across the centuries, they had stood as the first visible signs of home to any returning sailor. There was hardly a Secoran song that did not mention them. "I guess we don't ask questions of things that simply *are*, do we, sir?"

Marshall clasped his hands behind his back, squaring his shoulders to mirror the yardarms of the great ship in the bay as his officer shot him a quick salute. The Commander was not wrong – the Banners of Secora simply were, and had always been. Like lines on a map, points on a compass. North.

"The *Albatross* is fully supplied and ready to depart whenever you are, sir. I trust your business with Elder Frum went well?"

"Well enough," said Marshall, seeming noncommittal. "Advise the crew that we will be departing shortly."

"Aye, sir," Calum turned without hesitation.

"Commander," the captain interrupted the execution of his own order with a look that could not quite be read. "You have family, don't you?"

The ringtail grinned. "You could say that, sir. A rather massive and obnoxiously-widespread family, really. Most of them are members of the Cleric, or the Health and Hospice Guilds. My aunt is the ship's surgeon, as you know. She and I were the only ones defiant enough to join the Navy." He said the last with amusement, clearly seeing no defiance whatsoever in his choice of career.

"Do you keep in touch?"

Calum shrugged. "Of course, sir. What family wouldn't?"

The captain frowned in response. "What family, indeed."

Recognizing that there was more to his captain's stoic demeanor, Calum opted for silence in the space that followed. He respected Marshall far too much to push the issue.

Settling on a more benign inquiry, he said, "I can't help noticing that your compass isn't pointing north."

The captain looked down at the thing as though having forgotten it was there. "It's never worked properly." Carefully and without expression, he placed it back into his pocket. "It was a gift from my father."

Calum winced internally.

Maybe the question wasn't so benign after all.

The captain had never spoken of his father. Not once, in all the years that Calum had known him. He assumed there was a reason for that.

Stooping to the ground, Marshall lifted a handful of sand and allowed it to slip through his fingers into the sea. Within seconds, the grains had been carried from his sight on an undertow that served to remind him of the things he could not control. He could imagine its journey beneath a fog that would not lift. He could follow its image as it drifted from the shore, past the harbor docks and the Banners reflected on the water's surface. Just as he could see it coming to rest in the murky waters of an island he knew to be there, beyond his field of vision.

Understanding played around his eyes.

"Tell me, Commander," he stood with a new resolve, something of a smile in his voice. "Have you spent any time in the Archives?"

Calum shook his head, "I was never one for the books, sir."

"Even so... I'll wager you've heard the Legend of

Mosque Hill."

≈

Midnight had tolled. It was silent when Abner woke with a start and threw a nervous glance around the room. Just as he'd begun to close his eyes once again, he noticed the unlatched window and the catch in the silence.

He was not alone in the night.

"BOO!"

Abner screamed and fell face-first to the floor, a mountain of blankets landing on top of him.

As if to add insult to embarrassment, the form at the foot of his bed burst into laughter, sparking a flutter of recognition – and anger – in the old badger's eyes.

"Oh, Abner," the shadow chuckled. "I've missed your clumsy carriage – you have no idea how much!"

"McKinley, you rotten son of a sea cook!" Elder Frum pulled himself upright. Shoving the blankets from his face in a huff, he resisted the urge to direct a vindictive kick at the outlaw whose sinewy silhouette was still doubled over in laughter. "Haven't you the decency to knock? At least *some* of the time?!"

"I fail to see how that would produce a desirable response. I think you may be missing the entire point here." The otter leapt into view, wrapping a familiar arm around the Elder's shoulders in feigned friendship. "See, the *point* is to scare the holy living bejeezus out of you so that I can get my giggles from that wonderful look of horror on your furry old face. It's what I live for. If I can't have it, well then… what good are ya?"

Shoving away from him, Abner exhaled indignantly through his whiskers and moved to close the window against the mist. "No good at all. So maybe you and I should just call it a day and go our separate ways. Okay? Okay."

"Besides," McKinley ignored his suggestion entirely,

leaping to the corner bedpost and perching upon it like an agile bird. "We wouldn't want Captain Marshall to catch wind of our involvement, would we? He doesn't seem to like me much."

"I can't even begin to imagine why," the badger hefted the blankets from the floor and threw them in McKinley's direction.

With twice the virility Abner could ever recall owning, the Marauder moved from their path with seamless ease and looked to the Elder in confusion. "What must that say about you? Being my coconspirator and all?"

"I don't like you either, you slug."

"Aww, and after all we've done for one another? We've made such a team, working toward one other's selfish goals, thwarting the do-gooders and their good-doing deeds." McKinley's face underwent a theatrical change from wounded to demanding. "Marshall's been here, am I right? I can smell the lingering stench of superiority. It's so strong, I could vomit."

"Vomit away." Abner sneered. "*I'm* not cleaning it up."

"So now the codger thinks himself a comedian. That does it, next time I drop anchor in your village, I'm attaching you to it." He paused. "The anchor, not the village. But we're off topic here. I came about the artifact."

The Elder rolled his eyes and straightened his bed, preparing to return to it regardless of the intruder's presence. "I showed him the bloomin' thing, as you asked. You were right, he knew exactly what it was. He even opened it."

"Opened it?" This time, McKinley's confusion was genuine.

"Didn't know it did that, did you?" Abner gave him an impudent smile.

"Of course I did."

"No, you didn't." The Elder's grin widened.

"Okay, I didn't." The intruder folded his arms and slumped against the wall, looking impudent. "What was in it, then?"

"A note." Abner climbed into bed with an uninterested yawn. "He couldn't make sense of it here but, as I hear it, he's en route to the capitol to speak with the Queen. So maybe he made your discovery for you after all. If you want to catch up with him, you'll have to do it there. Which means you'll have to leave. Now."

"Right, right," the Marauder's enthusiasm was underwhelming. "I should probably go, then."

Pulling the blankets snugly beneath his chin, the Elder closed his eyes and grunted in agreement. The room was silent for far too long. When he deigned to open one eye in order to test the stillness, McKinley's face was inches from his own.

"Just so we're clear," the otter said in hushed tones. "You didn't give super-special Navy boy any reason to suspect anything, did you?"

Deadpan, Abner matched his self-amused smirk with an even voice, "Actually, I did. I told him all about you and your plans to piggyback on his efforts, to ingeniously steal his thunder along with your fortune and sail into the sunset as the greatest pirate in Secoran history. He just laughed."

McKinley pulled back with a sidelong grin. "See?" he said jovially, patting the Elder on the cheek. "We go together so well. The Marauder and the Comedian. You're a riot, really. How have I ever gotten along without you?"

Abner sighed, "That question confounds me more than you could possibly imagine."

With no preparation and no warning, the Marauder rocketed himself over the badger's head and onto the sill, knocking the window open yet again with a flick of his tail. "I just hope for your sake he takes me where I want to go."

"Or what?" The Elder growled, sitting upright and glaring at the outlaw as he was enveloped by the mist and the night beyond. "You'll make good on your pathetic threats to end my suffering? Go ahead, kill me. I'd prefer it to being forced to deal with you."

Even from the shadows, the distaste on McKinley's face was quite visible.

"What?" He said before launching himself into the vaporous night. "Of course not I'm not going to kill you. What sort of monster do you take me for? But you'll wake up to my gorgeous mug every night for the remainder of your natural life."

Abner leapt from the bed and leaned after him into the dark yelling, "I shudder at the thought!"

Then he slammed the window shut with a bang, this time making certain that it was well and fully latched.

≈

From this house, a candlestick.

That is what they had said. But where was it?

The bony thief had searched everywhere. They'd not said that it was hidden, had they? They usually *said* that it was hidden, when it was hidden.

Quietly stamping his feet in the dark, the thief could feel the wooden floor through the holes in his shoes. There was no give. No phony boards or secret coves in which to hide a small and valuable thing. So where was it?

Ah! There! By the fireplace.

He nearly squealed in delight as he snatched it from the dark.

He could have sworn he'd looked there before, and yet, there it was. Solid silver, for sure. Carved round-about with the same strange markings as the other items from the other houses. With the other purposes. Or was it the same purpose? They hadn't said.

It was pretty and shiny.

Still, he swore it wasn't there before.

Maybe they were playing a game with him. How fun!

Suddenly, from the floor above, there was a rustling of

sheets, a squeaking as of someone shifting in a rusty cot. Had they heard? Would they come running? Oh, he knew what to do if they did, the thief grinned grossly, licking his lips.

Moments later, he heard a tiny cough, but nothing more.

That's right, the sick girl. They had mentioned the sick girl.

But he was here for the candlestick.

Stuffing it into the large canvas sack, he slung the clanking bag over his shoulder and darted into the alley behind the building, not even bothering to close the door behind himself as he ran.

There was more to do.

Always more to do…

2
THE HOUSES HAVE SECRETS

Secora Tor was hardly all about politics. As the oldest city in the kingdom, it was far too full of history and elegance to be bothered by the petty day-to-day bickering of its leading inhabitants. Unfortunately, and despite the best efforts of noble Queen Victorie Prideaux, the city's high-ranking officials would never let something so simple as grand architecture stand in the way of ambition.

And, if there was one thing Marshall had learned in the Nobles Circle, it was that *politics* were all about Secora Tor.

"I still find it hard to believe you were ever in the Nobles Circle," Commander Calum said, as though reading his thoughts.

"You wouldn't be alone in that." Never breaking his smooth, military stride, Marshall tipped his head to the officials in the palace courtyard. They each looked immediately away, as though intimidated. Their reaction shouldn't have come as a surprise to Calum. He knew the captain had a reputation as a powerhouse in the political realm – a plainspoken realist whose loyalty to the crown hadn't gone unnoticed or unrewarded. Even so, the commander couldn't help but marvel at the way these influential people moved from Marshall's path.

Like ants fleeing from a fire.

"So, if I'm to understand correctly, sir, the Mosque Hill Fortune – the greatest treasure ever uncovered – is more than just a legend? Is that why we're here? To tell the queen?"

"The Fortune is real enough, Commander, I can promise you that. It sounds implausible, and the Archives are certainly sketchy on the details, but Masguard was not in the habit of chasing things he could not catch." Marshall nodded to the guards at the gate. They stepped aside and waved him through without question. "Her Majesty already knows this. We are here to find out what Mosque Hill itself really means to Secora."

"Sir?" Calum asked in confusion.

Marshall paused before the enormous wooden doors at the end of the palace hall. Beyond, the voices of a court in turmoil beat against the walls with a low and steady rhythm, as if to sound their arrival. With his hat held firm beneath his left arm, Marshall rested his free hand on the hilt of his sword and nodded once again to the guards.

"The quest for the Mosque Hill Fortune was Masguard's final endeavor," he explained as the armored men leapt to comply with his unspoken command. "And it was not an undertaking of personal interest. It was a mandate from the crown."

"The former queen, Constance Prideaux," Calum nodded in understanding. "She ordered the mission."

"Indeed," Marshall affirmed. "If the records are to be believed, it was the only order she ever gave him. An order he followed without objection or hesitation. I cannot believe that he – or his crew, for that matter – would ever have been willing to die for something so trivial as an Ancient treasure."

The Commander looked thoughtful, as though preparing to respond.

He didn't get the chance.

With a heave of effort, the guards pulled at the doors and the court's chaos hit them at full volume. Deafening shouts blasted back and forth like opposing winds; answers or objections to the weasel standing at the center of the great chamber.

At a break in the commotion, one cry rose above all the others.

"*Treason!*"

Everyone turned to stare at the old official as Marshall and Calum seated themselves unnoticed on the outskirts of the room.

"Your words border on treason, Putris!" The hound stood angrily from his place at the front of the chamber. Calum recognized him as Drumlin, the mayor of a local village – not someone who'd ordinarily have any sway over council proceedings.

But then, the vibe in the palace was far from ordinary.

The weasel turned, baring his teeth in a smile that was as sinister as it was condescending, "Under article seven of the Ancient Code – the very same law that your Queen is asking you to overturn – ownership of the scepter trumps any and all claims to the throne. The bearer is to become ruler of the kingdom, as chosen by Fate. It is one of Secora's oldest and most traditional mandates, handed down to us by our most revered ancestral society. There has never been an allowable exception to their decree. Do you count yourself so grand in your position as mayor that you would dispute the will of the Ancients? The very will of destiny itself?"

"This isn't about destiny, runt. It's a blind grab for power. Everyone knows it. And we deal in the *law* here, not in speculation," Mayor Drumlin drove his cane into the floor for emphasis.

"The law?" Putris drew a seething breath and clicked his claws one against the other, a subtle but threatening recognition of the mayor's insult. "Should the Baron succeed, he will be rightly and *legally* crowned. I am casting my vote for the future. You would be wise to do the same. For hear me now and hear me well. He will remember those who stood with him," there was a slight pause as he looked around the room, then pointedly brought his gaze back to the mayor, "And there will be a special place in his wrath for those who did not. You know the Baron, and you know his ways. Will you count him as an enemy by striking down the Ancient Code? Because I certainly won't. It is not treason. It is practicality."

From the end of the red carpet that stretched along the marble floor, a serene but powerful voice rose up to fill the chamber. All eyes turned to the female wolf seated on the throne.

The room fell silent at her word.

"I sent for Von Ulric. As highly as my cousin may think of himself, he is not king yet. Why did he defy me by sending you in his place?" Her brilliant yellow gaze bore through Putris' defiance like a bolt of lightning through tinder. He wilted noticeably.

Clearing his throat, the weasel tugged at his robe and stepped forward, seeming desperate to regain his composure. "I was not sent by Von Ulric, Your Majesty. I am but a voice of the people, expressing their convictions." Her gaze hardened on him and he sputtered, "If Your Majesty would be so kind as to recall, I did say that the Baron has already set sail on his quest to retrieve the Scepter of the Ancients."

"Indeed, you did. And I dismissed the statement as absurd." Betraying neither emotion nor intent, her words were hard and flat – like an anvil. "Tell me why I should not do so again."

Putris' false smile returned.

"Several nights ago, the Baron was visited by a Voice of Fate." The weasel let the statement hang on the air just long enough to create a stir, then he turned from the throne to direct his words into a rapt crowd. "The Voice imparted a tale of woe and intrigue, stating that the scepter, once believed to be a lost instrument of destiny, wasn't lost at all. It was hidden centuries past, and intentionally so, by the last dynasty of Fate's choosing. In an effort to maintain permanent control of Secora, this house took it upon themselves to preempt the will of destiny with an act of greed and desecration. They buried the Scepter of the Ancients where none would ever find it – at the heart of an island so elusive that many believe it to be a free-floating landmass. That island, ladies and gentlemen of the court, was the legendary island of Mosque Hill. And the offending house," he turned again to face the queen, an accusing glint in his eye, "Was none other than the House of Prideaux."

The chamber exploded as noblemen leapt to their feet in furious debate.

"Scandal!" They cried.

"Lies and superstition!"

"Our leaders have betrayed us!"

"We cannot believe this!"

"Are we to refute the wills of destiny as they did?!"

Commander Calum looked to his captain in the chaos to find him strangely silent, even calm, though his mouth had drawn itself into a grim and determined line.

"Don't think that I would denigrate Her Majesty without proof," Putris was quick to address the detractors. Pulling a letter from the folds of his robe, he lifted it high so the wax seal on the envelope was visible to all. "I have here a signed confession by the official scribe of the former court. In it, he reveals that Queen Constance knew the whereabouts of the Scepter. More than that, immediately following the famous failed voyage of the explorer Masguard, she knowingly and willfully removed all information concerning his mission from the Archives. A grievous crime against the court and against the integrity of Secoran history. In light of this, the Baron's quest for the scepter is anything but absurd." Again, he smiled. That condescending, malicious smile. "Does Her Majesty find it so easy to dismiss my statements now?"

The queen's eyes narrowed in response.

The mayor hound rose again from his seat, this time addressing Putris with a little less certainty, "These are very serious allegations."

"Allegations to which your queen has not yet responded, mayor. Wouldn't you like to know where she stands?" The weasel never moved his gaze from the throne as the room fell quiet around him, waiting.

A long pause, and the snow-white wolf drew a heavy breath.

Then she opened her mouth to speak.

"Your Majesty, may I be heard?"

When he realized that the bold speaker was standing immediately to his left, Commander Calum looked up at his captain in surprise.

"What's this?" The weasel pulled his lips back in a snarl. "Captain Marshall, you are not an elected official. You aren't even the member of a recognized Guild, not any longer. You have no place here."

"Unless and until another rises to take my position, this hall is a place for *all* to have their say," the queen silenced him with a look. "The lack of a Guild does not deprive one of the ability to speak. He has a voice, and I would hear it."

"Thank you, Your Majesty," Marshall said.

Officials murmured one to another as the captain made his way to the center of the chamber. Once there, he stood toe to toe with the weasel, resting a hand lightly on the hilt of his rapier.

And again, Putris wilted.

"The issue before you today is not whether the accusations of a paid speaker are worthy of consideration, but whether the kingdom of Secora is best served by the wills of Article Seven. It is my opinion that this law is outdated and irrelevant." He met the weasel's dark eyes with an icy resolve. "Her Majesty's Navy supports this amendment. And we support the House of Prideaux. Your claims be drowned."

Taking an unconscious step backward, Putris forced himself to laugh. "You would speak for the whole of the military? Favored prodigy or not, Captain, I think you overestimate your influence."

At that, Calum stood partially from his seat and lifted a hand for recognition, offering, "Um, no. No, he doesn't."

The mayor hound chuckled.

Much of the court followed suit.

"It doesn't require a prodigy, or even one who has studied in the Archives, to tell you that rulers of integrity have been rare in our history," Marshall countered, evenly. "Among those few, Constance Prideaux stands as one of the most brilliant examples of the very sense of justice and decency that made Secora into one of the greatest societies our world has ever seen. I stand before you today, a dedicated serviceman, willing to lay down my life for this kingdom, as a direct result of her efforts. I guarantee that even you, Putris, cannot name a finer proponent of progress and equality than her daughter, Victorie Prideaux, whose reign has improved your lives in more ways than you likely know. For this, and much more, the queen has earned every ounce of my loyalty and my trust." Though his voice did not change at all from one statement to the next, the slight lowering of his head was enough to add emphasis to his closing words. "So believe me when I say that I will fight for no house but the House of Prideaux. And I will do as I must – whatever I must – to remain in that service."

Putris' already-dark eyes deepened to a shade of black that almost concealed the fear he felt.

Almost.

"I'm afraid I am not familiar with the rhetoric among military men." He struggled to maintain a steady voice. "If I didn't know any better, I would swear that sounded like a threat."

"A threat? Not at all. Merely concern for the *practicality* of your agenda." His voice fell as emotionless as his face. "The Baron will find it rather difficult to rule Secora without the support of its military, will he not?"

Putris threw his arm in the air with a pointed claw. "*That* is treason!" he bellowed. "You swore your oath to the crown of Secora, not to the one beneath it!"

"Should the kingdom fall under the rule of Baron Von Ulric, it will no longer be the Secora to which I gave my oath. And I *will* fight to maintain the honor of Secora as she stands. That is not treason, Putris." Marshall stepped forward, throwing the weasel's words back at his feet with a stoic glare. "It is allegiance."

The room erupted in hostility and scattered applause.

Desperate, Putris dove for the final card held up his sleeve.

"Tell me, Captain," he snarled. "Would you be as quick to offer your allegiances to a House not simply of liars, but of *murderers*?"

Marshall narrowed his eyes in suspicion.

Hazarding a step in his direction, Putris continued, "Remember that Constance Prideaux sought to remove all evidence of Masguard's final expedition. An expedition from which he, a seasoned explorer who'd survived far more dangerous ventures, never returned. Don't you find it odd? Doesn't it make you wonder how far the queen might have been willing to go in order to ensure that the crimes of her family were never discovered?"

"What are you attempting to suggest?" demanded the captain.

The weasel waited just long enough for the room to fall completely still before saying, "That she had the famous explorer, along with his crew, executed."

Gasps and appalled protestations echoed throughout the chamber. Even Commander Calum found himself looking to the throne in shock.

Could it be true?

Masguard the Relic-Hunter was Secora's most beloved icon. If the House of Prideaux was indeed involved in a scandal of this magnitude, it would not matter how removed, or how ignorant of the crime, Queen Victorie was. She would be ousted as a matter of national pride.

"I ask you, what other conclusion can be drawn? How can we offer fidelity to those who give us none? Will we follow where they would make casualties of our most celebrated citizens?" Glaring over the crowd in deviant victory, Putris' smile widened with every fearful glance, every dubious stare. He had them now. No defense she could offer would ever be enough to combat the doubts of a suspicious court.

They would crucify her with rumor.

Or, so he thought.

He, and everyone else in the room, turned in surprise when they realized that Captain Marshall, quite uncharacteristically… was *laughing*.

Even the queen sat forward in confusion.

The mayor hound stood once again and pointed with his cane as if to indicate Marshall's sudden lack of decorum. "I fail to see why this is so funny!"

Commander Calum shrugged when those nearest him looked his way for an explanation. "Don't look at me. I'm at as much of a loss as all of you."

At length, the captain managed to compose himself. "I apologize, but the notion of Masguard having been the victim of a political execution? *That* is your trump card? Bureaucratic revenge? The explorer was many things, but he was no fool. He did not trust easily or often, and if he'd any notion whatsoever that his queen was anything but genuine... My pity and yours on anyone brave enough to attempt a double-cross on him."

"How dare you?" the weasel spat.

The laughter threatened to bubble from Marshall's mouth a second time. "Again, I am sorry, but what a fiction! Executed by the queen? Not in this life, or in any of your imagining. It's possibly the most absurd thing I've ever heard a nobleman suggest. And that, in and of itself, is saying something."

Putris snarled as those in the room began to join in the captain's laughter. "Now you would claim even to know the mind of history's greatest explorer? Exactly who do you think you are, Captain?!"

The smile of amusement fell from Marshall's ever-stoic face.

With Abner's warning playing fresh in his thoughts, Captain Marshall glanced first to his queen, and then to the room's inhabitants. They were so perilously close to the edge, these politicians. So easily swayed. They would leap to either side of the argument, given the slightest inclination.

His caretaker would have a heart attack.

But, looking to his queen, the dutiful captain knew that some things were more important than personal safety or even the wills of an absent father.

At long last, he sighed. If these noblemen wanted a scandal... he would give them one.

"Who am I?" he said, his voice firm, authoritative, leaving no room for compromise or question. "I am Masguard's son."

Putris stepped away, as if in retreat.

Queen Prideaux leaned back in her seat and laced her fingers together, the hint of a smile on her fierce, canine features.

Marshall could swear he felt the prod of Abner's cane thumping on his chest.

And from the outskirts of the crowd, Calum shrugged again to those around him – as if to stave off their glares of accusation. "I didn't see that one coming, either."

"We're finished here!" Putris exclaimed in defeat, turning to storm from the room before this captain could bury him further.

"But I do have one more question, Putris." Marshall stopped him. "How does the Baron hope to find Mosque Hill without the Key?"

"What makes you think he does not have it?" the weasel snarled reluctantly over his shoulder.

"Because," Marshall clasped his hands behind his back and squared his shoulders, sealing his victory with a smile. "*I* have it."

≈

"The son of Masguard." The hall had been emptied of everyone but Marshall, Calum, and a single advisor in the corner of the room. And, of course, the regal queen, who smiled and shook her head in a familiar gesture. "That was quite the revelation, Captain."

Though he said nothing, Commander Calum's agreement with the monarch could practically be felt. He was in shock, certainly.

The queen was not.

"If I may say, Your Majesty," Marshall noted, "You do not seem surprised."

"Surprised? No." She stood, descending the steps as though preparing to conquer the floor, her blue cloak trailing behind her like an ocean tide. "Masguard was my mother's oldest and dearest friend, Captain. Whatever secrets he once kept, by the end, he couldn't help but share them. One of the beneficial hazards of friendship, I suppose." For the briefest instant, the queen looked markedly emotional. It passed quickly. "So yes, of course, I know who you are. I've always known."

Marshall shifted ever so slightly on his feet. "Then, my success… in the Navy…"

"Was well-earned," she finished for him. "Granted on your own merits and nothing beyond. I would never pander, Captain, not even to a cherished line of nobility. If I were the sort to engage in such a thing, I would hardly be worthy of your devotion, isn't that true?"

The captain responded only with an appreciative nod of his head.

"I can't thank you enough for intervening when you did," she continued. "Sending Putris to masquerade as a voice of the people was a brilliant move on my cousin's part."

"The Baron is nothing if not politically aware," the queen's advisor tittered from his position. "He knew that Putris' words would bear an impact. Even though he was contested, the damage he caused…"

"Might have been much worse." The queen waved a dismissive hand. "I knew that introducing this bill would not be met with the approval of the court. Noblemen do not like being called upon to openly choose sides. It narrows their options."

"Surely they must see that this bill is in their own best interests," Calum said.

Marshall agreed, "It would be a devastating blow to Secora if the Baron were crowned in your place. The Scepter and the laws behind it are outdated. Ludicrously so."

"The same is true of many of Secora's laws, Captain. That doesn't prevent them from standing." The queen's mouth tightened. "The *Rules of Challenge*, the *Caste Proclamation*. These codes survive today on tradition alone. They may be counter to the progressive ideas that Secora is meant to stand for, but it is a delicate balance between progress and possibility. I cannot change the world without the will of the people, and many of them are not prepared to distance themselves from the old ways. If it were for the benefit of the kingdom, I would have no qualms with stepping aside, not even for an outdated law. However, I will not do so for the Baron. He is a malicious animal. The court knows this. But they fear him. Almost as much as they fear his foreign allies. They will not stand in his way if his claims are true."

"Then why will they not pass your amendment?" asked Calum.

"Because they're cowards," Marshall said flatly. "Easier to sweep the issue under the rug and bide their time than to cast a vote that might mark them for retribution. They'll take their chances in silence, and hope that his mission is unsuccessful."

"And if it isn't?" the commander asked. "What happens if he returns with the Scepter and they are forced to make him king?"

Queen and captain exchanged looks of steel and apprehension, each of them knowing the unpleasant answer to his questions.

Marshall was the one to finally give it.

"Civil war," he said.

Calum's reaction was silent, but severe. Secora was a symbol of peace. The kingdom hadn't known outright war in more than a century.

This could change everything. And not for the better.

The queen's advisor approached the trio at last. "Which brings us to the matter of the Key."

He was an odd-looking bird, to put it mildly. Wide-mouthed and stout, he blundered more than stepped as he made his way into view, where Marshall could plainly see the strange symbol dyed into the feathers of his right wing. He recognized it as the Ancient symbol for knowledge.

The bird was a member of the Order.

"My royal advisor, Eadric," the queen said, by way of introduction. "You are familiar with the upper echelons of the Scholars Guild?"

"Quite, Your Majesty." Though Marshall managed to keep his tone even, the bird chirped abruptly in response.

Clearly, the captain's bitterness was not lost on him.

"As we are familiar with *you*, Marshall. You were one of our most promising recruits. It is a shame you left us when you did. And…in the manner that you did."

"Isn't it, though?" Marshall tipped his head coolly.

"But please refer to me as Captain."

"Of course… Captain. *May knowledge light your path.*" Eadric offered the customary Scholar's greeting and extended a wing, along with a slight bow. Something about the way he performed the gesture made it seem insincere, at best.

Marshall exchanged glances with his first officer, who lifted a dubious brow.

"And yours," the captain managed to respond, pulling the folded bit of parchment from his pocket. "But, to the matter at hand. The Key was found off the coast of Vernos, a year ago. The town Elder is an old acquaintance. He brought it to my attention."

"Where is the Key now?" The queen asked.

"On my ship, Your Majesty."

"You didn't bring it with you?" Eadric puffed his feathers in disapproval.

Marshall gave him a harsh stare. "You'll forgive me, but waltzing through the streets with an Ancient artifact, one dearly coveted by Secora's gravest enemy, seemed a rather poor idea. It is well guarded where it is. I did, however, bring its contents." He held up the note.

Eadric's pompous demeanor gave way to curiosity as he eyed the thing in Marshall's hand.

"May I?" he demanded, more than asked.

Marshall watched as the strange bird puzzled over the rhyme. After a long moment, the advisor shook his head and passed it to the queen.

"This is Masguard's seal, is it not?" she said.

Marshall nodded, "Aye, Your Majesty."

"The message is quite cryptic," she glanced expectantly at her advisor. "What does it mean?"

"I…" Eadric said with an uncertain voice. "Well, Your Majesty, it's… Quite clear that this is a… Well, the last two words are capitalized…"

"You aren't meant to understand it, Eadric," Marshall interrupted, sparing him further embarrassment.

"Masguard's entire point in writing this message was to narrow his audience. He didn't want just anyone stumbling across the Gateway."

Calum raised his hand, "At the risk of sounding clueless, sir, what in Fate's name is that?"

"A metaphor, Commander," Eadric piped up a little too quickly, seeming grateful for the opportunity to look more learned than someone. "The Key opens the Gateway, which in turn opens the road to Mosque Hill."

"It's a puzzle?"

"Of sorts," Marshall agreed. "It might be more accurate to call it a reference."

"But to what?" Again, Eadric shook his head.

The captain looked to their confused faces then sighed in resignation, saying:

"Forever Isle, forever moans,
'Stay ship, won't you stay?
Come rest your wooden bones
In my old and murky bay.
Button up your sails,
For you cannot swim away.
I've got you by the tail.
Stay here, *ever stay*.'"

"It's a nursery rhyme," Marshall explained, when his words triggered no response. "An island to the north of Vernos, now known as Pelham Point. It is surrounded by a rather hazardous stretch of sea and shoal. Prior to the construction of its lighthouse, the locals referred to it as 'Forever Isle,' in honor of the numerous ships to have run aground on its sandbars or crashed on its rocky shores, never to return. Children wrote poems about it, painting it as something of an oceanic boogeyman."

Eadric stared at him.

"But I've never heard this *poem*," he bit the last word scornfully.

Marshall shrugged. "That doesn't surprise me in the least, Advisor."

"It *should*," he continued, adamantly. "History – *this history* in particular – is my specialty, Captain. And I know for a fact that Pelham's lighthouse was constructed centuries ago. Do you expect me to believe that you have access to historical lore that isn't available within the Archives?"

Marshall met his scrutinizing glare with indifference.

Abner would have slapped this pretentious bird.

"I had older and wiser teachers than those provided by the Scholars Guild, Eadric. Believe it or not, as you will. It is the truth," the captain said, pointing to the parchment now in the queen's hand. "This is the Key, and Pelham Point, the Gateway."

Victorie stood beside her throne, drumming her fingers on the edge, lost in thought.

"Forever Isle. That is where it will begin," she said quietly, as if to herself. "That seems fitting, for some reason." Then, glancing to those in the room as though having forgotten that they were there, she ordered, "Eadric, I believe we have an item within the royal treasury that was meant for our captain. Please retrieve it. Commander," she turned to Calum, "If you would be so kind as to return to your ship and prepare the hold for a rather delicate package, I'll have a delivery sent your way by nightfall."

"Certainly, Your Majesty." He bowed. "May I ask the dimensions of the package? We are fully loaded at the moment."

The queen paused before saying, "You... may wish to clear the hold entirely, Commander."

Calum looked from her to Marshall and back again. Clearly, that was no small request.

"I'll do my best," he said at last and without complaint before turning to leave. "If I may speak freely, Your Majesty?"

"Please do." The queen tipped her head graciously.

"Putris may paint himself as a voice of the people, but he's the furthest thing from it. Your people are loyal to you, even if your politicians are not."

She smiled. "That humbles me more than you know, Commander. Thank you."

The commander gave his captain a quick salute before leaving the room.

Marshall glanced around to note that Eadric had already gone, without having pardoned himself, or acknowledging his queen's order.

"Your advisor, he is… new, I take it?"

Victorie chuckled behind closed lips. "Do not be concerned, Captain. I have not been swayed by the wills of the Scholars Guild. Eadric is something of an expert in the lore surrounding both the Mosque Hill Fortune and the Scepter of the Ancients. He advises me on those matters alone. Nothing more." Her silver-blue cloak slid soundlessly along the floor behind her as she moved. "Will you walk with me?"

"Certainly, Your Majesty." Marshall bowed.

They exited onto an open terrace overlooking the bay. Though the mist prevented them from seeing anything below, the vast balcony itself was a testament to the strength and grandeur of the palace, with intricately carved banisters and glittering blue stone. Marshall couldn't help but revel in the look and feel of this place, so like his ship. Regal. Detached.

Lonely.

"I remember him, you know. Your father." She paused as if to ponder the low-lying haze on the Bannered Shore. "I was quite young and surrounded by people of supposed import. But he made an impression. He burned with purpose. When he spoke, people listened. And where he led, others followed." With a sigh, she leaned forward and placed her hands on the rail. "What they are saying is true. My ancestors were responsible for the loss of the Scepter."

She glanced back at him with a smile. "Now it is my turn to note that you do not seem surprised."

Marshall seemed hesitant to respond. "Secora has seen this mist once before, during the reign of your mother. It appeared shortly before Masguard's final mission and dispersed in the months following his disappearance. Now its return coincides with the discovery of the Key and the proposal of your amendment. Queen Constance would not have sent my father on a perilous mission to retrieve a handful of petty treasure. Nor would you introduce an equally perilous bill without cause. The conclusion was a leap, certainly, but not an impossible one."

"For many, it would indeed be impossible. You're more like your father than you know."

Marshall tipped his head in thanks, but said no more.

"My mother could not abide the knowledge that her throne had come to her through deception," the queen explained. "But she knew she could not pass that knowledge to the public. Not because it put her rule at risk, but because she feared for my safety. The Baron had already come to power in his sector of the kingdom, and he had made his intentions known. He'd even used the threat of my abduction to take down the last of the Secoran Knights."

"The Massacre. That was Von Ulric?" Marshall's look bordered on disgust.

The queen nodded. "We could never prove it publicly, but it was enough to teach us that he would exploit any opportunity to seize the throne, and eliminate me in the process. That is why my mother called out to her friend for help, in secret. She asked Masguard to venture in search of the Scepter. To right a wrong by returning it to the sea, where it belongs, as a true instrument of Fate. You know well the result of that mission."

Just then, her advisor returned with a small, clasped box. Clearly, this was not the delivery she'd sent Calum to prepare for.

"What you do not know," she went on, "is that Masguard was able to send a final missive to his sovereign. On his order, a fearsome bird came to the capitol – large and terrifying, a force unlike anything we'd ever seen. He offered a tale of bravery and wonders that few would believe. He also brought this." She opened the box and lifted its contents to the light. It was a pendant – or part of one, at least. It was broken and tainted, gold suspended on a silver chain. "Masguard wanted you to have it. But only if the mists returned. As you can see, they have done that."

She gestured to the weather, but Marshall's eyes were fixed on the broken medallion.

He swallowed, "Do you know what happened in the end? To my father?"

An expression that Marshall could not read passed just behind Victorie's eyes, but only for a moment. "I'm sorry, but no. The bird left without explaining what had become of those who are now gone. We couldn't have stopped him if we'd tried. He said only that Mosque Hill would be waiting for the one who dared to follow." Reverently, she coiled the partial pendant in her palm and handed it to Marshall. "I now find myself in the same position as my mother. Forced to ask the most difficult thing I've ever asked of the dearest friend I have. Marshall, I need you to follow in your father's footsteps. To reach the Scepter before the Baron can ever set foot on Mosque Hill. All of Secora may depend upon it."

Marshall was quiet as he wrapped his hand around the marred gold. Masguard sent a necklace but no message? No words of comfort for a lost and lonely child? That left questions – so many questions. But standing here beneath his queen's request, Marshall's sense of duty overrode them all. Steeling himself, he returned his gaze to hers, "The Baron is pushing our enemies to ally against us, isn't he? That is why you called the alert. He's positioning himself for the threat of attack, to bully the court into accepting his rule once he returns."

The queen nodded. "The Baron has spies in every corner of Secoran politics. So he knows well where you stand, Captain. He knows also that my armada will gladly force the law aside in order stand with you. As I said, you are your father's son. So, where you lead..." She let the statement stand unfinished. "But the bloodshed of my people is not a sacrifice I am willing to make. Not yet. That is why I must ask this of you. That is why you must succeed."

With a final glance at the necklace in his hand, the captain bowed low. "I understand, Your Majesty. If the Baron lays a hand on the Scepter, it will be on my life."

"I would very much like to avoid that outcome." She smiled. "Still, there will be many who seek to thwart your mission, should they learn of your intent. Some of them you will know. Others, you may not. What I send to your ship should provide you with an advantage they'll not be able to predict. But is there anything more that you will require before you depart, Captain?"

Marshall's inhalation carried purpose. In light of all of this, it seemed a petty thing to ask. But he knew he would not get another chance.

"There is one thing, if Your Majesty would be so kind as to indulge a personal request."

"You need but ask."

"Vernos has had some difficulties lately. It could use some added security." He said, earning a chirp of irritated surprise from Eadric.

The queen eyed him for a long time before answering.

"I will send a contingent of troops immediately," she agreed at last, without further question.

Again, Marshall bowed, this time in gratitude. Then he donned his hat with the hint of a smile as he turned to take his leave. "Quite against his character, the town's Elder will thank you for it."

He hadn't gone more than a few steps before she stopped him with an uneasy expression. "There is one more thing I would ask of you as well, Captain."

Marshall's smooth military stride halted on the instant.

"And this request, I think," she continued in an apologetic tone, "You will likely *not* thank me for…"

≈

Escorting Eadric to the docks was like pulling teeth. It wasn't enough that he'd taken the better part of the evening gathering his things, or that he'd expected the captain to assist in the hauling of his absurd amount of finery. Despite repeated reminders that they were on a schedule, the kookaburra had meandered the streets at a snail's pace, glaring through shop windows and muttering judgmental statements over everyone they passed, as though unaware that most mammals had hearing far better than his own. If Marshall were the impatient sort, he'd have dumped the pious official in a trash bin.

Why the queen had insisted on his presence was a mystery.

"I will of course require a room that reflects my status," the bird mumbled between sniffs of annoyance. "Can't have me lodging with the crew or any such nonsense."

"Certainly not," Marshall answered stiffly. *They'd tolerate you no more easily than I.*

"And I'll not be partaking in any of those dreadful rations, so you'd better have some real food onboard this…" Eadric's voice trailed into something a little less petulant as they passed through the main arch in the city walls and the *Albatross* came into view. "This… sufficiently impressive ship… of yours."

Marshall offered no response, but he couldn't help but smile at the insufferable bird's reaction.

As usual, the crew was hard at work, swabbing the deck, testing the lines, and performing basic maintenance. Commander Calum stood near the ramp, directing the flow of traffic as the hold was emptied per the queen's instructions. And from the uppermost topmasts, a collie accompanied their actions by singing in a beautiful and boisterous tone:

"Welcome to the *Albatross*,
A ship beyond compare.
Wherever you roam,
You're never alone,
If her sails take you there.

For helpless and weak,
For noble and meek,
Forever she'll stand at your side,
But criminals flee,
Over land, over sea,
She'll bury your dust in the brine.

A hero of war,
A banner for peace,
She's soldier, Secora, and queen.
She's mother and home,
She's all that I know,
And everything in between.
Hoist her flag high,
Let it be a light,
A clarion plea to the just.
The *Albatross* calls.
So, come one, come all,
I'll sail her alone if I must.

If you fear wooden scales,
Or the fire on the sails,
Of the ocean's fiercest dragon.
You haven't the strength
To stand here at length,
Find yourself another wagon.

But come ye brave sailors,
Bluejackets, and tars,
Abandon these shores,
And your strife.
Unfurl her sheets
And dust off your feet,
You're in for the ride of your life."

There was a brief pause in the bustle as a round of cheers and applause rose up from the deck. Then the collie bowed and, just like that, they all returned to work.

"Ryder is my First Lieutenant." Marshall gestured to her with no small amount of pride.

Eadric stared with his beak parted for several moments. "She gave your ship… a theme song?"

Never breaking his steady stride, the captain shrugged and said, "It's her way."

"Captain on deck!" Calum called out with a sharp salute.

"Commander," Marshall acknowledged, "All's well?"

"Indeed, sir. As you can see, we're nearly finished. We've had to offload all non-essential supplies, though, so here's hoping we don't run into anything unexpected. The queen's shipment…?"

"Will be delivered within the hour, Commander," Marshall answered. "And I want the ship cleared by then. Once the hold is empty, grant shore leave to the entire crew."

"For the evening, sir?" If Calum was at all perplexed by the unconventional command, he didn't show it.

"For the night." The captain turned his brisk walk toward his cabin. "We may have a long road ahead of us, and my crew deserves some downtime." He paused before the door and looked meaningfully back at his crew. "Who knows when they'll get another chance?"

"I understand, sir. And, um…" The commander

lowered his voice and gestured to Eadric, who still stood at the top of the ramp, staring at the deck with something akin to horror. "What do we do with him?"

Marshall drew a deep breath. "He's coming with us, I regret to say. And apparently, the queen's advisor requires… accommodations."

Calum sighed, "He can have my quarters, sir."

"Nonsense, Commander." First Lieutenant Ryder came alongside him. "He'll have mine."

The three turned to watch Eadric struggle with his mound of luggage. Grunting ineffectually, the bird called out to separate members of the crew, demanding assistance and threatening reprisal when they did not respond.

At least they weren't so unkind as to laugh in his face.

"Are you sure, Lieutenant?" The commander winced. "With that amount of pointless junk, he's liable to crush each and every one of your belongings without ever having noticed. And I doubt he'd feel bad about it."

The collie gave a sinister smile, baring a row of sharp teeth as she lifted her voice just enough for her words to rise above the din of the ship. "Not to worry, Commander. The advisor and I will just have to have a friendly chat about respect and boundaries."

There was nothing particularly threatening about *what* she said.

Only in the way she said it.

Eadric, who'd been hauling cartoonish-ly at an oversized suitcase, overheard her statement and froze in place.

Calum suppressed an outright laugh.

Ryder made her way across the deck to the stairwell and stood patiently at the top, clasping her hands behind her back in a way that very much mirrored the customary stance of her captain. As she watched Eadric with that same sinister smile, he couldn't help but wonder how one so fierce could have ever managed the sentimental and joyful chorus he'd heard only moments before.

She must have eaten a songstress at some point, he grimaced.

"Don't let the pretty fangs fool you, advisor." Calum clapped the bird on the back with a grin as he passed. "Once you get to know her... Ryder's really quite terrifying."

Captain Marshall

3
INTRUDERS

Careful Steps Kal pried the lid from the trash can. Dropping it to the cobblestones beneath the cathedral with all the subtlety of an overturned china cabinet, the young raccoon dove to her elbows in the refuse with a shake of her head. She couldn't believe some of the things people threw out. A bit of broken porcelain, an uneaten apple – these things were useful, for Fate's sake.

"Pfft, nobles," C.S. scoffed, all but falling from the haphazardly-stacked crates when a voice shot from the shadows.

"They are an obnoxious bunch, aren't they?"

She recovered quickly, forcing her voice to calm itself as she turned to the form in the mist and chided, "You're late."

"Couldn't be helped," he shrugged, showing a glint of metal from his uniform. "Marshall runs a tight ship. I'd think your employer would appreciate my caution."

"Maybe he will. Maybe he won't," the young raccoon shrugged in return, mocking him. "You know how the

Baron can be."

The informant cleared his throat and stepped forward – not enough to reveal himself, but enough for her to recognize the gesture for the threat that it was.

"It's C.S., isn't it?" He waited for her to nod before continuing. "Well you see, C.S. – I, in fact, *don't* know how the Baron can be. Because the Baron has never seen fit to meet me in person, has he? He keeps sending you to throw a bit of money at my feet and gather whatever information I've collected on the queen's impenetrable Armada. Which is hazardous business. So, between the danger and the disregard, you might understand if being scolded by a street urchin in an alley that smells like the tail end of an octopus isn't high on the list of things I'm willing to tolerate."

An expectant silence followed.

Next to her, the naval officer was practically a giant, and he was certain to be well-trained with the sword at his side. He could kill her with ease and leave her here among the refuse – it wasn't as if anyone would miss her.

So C.S. countered in the only way that she could.

Baring her teeth in a vicious snarl, the tiny raccoon lunged over boxes and garbage cans, pressing her face as close to the informant's as she dared.

"You don't like it?!" she hissed and howled all at the same time. "Then shove off and find another job, you filthy tar! You came to us, remember? So far, the information you've given hasn't been worth the coin you're getting in return. Now, if you want to be the one to explain to the Baron that you're doing something other than wasting his time, be my guest. But, until that day, you deal with *me*. And I don't *appreciate* it when you're late, you got that?!"

As if to punctuate her display of aggression, the cathedral's bell began to toll, a grand echo that swallowed the informant's surprised reaction. She had gambled on this same ruse many times in her short life. Sure, he was bigger, stronger, older – but would he be willing to test her if he thought he might lose his nose in the process?

She held her breath, careful to conceal her fear as she watched for his response.

Then the pealing of the bell subsided and the officer sighed.

Luckily, it seemed he liked his nose where it was, thank you very much.

"Now," she sniffed. "Where's the medallion?"

She could vaguely make out the line of his head as he shook it. "I couldn't get to it in time. I think she may have given it to the captain."

"So what? You can't steal it from *him*?"

"Not unless you want me to pry it from around his neck," he said.

C.S. sat back in confusion. "He's wearing it? He's *wearing* a priceless piece of jewelry formerly owned by Masguard the Relic Hunter? Doesn't something like that belong in a safe?"

The informant grunted and folded his arms over his chest. "Probably, but that's hardly any of my business. All I know is that it isn't exactly reachable."

C.S. felt her pulse begin to climb.

She could never return to the Baron with this news.

He would skin her alive.

"Could you get it from him, given more time?" She bit her lip.

"I doubt it. Besides, what would that accomplish? The *Albatross* ships out at dawn. Unless you mean for me to drop it in a bottle and toss it overboard."

She grunted in frustration. "Leave it to me, then. You're traveling to Pelham Point? I'll catch up with you after."

She could feel him eyeing her in the darkness, "Your species isn't exactly known for its swimming ability."

"No," she puffed her fur in indignation. "We're known for something else – something that's going to keep the two of us alive. So watch your tone. In the meantime, you're going to have to start pulling your weight."

"What did you have in mind?"

"Word is, Marshall's moved some heavy freight onto his ship," C.S. eyed him. "Funny you didn't mention that."

"The *Albatross* is *always* moving something, kid. I wasn't paid to watch the cargo."

"You're right. You were paid to retrieve the medallion. And you failed. Now we're *both* in hot water, get it?" Frustration bled through in every word. "So unless you're keen on the idea of being nailed to the ocean floor, you'll find out what was in that delivery. My guess is that it's something that might get in the Baron's way. If that's the case, and you value your life, you'll sabotage whatever it is. Are we clear?"

"I still don't understand how you plan to catch up with us," he said suspiciously. "Or what the Baron wants with some broken old trinket, for that matter."

"You're the one who's so pushy about meeting in the dark," C.S. gestured defiantly to their surroundings, the barely-there moonlight and ominous shadows that kept the informant's identity concealed. "You shouldn't whine over being made to stay there."

She leapt from the trash can and into the streets beyond, sighing relief as he grumbled after her, but did not follow.

"By the way…" The little raccoon known as Careful Steps turned in the street with a confused expression. "How in the world do you know what the tail end of an octopus smells like?"

At that, he gave a threatening step forward and she disappeared into the city, cackling with childish laughter.

≈

For the second night in a row, Abner woke to the sound of an intruder in his library. Kicking covers from the bed with a growl, he stormed into the adjoining den and yelled, "McKinley, I've had just about enough of – !"

The words died in his throat as he was thrown to the floor by a sea of rough hands. Shadows swarmed around him. A boot pressed against his windpipe and he clutched at the cruel leather, gasping for breath.

"Come now, Mr. Frum. Do keep calm, if you can." The form seated in the corner of the room struck a match in the darkness. Though Abner could not turn his head to see him directly, the intruder's beastly shadow fell across the floor near Abner's face, where it seemed he was speaking to the Elder, nose to nose. "I'd very much like to hear more about this *McKinley* character. You couldn't possibly mean McKinley the Marauder, now could you? I'd heard rumors that the two of you were affiliated. Never thought they could be true. How very interesting."

Abner's voice caught with fear and distaste alike. "Von Ulric."

"Oh, my reputation precedes me. Good," the shadow smiled, showing a row of dagger-like teeth that danced like demons in the lamplight. "That makes things easier."

"What do you want with me?" The Elder's demand sounded fragile, at best.

"To talk, Mr. Frum." The shadow splayed his massive hands in a peaceful gesture that was anything but. "Just to talk."

"Then let me up!" Abner clawed again at the boot against his throat. "I'm an old badger, for Fate's sake, what sort of threat can I possibly be?"

There was a slight pause before the shadow responded.

"That… is yet to be determined," he said, gesturing for the Elder's release.

Abner rose slowly and cast about for his cane. Only after finding it did he turn to eye the Baron in the flesh.

He regretted it immediately.

Von Ulric was a mountain. Tooth and claw and every horrible nightmare together in one fur. With eyes so cold that Abner could swear he felt himself freezing in place beneath their stare, the wolf seemed far too calm, too welcome in the shadows, to be anything less than a demon, or a ghost.

Abner swallowed, knowing well that the Baron was flesh and blood.

And that reality was the most terrifying thing of all.

"You're something of a mystery, aren't you, Mr. Frum? Elder, educator, learned sage. You might have done this little kingdom of yours a great service by joining any one of its Guilds and offering your knowledge to the world. Yet you only ever took one student. Why is that?"

The old badger's voice was a mix of resignation and defiance as he responded, "Perhaps he was the only student worth taking."

The Baron laughed – a closed-mouth laugh that sounded a little too much like the rumble before an avalanche. "Or perhaps *Masguard* asked it of you."

Abner hid his shock with an angry thump of his cane. "What are you talking about?"

Again, that horrid laugh. "Pretenses do not become you. But apparently they suited your student even less. The noble Captain Marshall confessed to his lineage today in Secora Tor."

A long silence followed, in which the Elder struggled to keep his breath from betraying him.

"You're lying," he said at last.

Von Ulric leaned forward in the shadows just enough for his monstrous teeth to glint in the firelight. "Am I?"

"Marshall wouldn't do that," Abner sputtered, as though trying to convince himself. "Even if he had, there's no way for you to have heard about it by now. We're too far from the capitol. Word doesn't travel that fast in the outer villages."

"Not for everyone, no. But they can't hear the Voice, like I can."

Now it was Abner's turn to laugh. "Finally fallen off

the deep end, have you? I suppose it was only a matter of time. Perhaps you could ask the voices to afflict someone a little smaller?" he gestured with his cane to the Baron's considerable bulk. "They'd do far less damage with a squirrel or maybe even an… ox."

"Voices?" Von Ulric said, sounding amused. "No. I don't hear 'voices,' Mr. Frum. I hear *a* Voice. *The* Voice. You've read the books, you know the tales. You are an educator. So educate me. Is it a product of insanity or of destiny when one is visited by a Voice of Fate?"

Brows lowered in wary scrutiny, Abner took an unconscious step backward. "A Voice of Fate? Visit you? Preposterous."

"Ever the skeptic. It brought me to your doorstep. It told me the truth about Marshall's dearly-departed father. It has set me on the path to recovering the Scepter of the Ancients. If I had been visited by anything else, Mr. Frum, I wouldn't be here."

Abner shook his head. "You don't know what you're talking about."

"Perhaps you could accompany me to my ship and verify my claim."

Again, Abner shook his head, much more adamantly than before. "No. No, I'm not going anywhere with you."

"My apologies, I must have phrased that poorly." Von Ulric lifted a hand in false benevolence and stepped into the light for the first time. A gray-black gargoyle whose ashen fur bristled around a neck that seemed bent in perpetual hunger or hate, the Baron's voice was low but titanic as he brought his face near Abner's and growled, "*I wasn't asking.*"

≈

"I still can't believe you get to live here." Careful Steps tipped her head back to stare up at the distant ceiling in wonder. "If this building were any more ornate, the Queen herself would be obligated to own it."

"I don't *get* to live here, I *have* to," a slip of an otter whined from her bed on the far side of the room. Her breath was ragged, labored. She looked as though she'd have complained a little more emphatically if only she had the strength. But a coughing fit rattled her tiny ribs as if to say her concerns were misplaced, at best. "It sucks, but I won't be stuck here forever. Dad says he's going to fix everything."

C.S. clinked her claws against one of a dozen exotic trinkets atop the dresser and rolled her eyes. "Dads always say that."

"He'll do it, though. Just you see."

The little raccoon swiveled on her chair, preparing to scoff out a remark about the reliability of noble parents. She stopped herself when she saw the much younger otter staring out of the window at the stars, looking so small, so lonely.

"I'm sure you're right," C.S. said at last, hopping from the chair and bounding across the room to sit closer to the sick girl. Maybe her impression of the otter's absent parents was unfair.

But she doubted it.

While the girl had never actually said anything about being of noble birth, C.S. could read between the lines with the best of them. This was the best care facility in the known world. It was as expensive as it was elite; the only hope for those with incurable diseases. That didn't change the fact that her parents had abandoned her here, out of sight, so their lives could continue unburdened by her condition.

The lousy truth was that only noblemen solved a problem by throwing money at it.

C.S. looked up to realize that the girl was staring at her apologetically.

"You don't have to keep coming here, you know," she said.

"I don't have to, I want to." The raccoon smiled cheekily. "You're like the baby sister I never had. Besides, you aren't nearly as depressing as you think you are." She plopped a small bag of candied nuts on the bedside table and ruffled the fur atop the otter's tiny head. "I'd better get going. My boss will kill me if I'm late."

"That's a lot funnier when it's a joke." The otter's concern was evident in her voice.

"It'll be fine." C.S. waved a hand in exasperation. "I know what I'm doing. Seriously, you're as bad as my mother would probably be, if I had one. Now, get some sleep. It's late."

The otter gave a weak smile and watched her friend leave through the back window with a farewell flick of her tail.

When the raccoon was gone, the sick girl turned to eye the darker corners of her room with a growing sense of unease. She could swear she felt the shadows moving.

Then, one of the shadows did just that.

In the moonlit wisp of flitting curtains, a cloaked figure stepped toward her bed. An intruder bearing hat and blade.

McKinley the Marauder.

The tiny otter sat bolt upright, as if to scream.

Instead, what escaped her mouth was a groan of irritation.

"Daaaad, were you spying on me *again*?!"

"What?" McKinley held up his hands innocently. "I was just waiting for your friend to leave, I swear. Can't have me scaring off visitors, can you?"

She rolled her eyes, but smiled all the same. "I don't think even you could scare her, dad."

"True enough." He lifted a brow and shot a glance to the window through which C.S. had disappeared. "She seems incorrigible that way. Reminds me of me at that age." In a single, smooth motion, the Marauder scraped a chair along the floor, flipped it about on one leg, and parked it alongside her bed. Seating himself, he wrapped both arms gingerly around his daughter and hugged her as tightly as he dared. "Maya, my dear, I've missed you so much!"

"I missed you too." She huddled against his chest. "Where have you been?"

"Silliest thing, really," he explained in an exaggerated 'pirate' voice. "Oi've been a-searchin' th' world fer me burrrried treasure, and ye know wot?"

"What?" Maya giggled.

"Daft ole poirate Oi am, Oi plumb fergot that Oi left it roight 'ere!" He tickled her sides as if to say there was gold in her gullet, then abruptly snapped his fingers. "Oh, that reminds me! I was away for more than a week. So, my darling, per our long-standing agreement, I come bearing gifts."

With a flick of his hand, he popped a perfect little seashell into the air.

He smiled when Maya caught it.

She was almost as quick as her father.

"It's so pretty." Turning it over in her tiny palms, Maya's appreciative grin turned to one of delight when it glinted in the moonlight like a gemstone.

The Marauder waved a dismissive hand. "What, this old thing? My cute little assumer, you're getting caught up in the wrapping paper. The real present is trapped inside." She gave him a skeptical glance, and then a smile when he protested. "No, really! Pull up an ear and have a listen," he placed its open end alongside her ear and watched her eyes widen in wonder at the ocean-like sound it contained. "One night, while I was away, I caught this noise running rampant on the decks of my fine ship. It was as wild as it was wily, but it was also a rather soothing sound, as you can tell. A sort of natural lullaby with a pinch of salt. Thinking of my lovely daughter, I politely asked whether it would be so kind as to share itself with you, to sing you to sleep, a few nights out of the year. Unfortunately for *it*, it refused – not realizing that *no one* refuses me on my ship!" McKinley leapt to his feet and drew his sword, turning to strike a dramatic blow to the empty space at his back. "My dear, there was a battle the likes of which few could imagine. It lasted for three days and seven nights when finally I lassoed it with my cloak, wrestled it to the ground, and forced it inside this shell."

"Haha, you caught it?!"

Her father shrugged. "Well, most of it. Unfortunately for *me*, some of it escaped and is still lurking on the decks of my ship. And Fate knows I'll probably **never** get it to shut up after this. But at least now, whenever you're lonely, whenever you miss me, all you have to do is listen. And know that you are hearing the same thing I am hearing. Then maybe the world won't be so big. And I won't be so far away."

Maya was quiet for a long while, looking down at the glittering shell with a very different sort of smile and leaving McKinley to wonder whether – were she a little older, a little more capable of that unexplained sadness that goes hand in hand with comfort – he might have seen tears in her little eyes.

"Thank you, dad," she said at last, giving him an impish glance. "Not bad for a *daft ole poirate*."

At that, the Marauder laughed aloud. "Sheesh, you're cheeky! Can't imagine where you got that. Now, how are you doing?"

"I'm okay, but the nurses have been in a fuss lately."

McKinley placed the shell on the dresser alongside Maya's other treasures, each one a beautiful but harsh reminder of all the time he'd spent away from her. He frowned when he realized that one of the trinkets appeared to be missing. A bracelet, unless his memory failed him.

It seemed Maya's friend was even more like him than he'd realized.

"Aren't nurses *always* fussy?" He tried to keep his voice light. There was no reason to upset her.

"Maybe a little," she laughed. "But this was different. Someone broke in."

McKinley tensed, the stolen trinket forgotten. "What happened?"

"Nothing, really," her lip protruded in confusion. "No one got hurt. They didn't even take very much, that was the weirdest part. Just some silly old candlestick. Still, the nurses were really bothered by it. Maybe I should share some of the ocean noise with them? To make them feel better?"

"Gasp!" The Marauder whipped about in a comic circle, clutching his hand to his heart as though he'd been struck, earning yet another giggle from his daughter. "You would divvy up that gorgeous lullaby between strangers?! For a candlestick?! Well I…! That's just…! Are you sure you've been taking your medicine? 'Cause that's just crazy talk, is what that is!"

Her giggling stopped on the instant.

"Yes, dad," she said a little too seriously. "I've been taking it. Honest, I have."

Lifting a dubious brow, McKinley folded his arms over his chest. "Uh-huh. You're too cute to be a rug, my darling, don't bother lying like one."

"It's just…" She wrung her hands. "Well, I have to take smaller portions now 'cause the nurses say it's nearly gone."

McKinley's arms fell to his sides. "Why don't they just buy more? They have the money, I've made sure of it."

Maya frowned. "They tried. The shipments from the Alchemists Guild aren't coming anymore and they keep turning the nurses away. I don't know why."

In the quiet that followed, the Marauder turned his back so that his daughter wouldn't see his expression darkening. "Well that's something I'll have to talk to them about."

"What about you?" She seemed desperate to change the subject. "Is your new plan working out?"

He turned back to her with a grin. "Amazingly, *yes*. I told you there was still a bit of magic left in this world. I'm going to find it. And when I do, my dear, it will make all of these trinkets seem like mothballs. You'll be well again – and free of this place forever, that's for sure."

"You swear?"

He placed one hand over his heart and one in the air as he vowed, "Pirates' honor."

"Pirates don't have any honor," she laughed.

McKinley did his best to look wounded. "This one does!"

"It's okay, dad, I believe you. And..." Maya hesitated. "And maybe then, once I'm better, I can be your daughter again?"

This time, McKinley's wounded expression was genuine. "You *are* my daughter," he said, more harshly than he meant. "You have *always been* my daughter."

She fell silent and stared at the floorboards.

Her father melted.

"Sweetheart." He sat on the edge of her bed and pulled her into his lap. "You understand why no one can know that I'm your father, don't you? It's just too dangerous."

Maya sighed. "For both of us. I know." They were quiet for a long while before she looked up at him with hopeful eyes and asked, "Dad, will you sing me to sleep?"

He pointed to the dresser. "But, that's why I brought you the seashell..."

"And it's lovely," she reassured, putting her hand in his. "But I want to hear a real song. The one mom used to sing when she tucked me in at night. I've almost forgotten the words." The sentence left her with a look of distress.

"Oh, my dear." McKinley's shoulders slumped a little as he put his chin atop her head. "I've nearly forgotten them, too. Do you remember the tune?"

Furrowing her tiny brow, Maya bit her lip and delved as far into memory as she could. At length, she started to hum a halting and uncertain refrain that eventually settled into something like a melody.

Recognizing a few of the notes, McKinley sang in an equally-faltering voice.

"I love you, my darling.
I love you, my girl.
I love you, my sunshine,
My starlight, my world.
And… and though you must go,
How I wish you could stay.
Rest your eyes, dear…
I… I…"

Through forgetfulness or emotion, McKinley's vocal tapered off until there were no more words, and Maya's melody hung alone on the air. She too was forced to end the song when her fragile ribs contracted in a coughing fit.

Her father held her through it, his eyes screwed shut against his daughter's pain.

When it passed, he kissed her forehead and whispered, "I'm going to fix you, my girl. I promise."

The brave smile she offered in return nearly dissolved him into tears.

"Don't worry, dad," she said. "I'm not broken yet."

They hugged then, carrying on with simple conversation, light-hearted banter, and fond farewells – each of them suppressing the gravity of the fear they plainly felt.

And, outside the hospital window, Careful Steps Kal swallowed similar emotions as she slipped away in the shadows, hoping neither of them would ever know just how much she'd overheard.

Or what that information might mean to her employer.

≈

The candlestick first. Yes, then the hammer.

The thief stood in his dinghy, tossing the contents of the canvas sack into the bay, one by one. He clapped his hands with glee as they sunk into the brine, those lovely shinies.

It was like rain falling to the ground.

Like candy from the sky.

They seemed pleased.

Ooh, a sword! That one had torn a hole in his sack. But nothing had spilled, nope. He'd been careful, as always. These things were important, they'd said. They wanted them, they'd said. So he couldn't risk losing them. Couldn't risk making them mad.

Almost there, they said. *We're almost done. A few more. Just a few.*

The robber giggled, kicking his old and bony feet on the floor of his raft and licking his lips. Done is good. Done is fun.

Turning his paddle in too-thin arms, he rowed farther from the bay. Even with the mist forming an impenetrable cloud on the water, he wasn't worried. They'd show him where to go.

Besides, they needed him. They wanted more shinies. And something else.

Something exciting.

He whistled a sailor's tune, cutting it with spastic mutterings and laughter as he made his way into the night, toward Pelham Point.

≈

Stepping back from his neatly-stacked display of poultices and potions, the shopkeeper gave a satisfied grin. He was still admiring his handiwork when the window exploded with an earsplitting *crash*!

Poultices and poultice-maker alike fell to the ground, the latter looking up in shock and dismay as McKinley stepped from the sill and dusted of his hands.

"Hi, Tom." The Marauder smiled casually and jabbed his thumb to the window, where the potions had been. "I realize you probably don't get many compliments in your line of work, but *that* was a lovely display. Truly. I can't tell you how much I love it when things shatter in neat succession like that. It's just... well, it's beautiful." Glass crunching beneath his feet, he hefted a nearby stool and hurled it through a second display over the beaver's shoulder. "I couldn't help but notice that your door was locked, though. In fact, according to your neighbors, it's been that way for several months now. And here I thought the Alchemists Guild went to such great lengths to ensure their shops were available at all hours. The Apothecaries too, for that matter. Seems a bit strange, doesn't it? To put such effort into a shop that never opens?" Voice still light, he swiped his arm along the counter, breaking beakers, vases, and vials before turning to the shopkeeper and asking, "So, what's the deal, Tom? Why is the Guild suddenly refusing service to the good citizens of Secora Tor?"

"I... we... " the beaver sputtered, making no attempt to rise from the floor. "We've had a... a complication in our supply lines. It... it was a theft! Surely you've heard about the increase in regional thefts, right? We've... we've been hit very hard, I'm afraid, so we can't afford to open our doors just now. But, but if you need something personally, we can always make an exception! A simple balm, perhaps? Maybe a nice bag of herbs for your travels?"

"A balm?" The Marauder pulled up short, twisting his mouth in irritation and moving to stand over the terrified beaver. "A *balm*? Me? Why would I need that? Do I look ill? Are you implying that *I look ill*?!"

"No! Not at all!" The shopkeeper lifted a hand in a hasty gesture, as if to shield himself.

"A bit warty, perhaps?! Does the *color of my fur offend you*?!"

"That's not what I meant, Mr. Marauder, I swear!"

McKinley raised his eyebrow and pointed an accusatory finger. "I certainly hope it isn't. 'Cause that wouldn't be very polite now would it, Tom?"

"No, sir, I meant nothing by it, sir! You look perfectly healthy!" His voice reached to desperate heights. "Uh, uh - dashing, even! A prime example of your species!"

Standing erect, McKinley straightened his cloak and sniffed. "Dashing. Yes. I like that. Couldn't have said it better myself. Here's the thing though, Tom. May I call you Tom?"

"Uh," the beaver stammered. "M-my name is Barlos, sir."

The Marauder waved his hand as though he hadn't heard and didn't care, "The thing is, Tom. I happen to know for a fact that your supplies are carried to you by sea. That's *my* turf, you understand. And nothing happens on *my* turf without *my* say-so. Thus, therefore, and thusly, if your inventory had in fact been stolen in transit..." He pressed his face close to Barlos' and wrapped a less-than-friendly arm around his shoulders. "I'd know about it."

"It... it's the truth, sir..." the beaver managed to say. "It really is. Maybe... maybe you just weren't paying attention?"

With a finger-wag of disapproval, McKinley stepped over the shopkeeper, drew his sword, and cut down the silk curtain separating the primary shop from the well-stocked storage area. "No, Tom. I pay attention. Enough to know that a certain overly-ambitious and terrifyingly-large Baron recently dumped a great deal of money into the Alchemists Guild. Why, he practically bought you up, along with the Apothecaries, and every other Guild-affiliated outlet in the capitol. Even the Farmers Guild. Can you believe that? The *Farmers Guild*. A lot of fat fingers in a lot of pointless pies, that one. If I didn't know any better, I'd say Von Ulric was appropriating capitol resources for himself, putting the squeeze on Secora's easiest targets and weakening the kingdom's ability to fight back when he starts his little war. But, I mean, I'm just a pirate. What do I know? What do you think, Tom?" He put his finger on the tip of his blade, as if to test the edge. "Do think carefully before you respond."

The shopkeeper held his gaze for a long time. "Please... you don't understand."

"*Make* me understand, Tom."

"My name is Barlos!" the beaver yelled aloud in frustration before he could think better of it. When McKinley turned to him with a cold stare, Barlos sagged in contrition, averting his eyes.

"I know your name." The Marauder's voice changed, carrying a low, hard edge that made an odd companion to his otherwise-jovial face. "As I said, I pay attention. But if I say your name, and then I have to hurt you, it makes it seem personal. And we don't want things to get personal, do we?"

Barlos took a long, slow breath. "I'm afraid of you, Mr. Marauder. I am. But the Baron... he's... he's so much more. I can't defy him, I can't. And I won't tell you anything. He's much scarier than you'll ever be."

McKinley very slowly sheathed his sword. His footsteps like the ticking of an ominous clock, he crossed the floor and lifted the beaver gently but firmly by his lapels. "Oh, Barlos. I really wish you hadn't said that. Because now, my next move? It's gonna seem so very predictable."

Without so much as a grunt of effort, the Marauder's hands shot forward and Barlos flew against the back wall. Two daggers, thrust through his fine silk coat just above the shoulders, halted his descent to the floor. He cried aloud in shock and kicked his legs, searching for purchase.

"I do so *hate* being predictable." McKinley scraped a stool across the floor and sat down, propping his feet up on an overturned cabinet and producing a third dagger from beneath his cloak. He flipped it deftly from blade to handle, handle to blade, until he was certain he had Barlos' full attention. "Truth be told, my guileless, guilded friend, I don't give a single barmy ballyhoo what the Baron's plans are. Because I don't care who runs this blasted kingdom, in the end. But when nobles like *you*, with your Guilds and your greed and your politics, get in the way of distributing desperately needed medications to places like, say, the children's hospital? Down by the wharf? Well, that kinda thing just…" Eyes on the opposite end of the room, McKinley threw the dagger as he spoke. It *thunked* into the wall over Barlos' head, separating a tuft of fur from his scalp. "It really rubs me the wrong way, you know?"

Barlos crossed his eyes to stare in disbelief at the knife handle. "The children's hospital?" he gasped. "That's what this is about?"

"I didn't say that." McKinley drew yet another dagger. "Did I say that?"

"No, no!" Barlos shook his head emphatically. "I was just jumping to conclusions, I'm sorry!"

"Pfft, a children's hospital, really? Look at me, Barlos. I'm a pirate, for Fate's sake. What do I care about a children's hospital? But, now that you bring it up…" he said the last part quickly. "You really shouldn't be putting your greed before the welfare of helpless kids, should you? I mean, I'm all for shifting loyalties, but that's… well, that's just awful. So, here's what you're going to do. You're going to resume shipments to that sainted place, even if you have to personally smuggle the vials beneath the Baron's very nose, one by one. Savvy?"

"Or what?" he whimpered. "You'll kill me?"

McKinley squared his shoulders in indignation. "What? No, for crying out loud, why does everyone always ask that? But I *will* feel obligated to inform the Baron that you've been supplying excess medications to Secora's standing armies. Which, I suppose, is as good as killing you."

Barlos shuddered at the thought. "He wouldn't believe

you."

McKinley smiled and hefted an intact box of herbs, one bearing the official stamp – not only of the Alchemists Guild – but of Barlos' individual outlet. "Wouldn't he, now?"

The beaver swallowed, knowing full well that the Marauder had him by the teeth.

"All right," he said at last. "I'll… I'll have the next round of meds to the hospital tomorrow morning."

"You'll do it tonight."

"Yes, tonight, that's what I meant."

He stood and slapped Barlos lightly on the cheek. "Good man! I knew you'd come around." Pulling his daggers from the shopkeeper's clothing, McKinley watched him tumble to the floor in an unceremonious heap, then knelt at the beaver's side, tightening his grip on the daggers in either hand. "Just remember… should you ever again decide to line your pockets on the backs of the small or the sick, I *will* be back. And then, Barlos, my friend, I might actually be forced to do some damage to this place."

With a disarming smile and a tip of his hat, the Marauder leapt again to the windowsill.

The beaver pulled himself from the floor with shaky knees and an even shakier voice. "Wait. Why? Why all of this concern? From a *pirate*?"

McKinley swept his gaze over the demolished shop and puffed his chest. "Consider it my good deed for the day."

Outside the shop, the Marauder waited in the shadows, out of sight, until the shopkeeper had gathered his supplies and set out for the hospital, true to his word. When Barlos was gone, McKinley leaned his head back against the cold stone of the building, letting out a breath of frustration before sagging forward in the darkness, feeling at once burdened and deflated.

Then, a movement in the fog.

A wisp of light.

Was someone there?

Pushing himself away from the wall, he stared down the street at a faint blue haze that flickered back and forth, like a firefly shrouded in smoke. He could swear he heard a tune, as of someone singing…

"I love you, my sunshine…
My starlight…
My world…. "

"Is someone there?" McKinley demanded aloud, hand on sword.

Upon the instant, sound and light both disappeared. The otter pirate shook his head, as if to clear it of demons.

"You're losing it, Mad Dog," he chided himself. "Jumping at shadows."

With a final, uncertain glance to the fog, he turned to the West, destined for a hidden inlet where his ship would be waiting to grant him rest and ale.

He clearly needed a bit of both.

≈

The Baron made no attempt to hide his purpose in Vernos.

Openly, through central streets, his company marched with the town's most important person in chains. Elder Frum stumbled in the darkness, screaming for help at every darkened window, a sudden and helpless prisoner of the Baron's wills. And no one dared lift a finger against it.

Staring up at the wolf's monstrous back, however, Abner couldn't really blame them.

"Why are you taking me?" He demanded in the strongest voice he could muster. "I'm nothing to you. Just an old man who once mentored someone important."

"Perhaps." The Baron shrugged his massive shoulders. "Or perhaps you're something more. I will know soon enough."

"This is isn't like you, Von Ulric," Abner said. "You've always been power-hungry. But never insane."

The Baron did not turn. He didn't laugh. He didn't growl. Eyes fixed on the road ahead, he made his way to the docks without speaking, and Abner was forced to follow on the tip of a sword. The old badger hesitated, even stumbled when he saw the ship itself. Whatever he might have been expecting, this streamlined vessel of understated elegance, light weaponry, and ebony wood certainly wasn't it.

"Is something wrong, Mr. Frum?" The wolf spoke over his shoulder as they boarded.

"I'm just... surprised by your ship, is all. It seems rather small for..." He looked up at the Baron's considerable bulk. "Someone like you."

"That's because it isn't *his* ship," a voice fell down from the rear of the ship. "It's mine."

Abner turned to see a long-limbed coyote descending the stairs. She was thin and scarred, with heavy bracelets on either arm and a coin-edged scarf on hips and head alike. "Do not be so quick to dismiss small things. Even tiny teeth are lethal, when the bite is well-placed."

She spoke with an accent that Abner recognized as Kathkan.

The Baron had allied himself with an empire of slavers.

"Lady Sira," Von Ulric acknowledged her with a slight tip of his muzzle – a gesture of formality, not of fealty.

Sliding a delicate claw beneath the Elder's chin, Lady Sira examined him, then lifted a dubious brow. "This is the one? Truly?"

The Baron shrugged slowly, as if to say it hardly mattered.

"Well now it is my turn to be surprised." Abruptly, she pulled her claw from beneath his chin. "You're rather frail for someone so..." She waved her hands as though searching for the right word, settling at last on, "*Necessary.*"

"What do you mean?" the old badger demanded. "Why am I even here?"

"Wait." Von Ulric's eyes were fixed on the fog.

"But I don't—" Abner tried to protest and found himself silenced by a raise of Von Ulric's hand.

"Just... wait."

At length, the fog began to close on the ship. It whirled and shifted like a living creature, casting about like a blind whelp until it could moor itself to something solid. Then a faint light rose from the water, just off the bow, and flickered its way onto the ship. Abner shied away as wisps of the light reached to touch his face, but found himself held fast by Lady Sira's guards.

He closed his eyes and winced at the sensation of ice-cold hands and a voice that echoed around him, whispering out an accusation that sounded more like a name.

"*Old blood....*"

When he opened his eyes, the light was gone, and the mists were still once more.

Von Ulric smiled, showing spear-like teeth. "The Voice confirms it. You're just what we were looking for, Mr. Frum."

The Elder's mouth hung open in shock. "The Voice? Is that what you said? Bloody destiny, Von Ulric, do you think that... that... *thing* is a Voice of Fate?!"

"Take him below," the Baron ordered Sira's men, ignoring the Elder's cries of distress.

"No! Please, you have to listen to me!" The Elder looked from one crewman to another, desperately pleading to any who could hear. "Please, you don't understand! You don't know what this is! Lady Sira! *ANYONE!*"

Expressionless, the lithe coyote watched him with a careful eye as he was dragged to the lower decks, where he would be gagged and caged like so many before him.

But not before his final cry rose up to echo throughout the ship.

"*He's going to kill us all!*"

4
LIGHTHOUSE / MADHOUSE

It would be an understatement to say that Eadric was not well-liked. Since gaining passage on the *Albatross*, the queen's advisor had dismissed his quarters as unsatisfactory, the crew as incompetent, and the captain himself as a poor conversationalist and dinner companion. A suspicious person might think he was going out of his way to alienate everyone around him, but the truth was that the insufferable bird couldn't help it. He'd spent years cultivating a cloud of haughtiness. It served him well in a world where scholars were seen as the gatekeepers of history, whose disdain, disregard, or general malaise could prompt a less-than-favorable footnote on a person's permanent legacy. What he hadn't realized was that neither ship nor sailor gave a crab's leg what future generations might have to say about their importance. They had a job to do. And Eadric, for the most part, was putting himself in the way.

"Marshall." The kookaburra chirped abruptly as he came to a clumsy landing on the rail near Marshall's arm. "I demand that the imposter who calls himself a cook be put off this ship, post-haste."

Lieutenant Ryder joined her captain in staring through the fog at the approaching coastline. "He's making demands now, is he?"

"Post-haste, no less." Marshall arched an irritated brow.

Eadric sniffed and puffed his feathers. "Go ahead, make light of a serious matter. But I know what happens on these ships. And I'm telling you, that galley of yours is a health hazard just waiting to happen. When I expressed these concerns to your cook, he had me removed and barred from – and I quote – '*his kitchens.*' Can you imagine the audacity?"

"Indeed I can," Marshall replied, stone-faced.

"Positive thoughts, sir," Ryder reminded in an equally-stoic tone.

"Were that not enough," the advisor went on as though he hadn't heard. "He outrageously believes that I should have to adhere to the navy's pedestrian system of rationing. I'm no commoner, Marshall. I'll not be treated as one."

"Certainly not," the captain said.

"For shame," Ryder agreed.

Eadric looked from one to the other until it finally sunk in that they were making fun of him. "Do you allow all of your people to behave so... *brazenly*... with those who are clearly above their station? Do they speak to you in this manner, as well?"

At that, Ryder turned to lean on the rail with a glare. "The captain has earned a little something called *due deference*, advisor. So we speak to him, ever and always, with the highest of respect. For example, were any of us to seek permission to hurl a certain pretentious windbag from the deck by his tail feathers, we would approach him with *sir* and leave with *please*. We're very well-mannered *pedestrians* that way."

Chirping in alarm, Eadric took a skittish hop back on the rail.

Marshall coughed, suppressing his amusement. "Positive thoughts, Lieutenant."

"Oh, the thought becomes more positive by the moment, sir." Her teeth glinted with every word.

"Captain." They were interrupted by a uniformed young fennec before the situation could escalate. "Helmsman says we're as close as we can draw to Pelham Point. Any farther and we put the *Albatross* at risk. Should we ready a raft from here, sir?"

Seeming grateful for the chance to answer an honest question, Marshall gave the ensign a nod. "That would be appreciated, Mr. Wexler."

With a final glare in Eadric's direction, Ryder turned and placed a hand on the hilt of her sword. "Sir, if you require a security escort…"

"Also appreciated, but unnecessary." Marshall waved a hand. "The Baron's forces haven't shown any interest in Pelham Point thus far. And by all accounts, this island only has one inhabitant – a doddering old commodore who watches after the lighthouse. I have some experience with the type. You may invite Commander Calum to join me ashore at his convenience, however."

"Aye, sir."

Ensign and Lieutenant both offered quick salutes and turned to their ordered duties.

When Eadric thought they were beyond earshot, he sidled closer to Marshall on the rail, tipped his beak in the fennec's direction, and whispered, "About your young ensign… Far be it for me to condemn your tolerance of the commoner species, Marshall, but a fox? Don't you think it quite imprudent to have one of his kind aboard? Pirates may consider them lucky, but foxes of any species are unpredictable and ambiguous, even in the best of circumstances. They're not to be trusted, Marshall. I would think that you, of all people, would know better."

Ryder and Wexler turned on the instant. Wexler's ears drooped in embarrassment, while Ryder looked for all the world as though she was fighting to keep her hand away from her sword.

Once again, the hard-of-hearing bird had misjudged the superior abilities of those around him.

With controlled movements, Captain Marshall clasped his hands behind his back and pulled himself upright, drawing a too-calm breath. "I, of all people?"

Oblivious to their reactions, Eadric shrugged, "Well, yes. As a well-educated member of... of..." Seeing the glint of steel in Marshall's eye, he trailed off and looked around the deck, having finally noticed that all work had ceased. Every topside member of the crew now stood facing him in a stance that – while not precisely threatening – bristled with anger and expectation.

Several long moments followed in which Eadric seemed as uncomfortable as he'd likely ever been in his life.

"Marshall," Now speaking in something of a stage whisper, he cleared his throat in an attempt to explain, "My intentions were simply to compliment your... broadmindedness. It's uncustomary, certainly, but that's not to say that it isn't admirable..."

Again, the advisor's sentence fell away as the whole of the crew took a step toward him.

From the other side of the deck, Ryder placed a protective hand on Wexler's shoulder and seethed, "We can still hear you, Eadric."

He parted his beak to reply, but the captain cut him off with the mere tilt of his head. "Enough. That the Scholars Guild would see fit to promote someone like you does not surprise me. They are rather fond of empty hierarchies, and prejudice plays into that notion all too well. But I still find myself puzzled by the queen's decision to place you on board my ship. Remind me again, Advisor, why are you here?"

He hesitated, seeming reluctant to speak. "Well... primarily... because the queen believed someone should be present to record your journey."

"And, in your time as a scholar, has no one bothered to instruct you on the differences between recording and inciting?" Eadric looked as though he were about to respond, but Marshall stopped him with an even tone. "Then allow me to assist. One includes a great deal of purpose-driven writing and little else. The other includes a great deal of pointless speech and little else. I'm sure you can suss out for yourself which is which. To help you remember, I will ask that you practice only one of them at a time. Bear in mind that the queen's instructions were on the recording end, so choosing to practice its alternate would probably be ill-advised."

Aghast, Eadric puffed his feathers and made an awkward squawking sound as if in protest. "What's this? You're disallowing me from *talking*?"

When the captain turned to face him directly, Eadric flinched at the look in his eyes. "Indeed, that is precisely what I'm doing. It's become apparent that you're not ready for the burden of decency, and it seems rather unfair to foist your inadequacies onto the rest of the crew, don't you think?"

"But Marshall…"

"*Captain*," Marshall corrected evenly. Were it not for the intensity in his eyes, he might have been speaking of afternoon tea. "Unlike the titles bestowed upon noblemen simply for being, it is one I worked hard to attain. I expect you to use it."

"I…" Eadric averted his eyes. "Yes… Captain."

"Most excellent. Should we return safely to Secora Tor, you may resume your self-importance at your leisure. But out here, the *Albatross* is a sovereign nation. *No one* outranks me. So when I ask you to hold your tongue, you will do so. And you will treat each and every member of my crew with the respect that they have earned, or this will be a very difficult voyage for you indeed. Do you understand?"

Eadric's expression had changed. He looked as though he hadn't heard much beyond a single phrase. "*Should* we return? What do you mean *should*?"

Apparently it hadn't occurred to the sedentary advisor that anything could actually go wrong on an expedition such as this.

Content to leave Eadric's fears unanswered, Marshall turned from the prow. "Ensign Wexler, would you be so kind as to surrender your duties to the advisor for the day? If his purpose is to record our activities, it would be a shame to deny him a personal look at what it takes to earn one's keep aboard an honest vessel."

Wexler saluted, while Ryder smiled ominously and offered, "Sir, I'd like to oversee this particular detail, if I may."

"Brilliant suggestion." The captain turned to Eadric. "What do you think, Advisor?"

The bird looked from Marshall to Ryder and back again, sputtering incoherently, "I... well I... but... "

Pivoting in smooth military fashion, Marshall walked away and concluded for him, "He'd be thrilled."

Ryder bumped Wexler's shoulder with her elbow in a friendly show of support that made his ears perk forward at last.

"Thrilled?" She laughed. "Why, he looks positively inspired."

≈

In his cabin, Marshall closed the door and shook his head. His dedication to the queen notwithstanding, he could easily see fit to maroon Eadric on the rocks of the Manus with limited rations and a compass he likely couldn't read.

Winged or not, it would be a rough flight back to the capitol if he couldn't find his way.

Grabbing his overcoat from the back of a chair,

Marshall flinched at the unexpected *clank* of something dropping to the floor from his pocket. It clattered from his field of sight before he could see what it was.

One knee on the floor, he stooped beside the desk and saw his father's compass lying in the shadows beneath, tipped on its side as though facing him.

When he reached for it, the needle began to spin.

Marshall recoiled.

He felt the temperature in the room drop and looked around for an open window, but all were closed as tightly as when he'd entered.

Chiding himself, he drew a steadying breath, which he inadvertently held as he knelt again and reached for the still-spinning compass. With some coaxing at the tips of his fingers, he managed to finagle it close enough to reach, though its edges made a rather horrid scraping sound when he pulled it across the floor. As it drew closer, the needle began to spin even faster, unnerving him. He released his held breath and it fogged up the glass. Then, abruptly, the needle stopped. Quite against his better judgment, Marshall looked to the right, where the needle was pointing.

And, from beneath his desk, he saw the faint outline of bare feet.

"*...Son of Masguard.*"

In a burst of instinctive movement, Marshall rolled away from the desk and onto his feet, sword drawn, ready for anything.

The compass skittered across the floor in the opposite direction.

But the room was empty.

Muscles still tense, Captain Marshall pulled himself upright and sheathed his sword. In slow, deliberate strides, he moved to pick up the compass – which sat harmlessly against the wall, back to its normal state of brokenness, as though nothing at all had happened. He turned it over in his hand, then gave a second, sweeping glance to the room and donned his coat.

The mystery be drowned.

He had duties to perform.

≈

"You'll never take me alive, I say!"

Marshall flinched at the sound of glass breaking against the interior of the locked cottage door.

"Commodore!" he somehow managed to yell over the racket. "I am a captain with the queen's navy! I mean you no harm – I simply wish to speak with you!"

A string of squawks and curses burst through the boarded windows in response, but the door remained solidly bolted. Exhaling in frustration, Marshall returned his politely-removed hat to his head and squinted up at the adjoining lighthouse.

Maybe he should have brought that security escort after all.

"Has he threatened to blow it up yet?" Commander Gray Calum gestured to the building in broad amusement as he approached.

"Not yet," Marshall replied with a roll of his eyes. "But I do have his firmest assurances that members of a covert military alliance have coded the beacon to transmit messages into outer space."

Gray scratched the fur beneath his chin and stymied an outright laugh. "I'm assuming he can prove this?"

"He'll swallow the evidence if we make any attempts at force." Marshall nodded as if to stress the gravity of the situation. "I take it the two of you have met?"

"I've had the misfortune once or twice, yes. My aunt treated him for a broken wing a while back. It was several years ago, but you might say it made an impression." He paused and lifted a hand to the ongoing ruckus. "I'm sure you can see why."

Marshall raised an eyebrow. "You might have warned

me."

"I *would* have if you hadn't shoved off in such an all-fired hurry," Gray countered in false indignation.

"I had no choice." Marshall squared his shoulders. "One more minute with Her Majesty's advisor and I'd have been threatening to blow up the lighthouse."

"I sympathize, sir. How any member of a species with the word 'kook' in their name can act so haughty is beyond me. But leaving him with Ryder? She may eat him."

The captain shrugged. "One can always hope."

Tipping their heads back to examine the full height of the building, the two sighed over their current predicament.

"Are you..." Gray was the first to break the silence, but his words were hesitant. "Are you certain that's the only reason you were in a rush, sir? Getting away from Eadric?"

Marshall shot a quick, noncommittal glance from the corner of his eye. "Would there be another reason?"

"Well, I don't know, sir. You just seemed a little perturbed when you left your cabin, is all."

With a thoughtful sniff, Marshall turned to face his first officer directly. "And you seemed likewise agitated when you came from below decks. What were you doing down there, Commander?"

Now it was Gray's turn to shift his eyes. "I... nothing worth noting, sir. I was just taking care of something, is all. Forget I mentioned it."

"Very well." Marshall's scrutiny disappeared on the instant as he jutted his jaw to the cottage door. "Are you ready, then?"

"For?"

"An attempt at force, naturally."

Gray laughed, "Oh, you know me, sir. I only took this job so I could knock things down. On three?"

"One." Marshall began in lieu of agreement, standing calmly as his first officer dug in his feet.

"Two." They counted together.

On "Three!" they launched themselves forward in unison, slamming their full weight against the cottage door. It exploded inward with a *crash* that stunned even the overexcited Commodore into silence. Marshall carried his momentum into an expert roll that brought him to his feet while Gray struggled to make heads or tails of up. By the time he managed to pull himself from the floor, his captain had already brushed clean his uniform and now stood staring pointedly at a particular cluster of shadows in the rafters overhead.

"You can come down from there," Marshall said. "We mean you no harm."

For the longest time, the only response came in the form of ruffling feathers and creaking wood. Then there was a loud squawk of irritation as the monocle-wearing gull dropped to a lower beam for a better look. He stretched and strained his neck, quirking his head in rapid movements to eye them up and down.

"Rubbish!" The Commodore stomped his feet and screamed at last. "You mean me no harm? Broken down my door, you have! Come bearing weapons! Lies! Get out!"

"Calm down, you suspicious old bird." Gray stepped forward and gestured to his uniform. "As you can see, we're seafaring soldiers – *of course* we're armed. And the door was your fault. If you'd let us in when first we arrived…"

"You look familiar," the gull interrupted with an accusing glare, hopping closer on the beam and tipping until he was practically upside down. "Have you tried to kill me before?"

Holding his gaze, Gray slumped in a heavy sigh. "No, Commodore." His words came out in tired monotone. "I've never tried to kill you."

"You must be thinking of his aunt," Marshall supplied with a hint of amusement in his voice.

His helpful statement must have triggered a memory, for the Commodore erupted from his beam in alarm, crying, "Not the surgeon!"

Marshall raised his eyebrow in his first officer's direction.

"As I said, she fixed his wing," Gray tried to explain, seeming both baffled and embarrassed. "Loony up there fell out of a window and refused to flap his left wing. Just the left one, mind you."

"*There was a grasshopper on it!*" The Commodore shouted indignantly, as though grasshoppers were sufficient explanation for anything at all.

Marshall and Calum shared a look of consternation.

Suddenly, Her Majesty's advisor didn't seem so bad.

"Commodore." Marshall's authoritative tone sought to bring an end to the madness. "I can promise you that we are here on an honest errand. Neither of us poses any threat to you, your cottage, or your lighthouse. We were led here by an artifact. The Key to Mosque Hill. Surely you've heard of it?"

At the mention of the Key, the gull shifted, turning to eye them warily over one shoulder as he stammered, "Key? What? No... no I... I haven't done anything wrong."

"No one is suggesting that." Captain Marshall lifted his hand in a calming gesture.

"And what else can be suggested by the presence of the queen's men?!"

Gray's exhalation was more of a low growl. "Dash it all, Commodore, you professed to being a queen's man once too, don't you remember? You had duty and purpose, and if there is any of it remaining in that scrambled egg you call a head, then you'll help us."

"What, what?" The bird whirled on them. "No... Rubbish! Lies and rubbish! You can't have it!"

With that, the Commodore pelted them with a volley of woodchips and rafter dust. When they crouched to protect themselves from the assault, he dropped from the rafters, snapped open his wings, and darted over their heads into the adjacent lighthouse, locking the door at his back.

Dusting themselves off yet again, the two stood and sighed.

"Well, I think it's safe to say he knows something."

Marshall nodded in partial agreement, drawing his fine sword and turning for the door. Hefting a chair with his free hand, he brought it crashing down on the handle and simultaneously planted his foot in the center of the door. It gave way with a splintering sound, dropping the doorknob to the floor beneath his feet. The open-beaked Commodore stared up at him with wide eyes – too stunned to react before the captain grabbed him by the ascot and hoisted him from the ground without any effort at all.

The entire display couldn't have lasted more than a second.

"I regret that our exchange has taken this turn, Commodore. As I have said – three times now – we didn't come here to harm you. But I'm afraid your paranoid fears have spawned something of a self-fulfilling prophecy. You see, my queen and my kingdom will soon be in jeopardy. We came here to put a stop to it. And whatever it is that you know regarding the Key, the Gateway, or the location of Mosque Hill may be enough to prevent the downfall of a civilization. I cannot believe that you are so dedicated to your delusions that you would risk the fate of Secora simply to prove their efficacy. So I will ask you for the final time to calm down and give us a chance at a civil conversation before this goes any further." Though Marshall's sword was held loosely in his hand with the point to the floor, the slight tension in the muscle of his arm was enough to add, *I will use this, if I must.*

The commodore's eyes flitted to the sword. After a minute or so of pointless struggle, the bird tipped his beak in frightened compliance and Marshall lowered him onto the lighthouse stairs. He couldn't help but notice that the gull had fallen still, his gaze fixed on the chain and bit of metal protruding from Marshall's coat. With careful movements, the captain sheathed his sword and pulled his father's medallion from the inside of his vest.

"You're staring at this? You've seen this before?"

Quirking his head in an unreadable gesture, the commodore nodded.

Marshall's voice was strained. "Masguard was here?"

Again, the crazy bird nodded, this time reaching to brush the tarnished face of the pendant with wingtips that trembled in anxiety or reverence. "It's you... you are the child of the Wanderer. The lonely prodigy." His eyes turned to Marshall with a new respect. "Masguard's son."

Calum took an unconscious step back.

Marshall didn't move an inch.

"That news shouldn't have reached you yet," the commander objected. "Marshall's own crew hasn't even been told."

"Masguard," Marshall concluded. "My father told you to watch for me, didn't he? That you would know me by this medallion? He knew I would come."

"Yes," the gull nodded. "Knew you would come. Had to be you. *No one else to follow, for none will make the choice. Many more will search in vain, but one will heed the Voice.*" The commodore gave an uncomfortable shudder. "You are the one. The only one who can find it."

Marshall furrowed his brow. "Find what? The Gateway?"

In lieu of a response, the Commodore began to cough.

Then to regurgitate.

Though the captain seemed unperturbed, Gray averted his eyes and tried not to look disgusted.

"Are you alright?" Marshall asked. Surely he hadn't gripped the nutter's neck *that* hard?

But the Commodore looked neither pained nor embarrassed when he turned to them and hiccuped, a saliva-coated key in his outstretched wing.

"Oh, for crying out loud," the commander gagged and muttered beneath his breath. "He really *did* swallow the evidence."

Lifting a brow in Calum's direction, Marshall sighed and plucked the key from the slime with careful fingers. The Commodore turned to the stair at his back. There, he scratched furiously at one of the boards with clawed feet. After a great deal of effort, he hopped to a higher stair and gestured, having managed to pry the board loose.

"He left this." The gull hiccupped again. "Masguard. Left it for you."

When Marshall made no move to look, the Commodore frowned, flew behind him, and pushed. Though the bird was less than half his bodyweight, and nowhere near strong enough to move him by force, the captain stepped forward out of courtesy, earning a grin of spurious accomplishment from his host. Stooping to the step, he saw a small, latched chest, covered in dust. He brushed it off and lifted it to the stair above, where he placed the key in the lock and then pulled back, hesitant.

All around him were signs that these steps had scarcely been touched in more than a decade – the rusted metalwork, the cracks in the mortar. The commodore had no need of them. Nor did anyone else, for that matter, because no one ever came here.

No one, except Masguard.

The last person to kneel on this stair, over this chest, was his father.

Closing his eyes and drawing a deep breath, Marshall turned the key until it clicked in the lock.

"He wanted you to have it," the Commodore said as Marshall drew the map out of the chest and into the light. "Only you. Said you would need it, when you came. Wanted you to know where to find him."

It was that last sentence which caught the captain off-guard.

"What?" Marshall whipped around, map and chest forgotten on the stair behind him. "*What are you talking about?*" He stepped forward, his words insistent and determined in a way that made his earlier display seem weak, at best. The commodore fell back, butting himself against the shattered doorway, squawking and staring with wide eyes. At a gesture from Calum, Marshall drew himself upright and continued with a forced sense of calm, "Are you saying this map will take me to Masguard?"

Confused, the bird frowned. "No, the map will take you to Mosque Hill."

"Then…" Marshall seemed hesitant to ask. "Where is my father?"

At that, the commodore laughed and splayed his wings, as though the answer should have been obvious all along. "He is in your compass."

It took several moments for the disappointment to settle on Marshall's face. Then he swallowed and looked to the floor. Calum offered a nod of sympathy as the captain turned to gather map and chest alike, sparing an extra moment to return the displaced board to its proper location.

"Thank you for the map, Commodore." The stoic, military clip having returned to his voice, Marshall stood and tipped his head to the keeper of the lighthouse. "You have my word that we will put it to good use."

"Your use," the bird shrugged, seeming sad. "Your business. No more secrets. Don't care."

The captain gave him a long and searching look, then turned to take his leave. "Indeed, then. Farewell."

Commander Calum moved to follow, but paused to clap the gull on the back as he passed. "You see, Commodore. You had nothing to worry about. We're leaving Pelham Point intact. Well," he glanced quickly and apologetically at the damaged entryway, concluding with a wince, "*mostly* intact."

"Pelham Point?" The Commodore stopped in his

tracks, quirking his head and gazing up at the lighthouse in much the same way that Calum had looked at the shattered door. "Not Pelham Point anymore. No. This… this is Forever Isle."

≈

On the deck of the *Albatross*, Gray moved to stand alongside Marshall at the prow.

"Well. You just can't buy entertainment like that, can you?" He said. "The Commodore wasn't always like that, you know. According to my aunt, he was practically respectable once." He smiled, hoping for some sign that the captain was interested in sharing his amusement. When none came, he bowed his head and moved as if to leave, offering, "The chest is in your cabin, sir, whenever you're ready for it."

Marshall stopped him.

"Does the lighthouse seem odd to you, Commander?"

Gray returned to his side and followed his line of sight to the burning lamp of warning that cut through the fog in an odd rhythm.

The commander leaned on the rail and squinted in confusion. "That's not a normal rotation for the beam, is it?"

Marshall shook his head, watching, counting.

It was a code.

Gray couldn't help but shiver when the captain deciphered its message aloud.

"Snuff out… the… son."

Then the lighthouse exploded in a ball of fire.

5
WHAT THE FATHER KNOWS

"*BOOYA!*" Mckinley's maniacal shout came from above the ship like a call to insanity. When the wind whipped just so, he could be seen through the mists holding to the mast with only one hand. Here and there, he leaned into the crisp morning air and howled to the salty clouds with all the stability of a free-flying pinwheel.

Far below, the majority of the crew went about their work, completely accustomed to his behavior.

But one among them watched his display with a terrified sort of fascination, hands clenched to his chest in bewilderment.

"Now I see why they call him Mad Dog..." the scraggly possum shook his pale head.

A nearby trio of raccoons lifted their gruff voices in turn, correcting him.

"Don't EVER call him that."

"'Specially not to 'is face."

"HATES that name, 'e does."

The possum hadn't even realized he'd spoken aloud. Truth be told, he'd been so caught up in his spectatorship that he hadn't noticed them working alongside him at all.

"Um," he looked away self-consciously. "I wasn't really planning on it."

"Good lad," the tallest of the three complimented. "Now, the Marauder's good, if you're after a moniker in a pinch. You can call him that."

"LOVES that'un."

"Thinks 'e worked hard fer it."

Furrowing his brow, the possum again turned his attention to the mop in his hands. "It's neither here nor there, I suppose. Not like I'll have much call to talk to him face to face. If ever I do, I'll probably stick with calling him *Captain*."

"*Cap'n*," the eldest confirmed. "Safe choice."

"Could always call him *sir*."

"Can't go wrong wi' *sir*."

"Shows respect."

"We never call 'im *sir*."

"'Cause we ain't respectful, is we?"

The tallest waved his hands at the two, shushing them. "You're new, aren't you, lad?"

Head spinning from the wall of words that seemed to hit him all at once, the possum forced himself to nod, but kept his eyes on the deck. "I'm Chimmy. Chimmy the Leech."

"Nice to meet you, Chimmy. My name's Lumber."

"Gil."

"Ormac."

Chimmy tipped his jaw in a weak greeting then tapped the bucket near his feet. "I, um, kinda have a lot of work to do here, guys."

Lumber chuckled, ignoring Chimmy's brush-off with a lighthearted jab. "And you'll be at it all day, at that rate."

"I'm doing my best," Chimmy countered defensively. "This is my first run on a ship."

Ormac tugged his eyepatch in surprise. "Aww, why diddun ya say so? None's ever taught ya the proper way te swab a deck?"

Gil gave him a playful shove. "By *proper* 'e means *easy*."

Lumber pointed at Gil. "And by *easy*, he means *awesome*."

The possum hunched his shoulders and shook his head, seeming annoyed that anyone would suggest his methods were somehow inadequate. "I guess not."

Gil rolled his shoulders and clapped his hands together. "Well, we'll jus' have te rectify that. Let us give ya a hand."

"No, it's alright, I got it."

"C'mon, lad," Lumber clapped him on the back and used his surprise to flip the mop deftly from his grip. Then he gestured to the topmasts. "Find a little humility and take your cues from the captain."

Chimmy gave a skeptical glance to the shadow overhead. "He doesn't exactly seem the humble type."

"No, no, no, not that part," Gil said. "'E ain't jus' up there for kicks, ye know. Well, partly, 'e is. But 'e's also keepin' an eye on Marshall's ship, see? It's th'only way te track 'em through the fog, at this distance."

"So… we're following them?" The possum sounded bored, clearly making no attempt to see any connection whatsoever.

"We're letting them do the heavy lifting for us," Lumber corrected, thumping the mop on the deck. "You see where I'm going with this?"

Chimmy looked timidly from one raccoon to the next. They were right, he supposed. It would be pretty foolish of him not to take them up on their offer. "Um, well. Alright then, I guess."

"Let's show 'im 'ow it's done, mates," Gil said with a wink, giving the bucket a nudge and tucking his toe beneath it.

With a whoop, a whistle, and a smile, the three sprang into action. Gil tipped the bucket on its side and leapt over it, landing on a soap-covered rag as Lumber tossed the mop to Ormac and mounted the bucket. They shot forward on a sudsy wave. Back and forth across the deck, they zigged and zagged until bucket and rag were dry. Then they threw themselves from the prow, earning a startled cry from Chimmy, who couldn't see their off-deck maneuver of forming an acrobatic, hand-to-ankle chain while wedging the mop's handle between rail posts as an anchor point. Whipping about in a downward arc, they filled the bucket and flipped back onto deck, rinsing and repeating until the whole of the ship was spick and span. In the space of a few minutes, the three once again stood before Chimmy, grinning from ear to ear and dripping from head to toe.

Aghast, the young possum stared, open-mouthed, until he found his voice. "That was the *easy* way?"

The trio looked one to the other.

Lumber shrugged. "Well… once you get the hang of it."

Chimmy was still gawping at them in disbelief when from the winds overhead came a boisterous laugh. "Amateurs!" When he was certain he could be seen, Captain McKinley gave a mock salute before releasing his hold on the mast and stepping into the open air with a grin that said: *while I appreciate your display of good-natured recklessness, I'm far more delighted that you've presented me with the opportunity to show you up. Stand by and thank you for playing.* Then he plummeted through the mist at breakneck speed. He maintained his free-fall until the last possible moment. Only then did his hands shoot toward a passing length of rope, bringing his descent to a sudden and short-lived halt. With unnatural grace, he swung forward, allowing the cord to slip between his hands as he dropped to a lower yardarm and somersaulted to the roof of his cabin. A final backflip planted him on the main deck, arms outstretched as if in anticipation of applause. He earned a golfclap or two, along with a few disparaging sighs. But poor Chimmy was practically beside himself with exasperation.

"You're all mad," he gasped before he could think

better of it.

His superiors stared back at him for a long moment.

Then, Gil chuckled outright, "Catches on quick, don't 'e?"

"Sharp as a tack, this one," Ormac agreed, returning the mop to its baffled owner.

"Though we prefer the term 'open to adventure.' Welcome to the *Negvar*, lad." Lumber nodded to his weathered companions and the three raccoons carried their shenanigans to the rear of the ship.

Suppressing a shudder of irritation, the possum bent his head to resume his duties, then noticed that Captain McKinley stood nearby, arms folded, brow raised.

"Chimmy, right?" He said, at length.

"Um... yes, sir."

"Chimmy the Leech?"

The possum nodded. "Yes, sir."

The Marauder began to circle him. "You're my new crewman?"

"Yes, sir."

He paused. "You're a possum."

Chimmy looked at him sidelong. "Yes, sir."

"Why do they call you the Leech, then?"

The new crewman shrugged, looking uncomfortable. "Um... well I – I don't know, sir."

McKinley screwed up his face. "Sounds rather off-putting."

Chimmy tightened his grip on the mop still in his hands. "I don't think it was ever meant as a compliment, sir."

"But," he resumed circling. "You introduce yourself as Chimmy *the Leech*."

"I suppose I do, sir, yes."

"So you must find some aspect of it... endearing?"

"Not really, sir, I just... maybe I'm used to the name. Force of habit and all."

"So you habitually refer to yourself with an off-putting

label because other people tell you to?"

"I…" The possum wrung his hands. "I guess I never thought much about it, sir."

"Well." McKinley stopped his pacing and placed his hands on his hips, looking disappointed. "This is never going to work, then, is it?"

Chimmy tensed. "H-have I done something wrong, sir?"

"Wrong? No." The Marauder shook his head in a very serious manner. "No, you're doing everything right, which is precisely the problem. You follow orders, even ludicrous ones. You're polite, quiet, unassuming. If I didn't know any better, I'd swear you had no idea whatsoever that this is *supposed* to be a pirate ship. We've no room for propriety here. So lighten up. Make a friend, one who will implore you to skip your duties from time to time. Have a mug too many and throw Tobb into the brine, if you can lift him." McKinley gestured to the rather rotund beaver whistling at the helm. "And, for Fate's sake, stop calling me *sir*. No one calls me *sir*."

"Sir?" A serene voice interrupted from behind.

"Except Amelia," the Marauder amended smoothly, turning to regard the cat with a deferential smile.

She smiled in return and tipped her elegant head. "The father is asking after you, if you aren't busy."

The Marauder donned his hat with an overstated sigh. "Oh, the unending demands of leadership. Keep an eye on Chimmy while I'm below, will you, Madame Ling? I'm concerned the poor lad hasn't the foggiest idea how to properly misbehave. I'd hate for his particular ailment to spread to the rest of the crew. Such a thing could carry dire consequences for us all."

"Indeed, sir."

Bowing out of his way in a peaceful manner, Amelia Ling joined Chimmy in watching the captain disappear belowdecks.

"This ship…" the possum said. "I don't belong here."

At that, the placid cat laughed. "No one belongs here."

"Then," Chimmy looked to her in confusion. "What's the point? Why join up at all? Why separate yourselves from the outside world like this?"

"Have you spent much time in the outside world?" She smiled down at him. "No one belongs there, either. The difference being, out there, everyone expects you to belong. To a family, to a Guild, to a group. Here, we know better. We are individuals with oddities and ill-fitting flaws – and we celebrate our misshapen personalities without having to put on a face for false acceptance."

"You're pirates." He said the words bluntly, almost distastefully, as though reminding her of something she may have forgotten.

She eyed him. "Yes, we are. But given the choice, I'd rather wedge myself a place among misfits who accept themselves for what they are. Wouldn't you?"

The possum stared up at her for a long moment, then rested the mop against the mast, stuffed his hands into his pockets and turned away, an odd expression on his hidden face.

"I guess so. I don't know." He shrugged as he walked away. "I'm probably the wrong person to ask."

≈

"Father?" Removing his hat, McKinley cracked the door to the dimly-lit room and peered into the darkness.

When he heard no response, he stepped inside.

On the far end of the room, he could just make out the silhouette of a fox kneeling before a candle, his head bent, hands clasped solemnly behind his back. The flame threw shadows from his shoulders that danced and sputtered like aimless weapons, making the cleric seem more dangerous than reserved, more kingly than priestly. The humble fox was whispering, intermittent words that McKinley tried not to hear – he knew they were not for him.

"…Heart and crux of Holy Fate… pass over my soul and make me clean…"

The pirate captain stepped forward and cleared his throat, but it was several moments more before the fox twitched his ears in recognition.

Then, his prayer concluded, Father Deagan Faiz lifted his head.

"Captain. Thank you for coming."

His voice was warm and regal. It filled the room with an ownership that made McKinley feel like a trespasser on his own boat. Despite the sloop in his muscled shoulders, and the humble way he held his ears pressed against his head, there was a deliberate strength to Faiz's movements as he stood and stepped away from the candle. That strength made him seem more like a fixture of nature than an individual. He was a rock, and he was a tower. Solid and calm as a frozen stream. As always, McKinley had to resist the urge to kneel or salute, struggling instead to keep his banter light. "If our history is any indication, it would have been foolish of me not to."

The cleric smiled, lifting his hand to an empty chair. He seated himself and, for a time, no words were spoken. The Marauder waited, mirroring the father's silence, fighting the urge to make a joke about the weather just to ease the tension.

The quiet made him uncomfortable.

And Faiz seemed far too torn for McKinley's liking.

"Forgive my hesitance, Captain," Faiz apologized at last. "This is difficult for me."

"I've never known you to shy away from a warning." The Marauder smiled, guessing the father's intent all too well. Not all foxes had the gift of foresight, if it could be called that, but there were enough of them to give credence to the idea that the sly species had one up on the rest of the world. It gave them a stigma in proper circles and made the Secoran underbelly vulnerable to an array of serial charlatans. But no self-respecting pirate would ever set sail without their token fox. Genuine or fraud, it hardly mattered. Among those honest few, Faiz had an unparalleled gift. If he called the captain to his quarters over every intuition or inkling, McKinley could well spend his life in these four walls. Faiz wasn't given to such drama. He would only call for the captain's private attention if something grave were afoot. McKinley leaned forward in his chair. "What's the deal?"

The cleric drew a breath and laced his fingers together. "You might call it... a conflict of interests."

McKinley studied Faiz. He knew of only one thing the father cared enough about for either conflict or interest to even be possible.

"When we started down this path, you told me it would lead you to your salvation – your one and only chance to atone for your past." Faiz winced noticeably, as though guilt had risen up to deal him a physical blow with McKinley's words. For mercy's sake, the Marauder might have ended it there, were he not already on the defensive. "It was almost as important to you as it was to me that we see this through. Now you're going to tell me to turn back, aren't you?" he asked, accusingly.

"Yes." Faiz forced himself into a deliberate nod. "Forgive me. But I must."

McKinley shook his head. "Too late, padre. We're on course, and we're not breaking it."

"Captain, please. You have to let this one go."

A hard glint entered the Marauder's eye. "That's not going to happen."

"It we continue on our current course, you will lose something. Something great and unrecoverable. I wouldn't have asked you here, were it not..."

"I know that," McKinley interrupted. "And I don't care. Everything comes with a risk. If there is a cost, let me carry it. I'm more than prepared..."

Faiz held up a gentle hand, interrupting him in turn. "No, you're not. You can't be. What you seek... the

Mosque Hill Fortune, the Secoran Captain... none of it is what you think. It won't end the way you think."

"Oh no? How's it going to end, then?" His words came almost as a challenge to the humble fox, who looked for all the world as though he were pleading for an alternative to the real answer, which he gave with a sigh of sincere regret.

"She's going to die, my friend."

For all the kindness with which they had been spoken, for all their sincerity and sorrow, Faiz's words fell like a fatal blow. McKinley blanched as though impaled. The moments before he reminded himself to breathe seemed infinite and nauseating.

Then he stepped away from the candle light, whispering, "... Who's going to die?"

Faiz remained seated, head still bowed while his words were cautious. "Your daughter..."

"No." McKinley pointed angrily. "You don't know her. No one knows about her."

Even as the argument left his mouth, the Marauder knew how hollow it sounded. Faiz knew the secret in everything.

And he was never wrong.

"Her days... they are numbered."

McKinley closed his eyes. "Shut up."

"Perhaps they would be better spent with you at her side."

"*I said SHUT UP!*" The words erupted from the pirate captain's chest as he lunged, dragging the much-taller Faiz to his feet and ripping his sword from its scabbard. "One more insolent word, and I'll cut that tongue from your sanctimonious mouth, do you understand me?! She's going to live! And no superstitious cleric is going to stand in the way of her cure by poisoning her father's sense of hope! Let me lose something great – let me lose *everything*! I'll make her well again if it kills me and everyone else on this rotted ship! I will cut a swath through this world in blood if there's even a chance that it might make her whole! Who the hell are you to stand in my way?!"

Faiz looked to the blade at his throat, no concern or surprise registering on his face, no judgment. He was only twelve years the captain's senior; though he looked for all the world as one who'd aged a thousand lifetimes for reality's one. Indeed, he seemed to be aging before McKinley's very eyes. Yet few could guess how easily he could overpower and disarm even the infamous Marauder. Fewer still would know that he would never try. Calmly, Faiz placed a hand on McKinley's shoulder.

Almost as if he were inviting the captain to strike.

"I am no one." He gave a slight, sad smile. "You can end me here, with no regrets, if that is your wish."

McKinley stepped back, somewhat rebuked, though his sword was still lifted. "My wish?" He smiled humorlessly in return. "A wish is precisely what I'm after, Father. Don't you know that? The Mosque Hill Fortune isn't just gold or jewels. It's a bloody miracle. It's knowledge gained and wishes granted. It's the only hope she has. I can't just turn away from that. How can you *ask me* to turn away from that?"

From anyone else, the sympathy in his voice would have been patronizing to the point of fury. "I can ask you to do it because it is the right thing to do. Do you really believe that you can save her with a wish? Are you truly putting all your faith into the idea of magic?"

"Is that so wrong?" There was a tightness to the skin around McKinley's eyes. It made his whisper seem like a desperate shout, more agony than insistence. "Is it so foolish to hunt for magic in an ordinary world? Maya's mother cared for me, though I was nothing. A scoundrel and a thief. She took my hand and saved me with a look. What was that, if not magic?"

"I believe you would call that... love." This time, Faiz's smile held more than sadness. "Though maybe you're right. Maybe there is no distinction between the two."

McKinley listened, drew several deep breaths, each one

more difficult than the last. "There must be." He said slowly, bitterly. "Because I've given Maya love and that hasn't fixed her. I've given medicine and money and tears... Magic must be separate, for it's all that's left. The only thing I haven't used up." He stepped back, his eyes trailing away to the darker corners of the room, looking at nothing. His sword sunk with every syllable, pulled down by the weight of his misery until it clattered to the floor. Its surrender was as hollow as its purpose had ever been. "I don't know what I'm doing anymore, Father. I don't know how it came to this. Maybe you're right. Maybe Mosque Hill is just a phantom star. Maybe I set my course by it in order to feel useful." He placed a shaking hand over his eyes, as if to shield the world around him from tears that were not there. "Maybe I'm just sailing forward because it's the only direction left to go."

Faiz pushed himself away from the wall, but said nothing.

"If only her mother were here," McKinley went on in an even quieter voice, as though wishing to himself, a private thought meant for no one. "Selene would know what to do, what to say. I'd give anything for her to be here in my place. I'd walk on water and trade my soul on the other side. But I can't bring her back, not even in memory or song, as my little Maya would have me do." He gave a sniff and a hollow laugh that sounded more like a stifled emotion. "I can't even keep my promise to her."

"What promise was that?"

"To protect our little girl. To keep her safe and whole. It was the only thing she ever asked of me. And I promised... with all my heart, I promised. But now... now..." McKinley sunk into the chair and leaned forward with his elbows on his knees, his head in his hands. "She's sick, Father. She's dying and, Fate forgive me, I can't let that happen. I can't fail her like that. *I can't lose them both.*"

Once again, Father Faiz sat. "You think you've let them down? Captain, her illness isn't your fault. It happened beyond your will to control it. Whether or not this feels like a punishment, you don't carry any blame and you don't need forgiveness. Not from Fate or any other force of nature. Not even from your wife." He leaned forward, meeting McKinley's reluctant gaze. "You know that this revelation comes at the cost of everything I was searching for. But I'm telling you this because you are my friend. You own more strength and determination than anyone I've ever known. I watch them drain from you with each passing day. I see you fading a piece at a time. It tears you apart to be away from her when she needs you most. If not for her, do this for yourself. You have earned the right to lay down your sword. To be there at her side... in the end."

McKinley was quiet, eyes closed as though he were waiting for his wandering resolve to return. "At her side?" He struggled to stand without the assistance of the wall, listening to the wind spin its familiar lullaby through the porthole. Then he smiled, a sad and heartfelt smile, hoping Maya was listening too. "Oh, Father. That would be the cruelest act of all. You don't know her. She's a fighter, like her mother. She's stronger than I am. I would only fall apart if I were with her. And that would kill her spirit as surely as anything. If she is to die, better that she do so with hope, feeling whatever strength I have left." He turned mechanically toward the door, willing his body to move forward.

Maybe because it was the only direction left to go.

"She has three months, at best. If our journey returns you before the third full moon, you may yet see her again. But it will come with a price – one you may not be willing to pay."

The captain looked back over his shoulder. "I told you, Father. I will pay *any* price."

"Captain," Faiz said slowly, as if to make certain that McKinley understood the full weight of consequence in this choice. "People are going to die."

Stiffly, the Marauder turned away to face the door, his features darkening in the shadows.

"*Then let them die.*"

Faiz said nothing more as the captain closed the door behind him, knowing how truly and bitterly he meant those words.

≈

McKinley ran his hands over his face, feeling numb. It wasn't the cold or the damp of the mist that gathered on his fur as he crossed the deck in a slow walk – bumping past Amelia and Chimmy alike, one looking concerned while the other acted somehow vindicated. It was exhaustion.

Pure emotional exhaustion.

He closed the door to his cabin and leaned his head on the door, then stood in the darkness for the longest time, trying to decide what he *should* be feeling.

Fury?

Regret?

Despair?

"All pointless," he said to the painting on the wall above his bed. "They'd just be pointless, wouldn't they, love? I'll trade them away, if I must." Then, quieter, he amended, as though reaching to be honest with himself – or perhaps the one in the painting. "If I can." He brushed his fingertips over oil and canvas and climbed into bed, boots and all. "Give me blind determination over hope, victory over possibility. I'll make it work, Selene. I'll keep my promise or die trying. Booya."

Then he fell into a deep, fatalistic sleep.

It begged a lesser commitment than any other means of escape.

≈

Chimmy picked idly at a plate of stale food. He was in the mess hall to hide, not to eat.

"'Aven't we scared ya off yet, lad?" A meaty hand clapped him on the back.

The possum jumped in his seat, settling back but not quite relaxing as Tobb, the grizzled beaver from the helm, helped himself to the empty chair on his left.

Amelia seated herself on his right. "Go easy on him, Master Tobb. The boy is still adjusting to life among the rough and unpredictable rabble."

Tobb grinned stupidly in response, giving Chimmy a friendly nudge. "Oi diddun mean nuttin' by it, ye know. And don' worry none 'bout the Cap'n neither. Loikes ta mess wi' the new ones, 'e does."

Chimmy lowered his head over his plate, gesturing with a dirty fork to the trio of raccoons on the far side of the hall. "And what's their excuse?"

The cat smiled.

Tobb laughed heartily.

"The Kota Brothers don' need no excuse. They is who they is. An' they seems te have a jolly good time bein' it."

Chimmy sat upright. "The... the Kota Brothers? As in... the Masters of the Thieves Guild?"

"Used ta be," Tobb nodded. "Don't ask 'em about it, though. Yer likely ta get yer head ripped off fer yer troubles."

"Wh-why?" The possum eyed the three sidelong, with a new respect.

"They're brothers," Amelia explained. "Dedication to family outweighs dedication to anything else, Guild or crew."

Again, the possum hunched back over his food, feigning interest but eating nothing.

Lumber seemed to take note of their interest and stood from his chair. "Hey lad, you're not sore about us nicking your duties, are you?"

Chimmy looked surprised, then shook his head.

"'Cause we was jus' tryin te help," said Gil.

"Weren't out te step on yer toes," offered Ormac.

"N-no." The possum lifted a limp hand. "It's n-not that, it's just…"

"Secora, right?" Lumber finished for him, lifting his tray and migrating to Chimmy's table. "Yeah, that place has us all on edge. Something's not right there, that's for sinkin' sure."

"Don' whine se much." Gil joined them. "I quite loike that the dolphin regs ain't passin' beyond the docks anymore. Makes it a lot less 'azardous to be a poirate, ye know."

"Corsair," Lumber corrected, soliciting a round of laughter from the mess hall over the more romantic term for their chosen profession.

"The shrouding o' the mist ain't se bad, neither," Gil went on. "A vessel can come and go almos' as she pleases wiffout risk o' capture."

Lumber scoffed, "Thus, our abundance of wealth, right?"

"'Spose that's roight and good and all o' that, but what's it what's got the regs in such a corner alluva sudden, anyhow?" Tobb looked uncomfortable. "Used te be a brave lot. Now they hugs te the shore loike their lives depend on it."

From the other side of the room, Ormac, who had not moved, took a long pull on his pipe and lifted his gruff voice. "Maybe the same thing what be makin' the whales run aground again." The mess hall went quiet as every crewman turned to find him peering almost maniacally from his single eye. "Whales is smart creatures, they is. Like the eagles and the gryphons, they passed our way o' understandin' a long time ago. They only go coast-side when sumpthin' we can't see er smell forces 'em to. Been decades since it 'appened – not since the last wave o' mists swept through this cursed kingdom have they thrown themselves te shore. But just this week, more'n five o' 'em done precisely that."

"Come on," Lumber attempted to argue. "Where did you even hear any of that?"

"Where d'ya think?" Ormac leaned forward. "Secora Tor. That rat hole where everythin's gone wrong and none wants te admit it. That place is the source o' it. The mists, they started roight there. Folk can't stop talkin' 'bout it."

"And what do they say?" Chimmy swallowed. "About the whales?"

"That they 'eard 'em screamin' in fear as they beached 'emselves."

Lumber glanced around the room, trying to calm the apprehensive fantasies of a superstitious crew. "Well that's hardly something for rumor. Certain death tends to put a fright into anybody, right Amelia?" He nudged the impassive cat, looking for support. "Don't mind him, Chimmy. It's just storytelling rhetoric. If those whales died at all, it was a blasted shame as well as an accident. And if they screamed, well… it was because they knew their fate, simple as that."

"Nah, mate," Ormac lifted his patch to stare through a blind eye at his rapt listeners. "They wasn't screamin' o'er what was before 'em. They were screamin' fer what was behind."

≈

The ladder creaked under Lady Sira's boots as she moved through the hungry belly of her ship. The walls around her moaned as if to signal their emptiness and she sighed, treading soundlessly through a sea of vacant chains that signaled her lack of revenue.

They held only one captive.

One might say business was going poorly.

"The *Havoc*," Lady Sira placed a palm against the charred wood and followed Abner's gaze to a patched hole in the hull. "She has seen better days, no?"

The Elder made no attempt to answer.

"It is sometimes difficult to remember she was once the envy of the Kathkan forces. Light, fast, elegant. Sadly," she paused, lifting her arms to indicate the battered beams surrounding them. "Secoran hands refuse to treat her with the dignity she so deserves."

Abner looked up at her at last, his eyes lingering on the many scars criss-crossing Sira's long arms and delicate face. "Are we still talking about your ship? Or are we talking about you?"

She laughed, moving to crouch before him with her elbows on her knees. "Do not try to get inside my head, aged thing. I assure you, you would not enjoy the trip." Lady Sira rapped him under the chin. "Now. Speak. What doom were you crying up there, on my deck? Something about the wolf is going to kill us?"

"Have you tried asking *the wolf*?" Abner mocked.

Lady Sira rolled her eyes. "He isn't so into the talking."

"Then maybe inviting him on board your ship wasn't such a good idea."

"I did not invite him." She looked insulted, then waved a nonchalant hand. "He invited himself. I liked his offer, so I let him stay. But you." She brought a claw near his face. "You, I think, know more of his plans than I do. This, I do not like. So what isn't he telling me?"

The Elder stared back at her, looking impudent and curious all at the same time. "What *has* he told you?"

"The wolf tells me that he seeks the throne and that this... what do you call it... *scepter* will give him rule of your sainted Secora."

"Which you support? You somehow think that a Baron-ruled Secora would be a *good thing*?" Abner looked genuinely surprised.

The lithe coyote shrugged, "I think the wolf will regard Kathkan enterprises with more sympathy than the current queen. My cargo will beg fewer questions and my ship will take fewer beatings. Good, bad, it does not matter. It is business."

The Elder seemed appalled. "You would see all of Secora burn just to make a profit? Through slaving, of all things?"

Lady Sira smiled, showing condescending teeth. "Your moral objections. They are so cute."

Abner scowled, "There are others out there with the very same objections. Younger, stronger, smarter people who will always stand in your way, regardless of what Secora has to say on the matter. Putting the Baron in charge of the law won't change it in their eyes. They'll still oppose you. They'll do it because it is right and just."

The coyote tipped her muzzle in annoyance. "You speak of your student, Captain Marshall."

Abner nodded. "Say what you will about the blighted boy, Marshall knows how to make a choice. In the end, law or no, he will come for you because it is the right thing to do."

"Yes, yes, yes." Lady Sira waved a bored hand. "He is a gem. Truly. But you have told me nothing that I care to hear. The spirit, the one the wolf brought from the sea. It called you something. *Old Blood*. What did it mean by that?"

As much as he could with the chains pulling at his arms Abner squared his shoulders, saying impudently, "I have no idea."

The coyote leaned closer, a deadly glint in her pretty eyes. "Come now." Her voice was flat and practical. "You do not wish to lie to me."

"I…" The old badger eyed her reluctantly. "I come from… a very old family. We were powerful once. Respected."

Lady Sira smiled. "Like my ship. Go on. Why does this Voice of Fate-?"

"*That* was *no* Voice of Fate," the Elder interrupted, insistent.

"Okay. Then what was it?"

"A wraith. A harbinger. It is a voice as well, I suppose, but one without an anchor. It may have even been a soul once, or a spirit, as you said. But it's forgotten itself now. Without a tie to the real world it's just... emptiness. An echo of death, and nothing warmer. You are fools to follow it."

"What might it want here, then? With you? With my ship?"

He studied her long and hard, then eased himself back against the wall. "No," he said bluntly, his chains clinking in resignation. "It doesn't matter what I say to you, Kathkan. You won't turn back because there's nothing in it for you. And you won't believe me because I'm nothing here. Another slave, whose only worth can be counted in what your monstrous partner is willing to pay you. Like you said, it's business. So go on. Have your little adventure. Play with the Fates and see what that gets you. Because you aren't getting a blighted thing out of me."

Slowly, gracefully, Lady Sira rose to her feet and clapped her hands.

At her command, a great white wolverine descended the stairs, one threatening foot at a time. The albino lumbered through the belly of the ship with bared teeth and red eyes until his shadow touched the Elder's feet.

Abner recoiled.

"Make him talk, Grogoch." Lady Sira turned away from the slavering beast as Abner tried to keep the fear from his face. "Make him tell me everything."

McKinley
The Marauder

6
WHAT THE ADVISOR DIDN'T MENTION

"**A**ll able hands to the shore! Prepare for rescue and assist! Idlers on the rails NOW!" Marshall bellowed as he leapt from the deck and into the brine, kicking off his boots on the fly.

Though his crew moved to immediate action, he knew the rafts would take several moments to ready.

Even at this distance, he could swim faster than they could be pulled, rowed, or drifted.

By the time his crew reached the coast, Marshall was already crouched among the smoldering ruins of the lighthouse, up to his elbows in ash and rubble.

"Sir!" Commander Calum sprinted to his side.

The captain's shoulders were tense with frustration when he turned to his first officer with only one thing to show for his furious digging.

A broken monocle.

"Blast it," Calum sighed. "Maybe he made it out in time."

Marshall looked up to the bit of empty sky that could be seen through the mist. The line of his mouth hardened. "And maybe he didn't," he said, laying the monocle on the remaining keystones and turning to survey the destruction.

Nothing stood but the foundation. Bits and pieces of the lighthouse were strewn across the shore like a dismembered pictogram – each part a smoldering and senseless memory without context, individual and useless.

As for the adjoining cabin, its thatched roof and thin timber construction had made for a brilliant but short-lived bonfire, almost as though its incineration had been planned.

"One thing's for certain, sir," Lieutenant Ryder called to them from the perimeter of the blast range. "The Commodore triggered the explosion himself."

"Reasoning, Lieutenant?" Marshall turned to face her.

She pointed with a gloved hand to where the tower had been only moments before. "The blast came from the lantern room. As the sole watchman of Pelham Point, the Commodore should have been the only one with access."

"The Commodore may have been unstable, but he was no fool," Calum argued. "He would know better than to blow a building from the top down. If he wanted to collapse the tower, wouldn't he have set the detonation at the foundation or supporting beams?"

"The tower only fell because it was in disrepair," Captain Marshall concluded, earning a nod of agreement from Ryder. "The beacon was his real target."

"The beacon?" Commander Calum lowered his voice and moved closer to the captain with a glance over his shoulder. "All that nonsense about space signals aside, he knew about the message. So, what, he was cutting off the code? Interrupting any chance that the intended target could ever see it?"

Marshall sighed, thinking back to the Commodore's parting words, noting that Pelham Point was once again destined to become Forever Isle, the stuff of nursery rhymes and ghost stories.

Pointless poetry.

"Maybe," the captain said.

"A pretty extreme response to such a cryptic bit of communication." Calum squinted in confusion. "What does that even mean? '*Snuff out the sun*?'"

"Son," Marshall corrected. "Ess. Oh. En."

Calum turned to him in confusion, then his eyes widened in understanding. "Snuff out *The Son*. You. The Son of Masguard. That message was calling for your execution?"

"Maybe," Marshall reiterated, seeming both unconcerned and deeply disturbed. He looked over the now-uninhabited island and its surrounding rocks, knowing that he couldn't leave these hazards unattended. Night was falling and the mists would not be kind to an unwary vessel. "Send a message to Vernos," he ordered. "Tell them what has happened here. Construction on a new lighthouse is to be initiated at once, even if I must pay for it myself. Any required funds should be obtained from the Town Elder on my behalf. In the meantime, pile the debris and set a blaze. The fire should burn through the night – long enough to give passing ships some warning. Let the lighthouse serve its purpose one last time. And Commander?"

"Aye sir?"

Marshall turned to march back down the shore, brushing off his uniform and biting angrily over his shoulder, "*Get me Eadric.*"

≈

Marshall's footsteps were even more militant than usual as he crossed the deck to his cabin. He pulled up short as he closed the door. In the waning light, the room looked cold and unfamiliar. The painting over his desk seemed accusatory.

You should have seen this coming…

But he hadn't.

He hadn't paid more than a moment's notice to the beacon before meeting with the Commodore. And he hadn't given the gull's words the attention he might have.

Marshall did *not* like failure. Not even the tacit sort.

With a sigh of frustration and a firm hand, he pushed the painting aside on its nail to reveal the safe embedded in the wall, where Calum had placed the Commodore's map. The captain had seen it clearly in the lighthouse. With his eidetic memory, that should have been enough, but there *must* have been something he missed. His father wouldn't have led him to it, were it not important.

Reaching for the rolled parchment, Marshall felt his eyes drawn to the back of the safe. There, tucked behind ledgers and logbooks, the Key to Mosque Hill sat idle in the most pretentious way. He could almost swear that it, too, was mocking him. He was about to close the door on its stony sneer when he felt an unexpected chill in the air.

Marshall paused.

The Key had been moved, he was sure of it.

…Or had it moved on its own?

Suddenly, a gust of wind burst through the door at his back. Mist washed through the room like an unwelcome wave as an ethereal voice echoed in his ear.

"*Son of Masguard!*"

Inhaling sharply in surprise, Marshall slammed the safe shut.

The room fell silent.

Instinct braced him for defense as his eyes darted from one corner to the next in anticipation of an intruder or yet another ghostly vision, but neither came.

There was no one there.

He barely had time to compose himself before Calum arrived with Eadric in tow. Oblivious to his unfortunate timing, the commander rapped politely on the frame and glanced to the door – it wasn't like his captain to leave it open.

"Captain!" Eadric dragged himself across the room and plopped into a chair, panting with exhaustion. Clearly, Ensign Wexler's duties had not been kind to him. "Never in my life have I been run to such a ragged length! Are you certain that lieutenant of yours isn't Kathkan? She'd make a very convincing slavedriv—"

"Advisor," Calum stopped him, placing a hand on his shoulder. "Believe it or not, the captain didn't call you here for a report on your chores."

"Well then, why —"

Marshall tossed the map on his desk by way of interruption, then sat down, lacing his fingers together on the desktop and waiting for the advisor to find his voice.

Silently, the captain hoped neither of his visitors would notice the battle-readied tension in his back.

"That's…" Eadric pointed to the parchment and leaned forward in his seat. "That's the Map to Mosque Hill. Isn't it? It was right there? In the lighthouse? This whole time?!"

"You knew about the map?" The captain angled his jaw in anger.

"Well…" The advisor shrugged. "*Knew* is, perhaps, the wrong word…"

Marshall held up a hand. "Spare the semantics. If you knew about the map, you must have known that the one guarding it was in grave peril. Yet you said nothing."

Eadric lifted an objecting feather. "As I said, I didn't know anything for certain. The map was an improbable rumor, at best. You've made it quite clear how you feel about rumor and —"

Slamming a palm on his desk, Marshall came to his feet. "Enough, Eadric. An island is in ruins and someone has died. These things happened because I, as the captain of this vessel and commander of this voyage, did not know enough about the situation to save them. Now, the queen sent you for a reason, and it certainly wasn't for the purposes of recording our mission." He gestured to the current – and very well maintained – logbook on his desk, not bothering to point out that Eadric had hardly lifted a quill since his arrival. "The *Albatross* isn't sailing an inch until you've filled me in on every fact, every detail, and every rumor surrounding our endeavor. I will not be left in the dark to wonder at my sanity, and I *will not* lose another person to your studied silence."

Eadric glanced back to Commander Calum, then to the map, then to the captain's immovable face and asked, "Why would you wonder at your sanity?"

Marshall pushed himself away from the desk and ran a hand over his eyes, shaking his head.

"Advisor, I think you may be missing the point," Calum interjected.

"No, no." Eadric stood and leaned across the desk. "This is about more than recent events. You're a naval man. You're accustomed to loss, whether you like it or not. But look at you. You've been rattled. You've seen one of them, haven't you?"

"Eadric, what are you talking about?" Calum asked, sounding annoyed, then redirected the question at someone more likely to give a sensible response. "Captain, what is he talking about?"

Marshall said nothing, but held Eadric's gaze across the desk.

The advisor clapped his wings in excitement. "You have! You've seen one! When did it happen? What did it say? You must tell me!"

The captain remained silent long enough for Calum's sense of curiosity to turn to unease. "Captain?" he asked, concern on his features. "Is he right, for once? Did you see something?"

Pulling himself upright, Marshall tugged ever so slightly at his collar, as though it were constricting his airways. "I don't know what I saw, Commander."

"You saw a harbinger!" Eadric supplied

enthusiastically.

Calum turned to him in confusion. "A what?"

"A harbinger of the flood," the advisor explained. "They rise from the sea before the storm. But they only come to those they know will listen. Those with the power to alter the course of destiny. If one of them came to you, well, it must be Fate!"

Having lost his tolerance for euphemism, Marshall raised an abrupt hand, saying, "Be clear, Advisor. In the grand scheme of things, what purpose could a hallucination ever serve?"

"More importantly," Calum said, creasing his brow. "What does Fate want with the captain?"

"Well, if the harbinger hasn't told him outright, I suppose we can't be certain of that, can we?" Eadric told the commander before turning to Marshall. "They aren't hallucinations. They are very real. These beings have consciousness. They are regarded as ocean-bound animations, so it's possible that they're simply undiscovered life forms. Frighteningly strange, perhaps, but they might be intelligent to a social degree. They might even be envoys or ambassadors from a hidden kingdom…"

"Or maybe they're scouts," the captain supplied with a hardened jaw. "But how do you know any of this?"

At that, Eadric practically rolled his eyes, retorting with condescension, "Captain. I am one of the highest ranking members of the Scholars Guild. How could I *not* know any of this?"

Marshall leveled a stony gaze at the pretentious bird. "If this were written in the Archives, *Advisor*," he stressed the word as if to remind Eadric of his place. "I would remember it."

"Oh, I don't doubt you in that," Eadric replied with a barely-concealed note of spite. "Perhaps you don't remember it because you never actually read it. You see, Captain, *this* was never *in* the Archives."

The captain leaned over his desk. "Explain."

A centuries-old construct of the Scholars Guild, the Archives existed for a singular purpose – to collect and preserve information. *Everything* was to be written and stored within its walls. And *every* Secoran was to be granted access.

A free distribution of knowledge.

It was perhaps the noblest endeavor in Secora's long existence.

The bird laughed at his naiveté. "Yes, yes, I know. The integrity of the Archives is paramount within the Guild, right? Freedom of understanding and access to history for all, and all that nonsense. But did you never wonder why the Guild established a separate, more elite version of itself *within* itself? Why it drew members like me from the ranks and elevated them above the rest?" He lifted a wing to show again the symbol dyed into his feathers. "What exactly do you think the Order is for, Captain? There are things in this world – important things – that should definitely be documented. And we *have* documented them, just as we were meant to. But not everyone has earned the right to these bits of knowledge. After all, the common people are unpredictable and easy to alarm. They do not need to know everything… Do they?"

There was a glint of enjoyment in Eadric's glare as he said those last words.

Marshall narrowed his eyes, his meaning clear.

Do not test me, Eadric.

The bird wilted.

"Perhaps," Calum stepped forward with a calming tone. "Now is not the best time for a political debate."

"Quite agreed," Eadric said quickly. "This isn't about politics. It isn't about the scepter or even the Fortune itself. This is about the workings of the world, the relationship we have with the way that things are."

Though Marshall said nothing, the way he held Eadric's gaze prodded the advisor into a more direct explanation.

"There is a *reason* the scepter has been held in such regard throughout the ages, and there is a *reason* the laws surrounding it have never been changed. The Scepter of the Ancients, Captain, isn't merely a symbol of power – it is a crossroads of power, a tether between land and sea. It opens a door, and whoever wields the scepter can either close it or hold it ajar in perpetuity."

"A door to what?" Marshall asked, unwavering.

"Well…" Eadric hesitated. "We… don't know. The legend is vague. It describes a barrier between water and air, one that strengthens and weakens like the ins and outs of the tide."

"The mists?" Calum speculated.

Eadric shrugged. "It's possible, but there's more. The barrier isn't permanent. With time, comes erosion. If it gives way, according to the legend, a flood will ensue. What this means in the literal sense, we can't say. But we know that the scepter is the only thing that can stop it."

"This is all sounding a little too much like a prophecy for my comfort…" Calum winced.

"It's not a prophecy," Eadric said insistently. "It's no more prophetic than a carpenter's warnings that your roof is about to cave. They knew what they were talking about when they wrote this down. Fate was their field of work and destiny was their machine. They understood its workings just as you understand this ship of yours, probably even more so."

"*They*." Marshall repeated. "You mean the Ancients."

"Indeed I do." Eadric nodded.

"And *they* were the ones who wrote of the significance of this map?"

"Indeed they did." Again, Eadric nodded, seeming proud.

"Then it seems *they* may have misled us all. This map is useless," Marshall said.

"Indeed it – …" Eadric beamed for an instant with his prepared reply, then immediately deflated. "Wait, what?

What are you saying?"

"I'm saying, Advisor, that *this* is no sea chart." He pointed to the rolled parchment. "At best, were it complete, this graph could pinpoint a single location on a stretch of land. But it is far from complete."

"But, but… " Eadric stammered, confused.

Marshall seated himself, folding his hands on the arms of his chair with an air of finality. "We're no closer to Mosque Hill than we were at the start."

"No." Adamantly, Eadric shook his feathered head, insisting, "No, no… that's not possible."

Marshall sighed. "Commander, if you would kindly return the advisor to his duties? I would enjoy some quiet while I consider how to proceed."

"Aye, sir." Calum saluted before tugging at the flustered bird's limp wing. "Come on, Advisor, there's work to be done."

At length, the kookaburra managed to pull himself from his disappointment long enough to whine, "*Still?*"

Calum shrugged. "Always."

Before they could open the door, Ensign Wexler entered with a troubled look on his face.

"Ensign?" The commander stepped back, pulling Eadric aside as the young fennec stepped into the room.

"Sirs." Wexler saluted. "Word has returned from Vernos."

Marshall leaned forward, his fingers still pressed to the surface of the desk as he waited for the ensign to continue.

"It's the Elder, sir. He's been abducted."

The muscles of his stoic face unmoved, Marshall sat slowly upright.

Shooting a glance to his captain, the commander asked, "Abducted? By whom?"

Wexler hesitated only momentarily. "By the Baron, sir."

Calum turned to Marshall. "Why would the Baron take the Elder, of all people?"

Though he took his time in answering, Marshall's eyes

126

fell immediately to Eadric. "Maybe for the same reason the queen sent him. Information."

Eadric pulled a dubious face. "Impossible. Any pertinent information is sealed. Elder Frum couldn't conceivably know anything worth telling in all of this."

Marshall brought his gaze to the eastern window with a shake of his head. "Don't be so certain."

Eadric opened his beak to argue, but Marshall cut him off in a firm tone.

"Unless you've any further warnings or details to impart, Advisor – most particularly those relevant to the saving of lives – that will be all."

Ensign and commander offered final salutes while Eadric allowed himself to be pulled from the room. Calum stared back in concern as he closed the door.

When they were gone, Marshall leaned back in his chair and closed his eyes.

Unconsciously, as though seeking solid comfort, his hand went to the compass in his pocket. He thumbed the latch for a moment before he even realized what he was doing.

Then, with slow deliberation, Marshall sat upright and placed the compass on the desk alongside the nonsensical map.

The Commodore's words echoed loudly in the back of his thoughts.

He is in your compass…

As he stared down at the needle, Marshall felt the muscles of his face softening into a near-smile.

At long last, things were beginning to make sense.

"Thank you, father," he whispered.

≈

Hours later, at the fore of the ship, Marshall drummed his fingers on the prow, watching the bonfire through the mist as the *Albatross* pulled away at last, into the night.

Unconsciously, he brought his gaze to the east, and to Vernos. He felt as though he should say something, at least in thought. But what could he say? Though his mission was moving forward at last, the place he had once called home was now abandoned, victimized, and haunted.

There were no words to commemorate that.

"So the Scholars Guild has information they keep hidden from the general public." Calum came alongside him. "I'd probably find it disturbing, were it not so very unsurprising."

Marshall nodded in agreement, then returned to his vigil.

"Is that why you dislike them so, sir?"

The captain offered no reply beyond a slight shrug of his shoulder.

"I realize it's none of my business, sir, it's just…" The commander chose his words carefully. "You were in a lot of Guilds. The Scholars are the only ones you seem to have any animosity for. Don't get me wrong, if Eadric is any indication, I'd be hard-pressed to get along with any of their members myself. But you're not exactly the grudge-holding type. Whatever your reasons, it must have been more than interpersonal discord. Was it the secrecy?"

Marshall studied his commander, then, with a sigh, he leaned on the rail and laced his fingers together. "It might have been, if I'd known the extent of it. Secrecy far too often begets dishonesty, for which I've no tolerance. When I joined, the Scholars each had a rather healthy lust for knowledge. One that I share in, even now. Unfortunately, they proved themselves willing to go to any lengths to obtain it. The more I advanced, the more I realized how much their yearnings had pushed them to deceit, to underhanded dealings and subversive goals. For all that their intentions may have started on a noble foot, the system they'd contrived had forced them too far in the opposite direction, fattening the deviant and self-serving while starving any honest intellectuals into submission.

They turned great minds into politicians by wearing them down. Students became spies and researchers became stockpilers of secrets that might have saved lives, were they known when they needed to be."

"As with the Commodore?"

The captain nodded and stared at his hands. "When they learned of my connection to the Elder, someone they thought untouchable, a brilliant historian and researcher without equal or incentive to join, they gave me an ultimatum: continue my advancement within the Guild by 'convincing' Abner to fall in line, or they would put my life – and, more importantly, his – at risk by revealing my identity to the whole of the kingdom."

"They knew?" Calum asked, surprised. "So what happened?"

"I *disagreed* with their offer."

It took a moment for the implications to set in. Then the commander laughed outright. His natural skill with a blade aside, Marshall had completed his education with the Warriors Guild long before ever setting foot in the Scholars Hall. Their too-sophisticated masses wouldn't have stood a chance. "I do hope they documented that!"

"Commander, when all was said and done, those were my very words to them."

"And the Elder? What did he have to say when he heard about all of this?"

The captain stood from the rail and clasped his hands behind his back, saying, "I never told him."

"Why not?"

"Because I never went back," Marshall sighed. "He was less than approving of my desire for a career. And I was less than proud of myself for the manner in which I left. I'd defied his wishes. Worse, I'd done so with no regard for the consequences. He was right, in the end – as he had been all along."

The captain again fell quiet.

"Sir," Calum eventually said in a consoling tone of

voice. "If the Baron took Abner for information, it's very likely that he's still alive."

The captain nodded. "Yes it is, Commander."

When Marshall offered nothing more, Calum nodded in understanding. "I suppose that doesn't make it any easier, though, does it?"

"No…" The captain said, his voice much quieter than before. "It doesn't, Commander. Though I appreciate your concern."

After a few more moments of silence, the commander turned to leave, then paused and looked over his shoulder. "Sir? Back at the palace… When you said you couldn't bring yourself to believe your father's crew might have been willing to die for some Ancient treasure. I never got the chance to say you were most certainly right. They wouldn't have. Not for gold or jewels or even for posterity." He squared his shoulders and firmed his jaw with certainty. "But they would have been willing to die for *him*."

Marshall opened his mouth to reply, but words failed him.

A mixture of emotion played behind his eyes.

Eventually, with effort, the captain bowed his head in a simple gesture.

Commander Calum nodded in kind, then retreated to his quarters while Marshall continued his watch over the ship, mirroring the nearby figurehead in a way that even he would never truly understand.

Strong, significant.

And wooden.

Never noticing the tiny raccoon hidden below the prow, out of sight.

≈

Done!

Several miles from Pelham Point, the giddy robber

stood in his brittle boat and clapped his bony hands with an elated grin.

Secora had taken note of his work. They'd tried to catch him, but they'd failed. For years and years, ever since he'd first been called to task. It hadn't been easy. So many trinkets and weapons and tools. So many tethers to tie and links to connect. And then the message. That had been important too. The faces in the mist had even opened the lighthouse door for him on that one. How nice! But now, finally, he was here. Watching the last of his carefully-collected items falling into the water. Down, down, down to the waiting hands of the ones who needed him.

He'd done well, he knew.

They were going to be so happy with him.

The mist began to close on his bobbing vessel. He clapped his hands at the waves, grinning in glee and anticipation. They were gentle, at first. Then, as the dinghy began to tip dangerously toward the surf, slopping water over the sides, the robber lifted his soaked feet and stopped smiling.

This wasn't fun.

This wasn't polite.

Didn't they know he had holes in his shoes?

Of course we know, they say. *We know everything.*

He didn't understand. They were supposed to be happy.

Oh, we are happy, they say. *We are. But you're done now. You should join us, now that you're done.*

He shook his head.

Nope. He belonged here. He didn't want to go, didn't want to join them.

That didn't sound fun at all.

Then, there in the dark, as the mist roared around him and his thrashing dinghy caved at last, throwing him into the grip of a sea with fingers and friendless faces, the hapless robber finally realized... they didn't care.

≈

"Son of Masguard…"

Marshall opened his eyes to a vacant room, his senses straining in the darkness. He was lucid as he sat upright and waited patiently.

He hadn't been sleeping.

"Son of Masguard." The female voice came again, thin and ethereal.

The captain came to his feet on the icy floorboards, peering with intent through the vapor formed by his breath. "What are you?"

The air seemed to gather and thicken before him, like a thought being collected.

"I am a song." A faint light appeared in the mist. *"An echo…"*

Marshall lifted his sword from the bedside table and stepped toward the transparent nebula as it struggled to form substance.

The haze shifted and sighed with his movement, saying warmly, *"There is… memory here. Peace. I envy you that. For I do not remember… it has been so long…"*

The captain focused. For a moment, he could swear he saw the faint outline of a face, staring back at him through the fog.

"Why have you come to me?" he asked in an even voice. "What is it that you want?"

The mist swelled and faded, then swelled once more.

Almost as if it were crying.

"To sleep… Peacefully, as you do," the unsteady face replied. *"To remember. And to wait in the arms of a memory, one worthy of forever. But they want… more. If they get what they want, my peace will be gone. As will yours, Son of Masguard. They rally. They rage. And it is you who must stop them."*

Marshall shook his head, sword still at his side. "What are you asking of me?"

"A solution. An end. Find the other. Open the way and drive

them back."

A flash of unease and consternation crossed the stoic captain's features. "What *other*? I don't–…"

Without warning, the face disappeared and the light receded.

Then came the echo of a single phrase, whispered in fear.

"*They know I am here!*"

In an empty room, free of mist or voice, Captain Marshall clutched his sword to his side, breathing heavily.

Too confused to notice the dispersing of the vapor from his breath.

Too unsettled to notice the warming of the floorboards.

7
SINKING SHIPS

Chimmy's hands were shaking as he turned the doorknob, not at all surprised to find the Marauder's room unlocked. The nimble captain was only the most notorious pirate in the Secoran Kingdom. It wasn't as if anyone would dare to enter his room without permission.

That would be crazy.

Head low, the possum poked his snout into the darkened cabin, nose and whiskers twitching in apprehension. When nothing stirred, he glanced over his shoulder, then ducked inside.

The pirate captain was lost in the kind of slumber that Chimmy hardly recognized, for he hadn't experienced it in ages, if at all.

Maybe the Marauder's too accustomed to guilt to be kept up by his misdeeds, he consoled himself bitterly as he recalled his recent nights on the *Negvar* – each of them a study in wakefulness. Pushing his resentment aside as best he could, the possum tip-toed across the room, pausing here and there to stare nervously at the rise and fall of

McKinley's chest. When he reached the captain's bedside, he froze.

This was madness.

He should turn back now, while he still had the chance.

You can do this, he drew a deep breath and held it, looping his fingers beneath the chain around McKinley's neck. *It's the right thing.*

He reached to unclasp the chain.

Then McKinley's hand clamped around his wrist like a livid vice. Chimmy cried out in shock and pain as he watched the momentary confusion on the Marauder's face turn to fury.

"Are you *thieving* from me, boy?" the pirate captain seethed, sitting upright to tower over him with readied muscles and a dangerous glare.

Terrified, Chimmy tried to pull away but found himself held fast.

"From *me*?!" With a thrust of his arm, the Marauder threw Chimmy to the opposite end of the room, far from the door. "You're bold, Leech, I'll give you that. But audacity has a time and a place. On a good day, I might chuckle over your inability to recognize that." His face darkened. "But a good day I *have not had*!"

The Marauder reached for his sword.

And found that it wasn't there.

His surprise gave Chimmy an opening, one the possum took as he lunged for a nearby lamp with no plan beyond wildly lashing out for escape. The heavy canister flew through the air, catching McKinley upside the head. Reacting from surprise rather than pain, McKinley stumbled just enough for Chimmy to haphazardly plant his shoulder into the captain's chest, knocking him to the floor.

There, with all of his slender might, Chimmy again hefted the lamp and threw it down on the back of McKinley's head.

The lamp shattered.

135

The Marauder fell limp.

Eventually, Chimmy the would-be thug stopped shaking. Then he leaned forward to jerk hesitantly at the chain around McKinley's neck until the old metal snapped free in his hands. The sudden give sent him off-balance and he stumbled away, tipping over furniture and pointing an angry finger to the Marauder's motionless form.

"Y-you had it coming!" he stammered in a voice of false commitment before bolting for the door with his prize, giving scarcely more than a second's thought to what he'd just done.

≈

Marshall practically danced across the deck of the *Albatross*, his sword slicing through the air in precise, measured movements. It was a rare exercise, this solo weapons drill – one so intricate and advanced that few members of the Warriors Guild ever got around to learning it.

Marshall had mastered it in two months.

Now, years after training, he found himself relying on the perfectly-controlled workout to bring order to his newly-chaotic reality. To silence questions and doubts. Maybe if he burned his muscles to exhaustion in a careful way, sleep wouldn't seem like an impossible task. As it was, there was no peace to be found in his cabin.

Despite what the blasted spirit had said.

At that, he stopped, driving the tip of his blade into the deck and leaving it to stand on its own as he turned to wipe his brow and stare at an unfriendly sea.

This wasn't getting him anywhere.

"Sir?"

Marshall turned to see his first lieutenant watching him from afar. Her brow was drawn together in concern. Clearly, she was unaccustomed to seeing her captain out of sorts.

"Is something bothering you?" Ryder asked.

Exhaling slowly, he said, "That seems a simple enough question, Lieutenant. But I'm afraid the answer is more complicated than you know."

"Forgive me sir." She bowed her head. "I didn't mean to intrude."

He waved a dismissive hand. "It's alright, Lieutenant. I'm simply reevaluating. I've found myself to be mistaken about a great many things regarding this mission."

"If you don't mind me saying so, sir, you've been correct about a great many things as well."

He arched a brow. "Such as?"

"The Baron's chances of success, for one," she offered. "You questioned Putris' claims in the Palace Hall, knowing that the scepter could not be found without first locating Mosque Hill, and that Mosque Hill could not be located without the Key, which he didn't have." She tipped her head, explaining, "Commander Calum told me, sir."

"Perhaps," he said. "But that is among the things to bother me. Why would the Baron claim possession of the Key in such a public forum? He gained very little by grandstanding on a lie."

At length, the collie gave him an examining look and said, "Except to spur the queen into sending you on this mission."

"Precisely," the captain concurred. "He knew I had it. But he had to be certain I would act on it. Because he needed me to open the Key and decipher its message. To lead him to the map. And now that I've done just that, a troubling thing has become abundantly clear. Something that *should* have been clear all along."

Her eyes widened in realization. "He isn't ahead of us at all."

"No, he isn't, Lieutenant." A glint of steel entered Marshall's eyes as he turned to pull his sword from the deck, concluding, "He's riding our tail!"

In one smooth motion, Marshall whirled in place,

ducking and bringing his blade around in a vertical arc. A *crack*! split the air as a flaming arrow fell to the deck in two pieces, having been severed in mid-flight, en route for the captain's skull.

From the mist beyond the rail, a ghostly shadow emerged, a ship. Small, but prepped for battle with a fully-armed crew, Von Ulric the Baron standing at the prow.

And it wasn't alone.

"*All hands to action stations!*" Marshall cried, bringing his crew to life even before the second ship rolled from the fog. Launching himself forward, he dodged swiftly through another volley of arrows. Though few of them took hold in any real target, the heat from countless tiny fires licked the moisture from the mainsail. A third volley, and it would burst into flames.

He felt the *Albatross* turning to port.

"Hold steady!" he bellowed, and was rewarded with a slight jerk of the ship as helm directed her forward once more.

One vessel behind and one across the starboard bow.

The Baron's strategy in attacking the naval vessel was clear.

He meant to herd her.

If the ship followed through on a leftward turn, having no guns facing aft, she would be at the mercy of both attackers with no way to return fire. The *Albatross* was big. She was strong. The temptation for any sailor would be to take the rearward hits and turn back for a full assault and a simple victory at range. But the Baron was no fool. He would never strike without the expectation of success.

Marshall bolted across the quarterdeck, commanding, "Ryder! Wexler!"

They fell instantly in line.

He pointed to the young ensign. "Get to fore and drop the starboard anchor!" Then to Ryder. "Sever the line once we're positioned to break between the two ships! Helm, hard to port on the Lieutenant's command! Let down and haul to run free the second we're clear! Gun crews, hold your fire! Wait for my order!"

No one questioned him.

Within seconds, the dominoes were stacked.

And in beautiful succession, they each began to fall.

The starboard anchor dropped and the ship jerked to the right like a fish on a hook, its hull sinking dangerously toward the surf. With a prepared shout, Ryder split the anchor's line and the helmsman followed suit, whipping the rudder into the turn just in time to keep them from capsizing. The crew set to work with the ship's halyards and the sails unfurled. Then they dug in their feet as the *Albatross* lurched forward at full speed.

It was fast and efficient – a militaristic symphony.

"Now!" Marshall ordered. "Let fly with everything we've got!"

As the *Albatross* shot between the enemy ships, her cannons erupted with simultaneous fire – leaving a deafening explosion of gunpowder and devastation in their wake. Only then did Marshall's crew recognize the reason he'd ordered the sails unfurled.

In the waters ahead, a third vessel was lying in wait, one that now scrambled and screamed as the greatest ship in Secoran waters barreled down on them.

They didn't stand a chance.

The oceans roiled and the wind was doused in splintered wood as the tiny ship was crushed beneath the naval boat's superior size and structure.

In less than a handful of seconds the *Albatross* had not only broken free of a carefully-laid trap, she'd drawn first blood and crippled her would-be captors.

Ryder looked to her captain in reverence. "Sir, *how did you know* there was another ship?"

Marshall had just opened his mouth to reply when the Baron's vessel came alongside them, shooting grappling hooks through the rails and into the crevices of the main deck.

139

Fate alive, but that ship was fast!
The captain gritted his teeth and caught Ryder's eye.
This wasn't over yet.

≈

It took a great deal of effort for McKinley to open his
eyes. And even when he managed to pry his lids apart, he
could scarcely focus on anything beyond the floor, where a
dark, sticky fluid pooled beneath his face. He could feel it
dripping warmly from his neck – though he couldn't be
certain whether it was oil or blood. A tentative touch of his
fingers revealed it to be both.

"Keep still, Captain," a gentle voice ordered.

The Marauder turned to see Father Faiz kneeling at his
side.

"You left your sword in my quarters. I came to return
it," the grizzled fox explained before he could ask, earning
a humorless grimace from the Marauder.

"Did you, now? Smashing timing on that front, Father.
Absolutely marvelo—" He bit off the word with a hiss of
pain as Faiz plucked a glass shard from the base of his
skull.

Pressing a folded kerchief to the open wound with
McKinley's hand firmly atop it, the cleric offered the
Marauder his weapon, hilt first.

Even in the darkness, McKinley couldn't help but
notice that it had been cleaned.

"Did you see him leave?" he asked as he came to his
feet, not bothering to sheath the sword.

"Yes," Faiz confirmed.

"Is he still on board?"

"I believe so." The father nodded once in a firm,
almost military manner.

"Well then," McKinley's voice was low and angry as he
turned for the door. "Let's go fetch the little Leech, shall
we?"

A few paces from the door, they each slowed to a halt, looking one to the other in uncertainty.

Something was wrong.

They felt the explosion before they heard it.

≈

Careful Steps Kal had been awake for many hours. Despite numerous attempts to get some sleep in a recessed bracket alongside the ship's figurehead, she found it difficult to relax. Not for lack of balance, as she had that in spades. She could curl up almost anywhere without fear of falling. The difficulty came when Captain Marshall stepped onto the main deck for his graceful version of sword practice. Quiet though his movements were, the mere thought of an accomplished military figure putting his not-inconsiderable skills on display was enough to make her stomach churn in anxiety.

Deep breaths, she reminded herself. *He doesn't know you're here.*

Screwing her eyes shut, C.S. leaned back on her tail, resolved to put the consequences from her thoughts. Sure, she might be caught. She might be throttled and clapped in irons. But there was nothing she could do about that now.

She had nearly convinced herself that an exposed sleep was better than none when a light appeared in the darkness, a flicker off the bow and just above the line of the sea. Several moments passed before she recognized it for what it was – fire.

No, no, this isn't happening!

She screamed internally as arrows rained over her head, drowning the ship in flames. Above her, able soldiers burst into movement, responding on instinct, their actions chaotic and rushed. Then Marshall's voice rose up, bringing order, building a machine where only scattered cogs had been. The ship became a focused weapon, one she shuddered to be a part of, even unintentionally. Her

141

former concerns seemed pointless as the anchor dropped to her right with a sudden rush of air, and she was thrown headlong over the end of the figurehead, scraping and clawing to catch herself just in time, with her feet dangling precariously over the sea. Then the cannons exploded, sending tremors through the wood. It shook with such violence that her tiny muscles cried out in desperation, proving no match. Her grip would fail her in seconds.

To make matters worse, an ominous shadow appeared through the fog ahead, staring down the bowsprit of the *Albatross* as if it were the spear of an angry beast.

It was another ship.

The orphan raccoon would be crushed between the two.

And there was nothing she could do about that, either.

For the first time in her young and difficult life, C.S. was well and truly afraid.

≈

Outside McKinley's cabin, Chimmy kept his head down and made for the life rafts, jumping at every sound, every movement, every odd whip of the wind.

Keep going, he told himself. *Almost there…*

"Chimmy, me lad!" a boisterous voice called from behind.

Oh no! He hunched his shoulders and pretended not to hear.

"Hey, new guy! Wait up!"

Reluctantly, Chimmy glanced over his shoulder to see the Kota brothers approaching with their affable brand of high energy.

Gil hopped alongside him, saying, "We hopes ye ain't sore at us fer that business earlier."

"We were only trying to help." Lumber nodded in agreement.

"N-no, it's fine," Chimmy mumbled as he kept

walking. "Don't worry about it."

Ormac gave a toothy grin. "Good, then. 'Cause we don' wanna give ye any trouble. Jus' welcomin' ya in our own way, is all."

"It's fine," Chimmy repeated, picking up his pace.

The rafts were so close.

Lumber jumped in front of him, walking backwards and forcing the possum to dial back his speed. "Where are you off to in such a hurry, anyway?"

Chimmy tried to step around the raccoon, craning his neck toward the prow, keeping his escape in sight. "N-nowhere," he insisted, a little too fervently.

At that, Lumber stopped altogether.

The Kota brothers shared curious glances, their jovial expressions bleeding away to show suspicion.

Catching a glint of light from the tarnished metal in Chimmy's hand, Gil pointed, asking, "What's that ye got there?"

"N-nothing," Chimmy pulled his hand away and turned to leave in the opposite direction, but Ormac grabbed him firmly by the arm, holding him in place.

"Is that the Cap'n's?" The one-eyed Kota demanded, looking both shocked and angry as the possum fumbled for an answer.

"N-no, no, of course not," he stammered, leaping in alarm when Gil caught his wrist and Lumber pulled the stolen item from his grip. "Hey! Give that back!"

Gil laughed. "Give it back, 'e says!"

"As if 'e'd any roight to it!" Ormac scoffed.

Lumber clucked his tongue, chiding, "Contrary to popular opinion, lad, possession's not the same thing as ownership. Stolen's stolen."

Chimmy lunged and pulled, screaming, "Yeah? And what do you care?! You're thieves, too!"

"Oh, aye, we're thieves," Lumber agreed, tossing the controversial object into the air.

"But we ain't crooks." Gil caught it and passed it to

Ormac, who nodded and gritted his teeth.

"*Thieves* have honor, we do," he said.

Lumber leaned in to Chimmy's face, accusing, "You clearly don't."

Gil moved closer as well. "So that makes you…"

"Nuthin' but a blighted *crook*," Ormac finished.

Folding his arms and pulling himself to his full height, Lumber planted his feet firmly in Chimmy's path, then said in a low voice, "We don't like crooks, do we boys?"

His brothers allowed a threatening pause before replying in unison, "No we don't, Lumber."

Eyes wide, the pale possum quivered with fear and no small amount of regret.

He'd almost made it.

Just then, the explosion he'd set only moments before sent the *Negvar* lurching to port. Taking advantage of their surprise and shaken balance, Chimmy made a desperate grab for the thing in Ormac's hand.

Then he *ran*.

≈

Breath held, C.S. prepared herself for the inevitable. Shaking from her ears to her toes, she tried her best not to cry. She didn't want to go out that way, not with tears in her eyes. As the shadow grew nearer, she tensed and turned her head. Maybe it wouldn't be so bad…

Then she felt a quiver in the wood overhead, one that was not the result of cannon fire or collision. She gasped in surprise as a strong hand gripped her by the scruff of her neck and towed her atop the figurehead. Clutching her to his chest, the uniformed officer turned and bolted for the ship, tumbling to the main deck just as the *Albatross* crashed into and over the enemy ship with a *crunch* that made the little raccoon cringe in sympathetic fragility.

When the adrenaline subsided, releasing her from her frozen state, she pushed away from her rescuer and stared up into the face of Commander Gray Calum.

"You," he said, as if in accusation, his familiar voice filling her with irritation rather than gratitude.

"You!" she bit back, coming to her feet and glancing warily at the otherwise-occupied crewmen nearby, wondering whether any among them recognized the traitor for what he was.

He scowled at her, demanding, "What in Fate's name are you doing here, kid?"

She folded her arms in a defensive gesture. "I told you I would catch up with you."

The commander pointed his finger in response, sounding far more exasperated than he had any right to be. "And *that* was your method? You could have been killed!"

"But I wasn't." She shrugged, then caught sight of Captain Marshall from the corner of her eye. "So, if you'll excuse me."

"Wait!" He stopped her with a shake of his head. "Where do you think you're going?"

Shrewdly, she watched Marshall disappear below decks. Before moving to follow, she glanced back to her savior and co-conspirator saying, "Presumably, you did your job. Now let me do mine!"

≈

Though the second ship was slower to right itself, it too had found its way alongside the *Albatross* and into grappling range.

"The smashers, sir!" Ryder pointed to the guns on either side of them. "If they pin us down…!"

Marshall nodded, grimly aware of the implications. Both ships – the Baron's in particular – were heavily fitted with carronades; brutal cannons designed to blast a wide and indiscriminate path through rigging and personnel alike. They were at their most lethal in a close-range battle where their target couldn't maneuver to mitigate the damage. With ships on either side, caught in a crossfire…

It would be a bloodbath.

"Return to the front of the ship, Lieutenant," he ordered before turning for the stairs. "Keep them clear of the forward hatch."

"Sir?"

Turning back, he explained, "They know they can't sink the *Albatross*, she's too much for them. They only attacked because they mean to board us. When that happens, do not break position and do not allow the forward hatch to become blocked. Is that understood?"

"Aye, sir!" Ryder snapped a salute and bolted to the fore of the ship, prodding the gun crews as she went.

Veins screaming, instincts cursing, and every ounce of his well-stocked mettle railing in protest, Marshall turned his back on the battle, destined for the lower decks. He was on the middle gun deck when the carronades opened fire.

And the world around him exploded in thunder.

The concussion rocked the ship. Marshall stumbled beneath the splintering of wood and the screams of those caught in the blast. He gritted his teeth as iron shattered the spaces around him, pelting him with hull fragments that cut through time and flesh like glass in a slow-motion salvo. Ignoring countless tiny wounds, he dragged himself to his feet with a growl and pressed on. Down and down until, after what seemed a lifetime of sound, he reached his destination.

The hatches had each been secured at the lowest level of the ship. A vital precaution, considering their cargo. Leaving the queen's advantage vulnerable to early release would have been unwise, to say the least.

He slowed to a stop at the front of the hold, surprised to see that they were already awake and staring back at him through the shadows with an unnerving silence. Wordlessly, Marshall released the forward hatch and tipped his head, waiting. For what seemed the longest time, they held his gaze with a distance, an alien austerity that left him wondering whether they hadn't changed their minds. Maybe they would turn on this miniscule thing and take their leave when they bloody well pleased. But no. At last, and returning a dutiful bow, they rose up on massive limbs and poured from the open hatches like unknowable nightmares.

Marshall drew a breath, hard-bitten and resolute. Then he turned to make for the stairs once more and found himself face to face... with a tiny raccoon.

Glancing over his shoulder as if to affirm the bizarre nature of this juxtaposition, he barely had time to look confused before she leapt past him at lightning speed. She ripped the medallion from around his neck in a single, swift movement and darting through the open hatch with an innocent smile.

Mouth open as if to speak, he stared after her for a brief and baffled moment.

Then he turned to follow her in the only way that he could.

Up the blighted stairs.

≈

The ocean responded violently to the blast. Bursting onto the main deck, McKinley saw half-aware sailors scrambling for a topside anchor as the ship careened beneath them. Despite the chaos, two things were immediately apparent.

One, Chimmy the Leech was boarding an escape raft to his left.

And two, Amelia Ling was far too near the railing to catch herself in time. She was pitched into the sea to his right.

Depending on the damage to the *Negvar*, any head start could spell success for the possum's efforts to betray them. He would escape with no repercussions, no reckoning, and no regrets. It would be a simple choice if only Amelia could swim.

But he knew that she could not.

He looked to his right.

Then to his left.

His decision had already been made, whether he liked it or not.

"*Blast!*" McKinley snarled through whiskers and bared teeth before turning right and darting for the rail.

His back arched into a dive as he cut through the air. He barely had time to see Chimmy's mouth part in gleeful triumph before plunging beyond the prow, slicing the surface of the water with a precision that would make even the dolphin regulators green with envy. Adept hands propelled him with impossible speed toward Amelia's convulsing form. When she saw him, she opened her mouth in an instinctive cry for help, sucking water into air-deprived lungs. She coughed and spasmed. Even as he closed his arms around her for rescue, her terrified struggle seemed beyond all rational control with flailing limbs striking at him in desperation. For a moment, she broke from his grasp and was ripped by rushing current toward a dark shadow along the belly of the boat.

Panic would drown her in seconds.

Forcefully, he launched himself after her, grabbing her by one wrist, then the other. Pinning her arms to her sides to keep her from thrashing, he muscled her through the water until they broke the surface, where she gasped in relief and clung to his chest, some semblance of her sanity restored.

Father Faiz was already at the rail, a lifeline in his hands.

The moment they appeared, the ready fox tossed the rope around Amelia's waist.

McKinley secured her tightly, then gestured for the exhausted cat to be towed onboard before submerging himself yet again with a roll of his tail.

In the darkness below, he moved toward the shadow and rush of current.

A massive hole grinned back at him from the keel of his ship. Vital beams parted with splintered edges to gnaw upon the water rushing into the hold like the teeth of a monstrous beast. He followed the tides through what was once the outer hull and only found air after he'd broken through the hatch to the middle deck. There, he gasped and slammed his fists into the floor. Water coursed in angry rivers from his cloak. His ship – his beloved *Negvar* – had been mutilated beyond repair.

Which left him without a means of moving forward.

Which meant his quest for Maya's cure… was over.

McKinley choked back a cry of despair, then shook his head, adamant and unremitting.

"No," he whispered in fury. "I'm not finished. Not yet!"

Through the deck and up the ladder he flew, launching himself the final feet onto the main deck with his teeth bared in a vicious snarl. Chimmy had nearly lowered his raft to sea.

Nearly.

"Kotas!" McKinley barked, drawing his sword. "Swab this deck! Port side! *Now!*"

The three raccoons leapt to action, running and throwing themselves from the rail as the Marauder catapulted into the rigging, swinging his sword and severing the forward support for Chimmy's raft. With only a single rope to hold its weight, the raft tumbled toward the sea, dumping Chimmy into the air, where he was caught mid-fall by the acrobatic Kota brothers. Using the very same move they'd so jovially employed only hours before, they swung around, tossing him back onto the *Negvar.*

And directly into the Marauder's murderous grip.

The possum tried to cry out, but the raw strength in McKinley's hands forced every inch of air from his lungs in a painful explosion – even before bearing him up and slamming him full-force into the mainmast. He gasped and whimpered over the claws that dug into his shoulder, drawing blood. The furious captain rummaged through the traitor's disheveled clothing until he found his stolen possession. Then, lifting the broken chain in a clenched fist, McKinley pressed his face close enough for Chimmy to feel the rage burning in his breath.

"This. Will cost you dearly, Leech." McKinley whirled and threw Chimmy to the deck at Lumber's feet, ordering through gritted teeth, "Bind this! Everyone else..." He paused, his voice lowering only slightly.

But enough to show the sting of an eminent loss.

"Abandon ship. The *Negvar* is going down."

8
A CAREFUL BETRAYAL

"*Come on!*" Ryder snarled to the mob surrounding her. Just as her captain had warned, the enemy ships had abandoned the carronades after the initial salvo. Much of their rigging had been shredded, along with an unthinkable number of the crew. Now the Baron's forces poured in angry masses over the rails, swarming the deck of the *Albatross* with swords and zeal. Despite their numbers, her captain had ordered her to keep them away from the forward hatch. And — feet apart, long-spear held ready — that was precisely was she was going to do. Wave upon wave of challengers had broken upon her already. Still she stood, fuming with the rage of a dedicated soldier, an obstacle that would not be moved.

The worst of it had been watching the Baron board. Marshall's men were well-trained — the best in the fleet — but such a thing hardly mattered against a force like Von Ulric. He moved like an avalanche, plowing across the deck with an indifference that made him seem otherworldly. Awful and unnatural at the same time. The jagged scimitar in his hand was used as an afterthought to add a bit of blood to the crushed bone and pummeled flesh in his rampage. He turned so violent that he even began using his teeth.

Her subordinates didn't have a hope against him.

Ryder squared her stance.

Do not break position, her captain had said.

Never one to disregard an order, the avid lieutenant hefted her spear. If she couldn't assist her crewmates by bringing herself to the Baron, she'd just have to bring the Baron to her. Stepping forward, she hurled the spear, whipping her entire body into the throw. In an impossibly straight and powerful line, it traveled the length of the deck, bound for the Baron's back. It was unlikely that the spear alone would kill him. But it would certainly get his attention.

Or it would have, had it reached its destination.

From the corner of her eye, Ryder caught a blur of scars and ornamental coins, rusty fur. Then the spear was smashed, struck from its flight by the crushing blow of a steel mace – a weapon held in the rather delicate hands of a long-limbed coyote. Landing in a crouch, the lithe Kathkan came to her feet as the Baron turned. Though his teeth were bared with an eye for revenge, she sent him back to his slaughter with an unhurried wave of her hand.

The two canines made eye contact.

Then the mob surrounding Ryder found the courage to rush her.

Forced to defend her position at close range, Ryder drew her sword, cursing the pointless loss of a weapon that could easier have kept them at a distance, away from the hatch. She whirled and swiped, covering as much distance as she could with every movement until the area was clear and the Baron's men lay prone at her feet. Ryder rolled them each from the hatch with a shove of her boot.

All the while, the coyote stared her down, seeming intrigued.

The battle roaring around her, she crossed the deck in

languid strides, stopping just short of Ryder's sword. There, she gave the lieutenant an approving once-over.

"Seeing you fight, I feel obligated to ask whether you wouldn't be interested in a job," she said in an accented tone.

Ryder felt her lips pulling back into a snarl. "Not remotely."

"A shame." The Kathkan shrugged, sounding bored. "But I expected as much. You Secorans are so predictable."

With a lightning flick of her arm, Ryder's sword shot forward and over the coyote's face, leaving another future scar on her cheek. She followed the blade with her fist, knocking the startled Kathkan back on the deck.

"Aren't we just?" she taunted, lifting an eyebrow.

The coyote righted herself with a laugh. Shaking off the wound as though it meant little enough to her, she took her time in drawing the mace that hung loosely from her hip. For a moment, she looked as though she meant to respond, but she didn't. Not with words.

With a calm face and feral movements, she flew at Ryder, weapon raised.

Ryder dodged, knocking her blow askew with a fast parry. The coyote's long arms carried a sinewy strength that the lieutenant was not prepared for. Her every lunge was vicious; every fall of her weapon like the drop of an anvil. Ryder ducked and pivoted and countered, avoiding blow after blow until the Kathkan's raw tenacity wore her to exhaustion.

Suddenly, there was a surge in the hatch beneath them. For the unfortunate fraction of a second, Ryder lost her footing.

It was more than the Kathkan needed.

The lieutenant felt a sickening *crunch*! as the mace came down on her shoulder. Bone and tendon ruptured beneath the skin and she crumbled, growling through gritted teeth to stymie an outright cry of pain.

And again, the coyote laughed.

"An excellent fighter, truly. But you try too hard to stay in control, I think," she purred to the lieutenant. "Commit to your movements and your sword will carry more weight."

As if to support her statement, the hatch pressed up against her feet, doing nothing to affect her stride.

It didn't open, either.

Speaking of weight...

Ryder looked down to realize that their combined weight was keeping the hatch in place. Whatever trick Marshall had up his sleeve could not be unleashed until Ryder cleared the area, as he'd commanded.

She glared up at the approaching Kathkan with renewed steel, knowing that she would not fall here.

Not until she'd followed through on her captain's order.

Turning swiftly on her side, Ryder swept her leg under the coyote's feet before rolling out of the way. Caught by surprise, the Kathkan toppled onto the corner of the hatch, remaining just long enough to see what peered up at her through the grate.

Her eyes widened.

She just had time to whisper "Impossible..." before the hatch exploded open, tossing her aside and spewing three winged silhouettes into the night sky.

≈

C.S. darted up the hatch with the captain's medallion clutched between her teeth, wondering at the creatures that had gone before her. Whatever they were, they were big. All along the walls were scuffs and gouges, claw marks that were wider than *she* was. She wondered whether she shouldn't stay below decks until she had a chance to scout the threat, but decided against it. Even with the detour, Marshall was only seconds behind her. If she wanted to avoid an encounter – which she did, at all costs – she'd have to climb the rigging and cross the yardarm to the Baron's ship before he reached the top of the stairs. Whatever was waiting overhead couldn't be any scarier than a naval icon with a grudge.

She flew into the rigging without a backward glance.

She hadn't gone more than a few steps before Commander Calum landed on the yardarm in front of her.

"What do you think you're doing?" he demanded.

"What does it look like?" She lifted the medallion into the air and sneered. "I'm getting out of here. And if you have a lick of sense, you'll do the same. Before Marshall comes up those stairs and kills us both."

"I don't think Marshall's the one you need to worry about," he said as a shadow floated across the nearby sail.

C.S. tensed and stared at the sky.

Three war-like shrieks pierced the air at such a volume that she winced and covered her ears. Pandemonium broke out when one of the Baron's men pointed with an open mouth, screaming an impossible name into the air, "Gryphons!"

"No way!" C.S. said with a stunned look on her face. "It can't be!"

Saying nothing, Calum watched them circle the ship slowly, with intent.

Almost as though they were looking for something.

"*That* was the cargo?!" she yelled in confusion. "You were supposed to take care of it!"

From high in the air, one of the massive creatures locked an avian eye on the tiny raccoon.

The commander gave her an odd, almost kindly look before plucking the medallion from her hands and saying, "That's exactly what I'm doing, kid."

At that, the gryphon dropped from the sky and dove straight for her.

"But… no! I – *help me*!" She screamed as it dragged her from the yardarm, leaving scores in the wood where she tried to maintain her grip but couldn't.

Calum watched her disappear into the mist, seeming remorseless, even satisfied. Then he leapt from the yardarm to the deck below. He pulled up short when he realized the Baron stood in front of him.

The wolf's coal-black eyes bore through him, shifting for an instant to the rigging, where C.S. had been only moments before.

"Leave her," Calum said, opening his hand to reveal the stolen pendant. "I have what you need."

Von Ulric bent his neck, lowering his head to peer sidelong at the commander. "And you are?"

Pulling himself upright, Calum forced some gusto into his words. "I'm your informant. Had you seen fit to meet me in person prior to now, you'd know that. This way."

Without looking to see whether the Baron had moved to follow, Calum strode past him through the fray and into the captain's cabin. He made a show of rummaging through the captain's desk, tossing papers aside and standing in exasperation when he came up empty.

"The map." He turned to Von Ulric. "It isn't here. Marshall must have hidden it."

Suspicious, the Baron bared his fangs. "He doesn't have a safe?"

"Not that I know of," Calum lied. "Even if he does, we hardly have the time to find it, let alone crack it open." He gestured outside, where the gryphons were making quick work of the Baron's men.

With a low rumble that caused Calum's fur to stand up on end, Von Ulric took a threatening step forward. "For your sake, Commander, I hope you have an alternative to me leaving this ship empty-handed."

Calum nodded faster than he meant to. "I may not be able to give you the map, but I have seen it. Take me with you and I'll reproduce it as best I can."

The Baron laughed. "You want to come with me?"

"I can't stay here." Calum lifted his hands to the room.

"Not after this. Marshall will skin me alive."

Von Ulric stared at him for a moment, seeming far too still to be paying any attention whatsoever to the massacre outside the door. Then he splayed his colossal claws in a falsely benevolent gesture and smiled, his teeth gleaming in the dim light like individual drops of saliva. "Very well. But you should know, Commander, that if you fail *me*... the punishment will be far, far worse."

"Yeah," Calum sighed, his voice quiet and resigned. "I get that."

He said no more as he led Von Ulric from the cabin and across the deck, easily avoiding combat because neither side knew whether or not he could be considered a target. His subordinates would not attack their commanding officer. And the intruders would not attack someone who seemed to be moving alongside their master.

It was a shameful immunity.

Calum swallowed his disgust just in time to find himself face to face with Captain Marshall.

≈

Marshall flew up the stairs and ran his gaze over the deck, searching for some sign of the thieving raccoon, but she was nowhere to be seen. He set his jaw, scarcely having time to savor his annoyance before he was rushed from ahead and behind.

Anger would have to wait.

Spinning back as he dropped to one knee, he swung his sword in a rapid circle, slashing across the shins of both attackers as they closed on his position. Stumbling, they collapsed onto one another's weapons and fell lifeless to the deck. Again, he was rushed. This time, he replied with brute force, leaping from the deck to plant his foot into his attacker's chest. The force of his blow sent the helpless creature flying into a nearby group. Entangled and off-balance, they tripped over the railing and into the sea. In a fluid motion, Marshall caught his enemy's abandoned cutlass with his foot and lifted it deftly into an open palm.

He was deadly enough with one sword.

With two, he was a blighted hurricane.

His arms moved in an articulate blur, gracefully dispatching foe after foe until dozens lay prone on the deck surrounding him.

Until the roar of battle had been forced to pay him a proper distance.

Until they didn't dare attack him further.

Tossing the secondhand cutlass aside, he turned to see Commander Calum staring at him with a look of horror. For a moment, he wondered why his first officer was doing nothing to assist the fight; why the Baron stood over the ringtail's shoulder but did not seem interested in using the opportunity to strike him down.

Then he saw the medallion in Calum's hand.

The officers shared a look.

"Gray…" Marshall shook his head. "Don't. Please."

"I'm sorry sir." Calum looked back at him with the utmost regret. "I have to."

Stunned beyond all ability to react, Marshall felt the blow to his chest, felt the snap of the chain as he reached for the medallion and pulled it free at the last second. He felt the painful crack of his ribs as he fell against one step, then another, and another. He felt the weakness in his arms as he tried to lift himself from the base of the stairs, only to sink trembling to the floor. But more than that, Captain Marshall felt the sting of an emotion he could not name as consciousness faded and blackness overtook him.

It felt suspiciously like… failure.

≈

"*NO!*" Ryder's cry rose above the din of an unfinished battle.

Overhead, creatures so rare that many considered them to be alive in legend only created furrows in the mist, blotting out the night with impossible wingspans. They circled and shrieked, drumming terror into queen's men and invaders alike. It was amazing. It was horrifying.

And the only thing in Ryder's attention was the image of her captain tumbling down the stairs – paid in terrible betrayal by none other than her superior, Commander Gray Calum. Of all the things to play out on the *Albatross*, that was the one to strike her most as unbelievable.

Shoulder screaming, she forced herself off the deck and stumbled into a run. Not bothering to ensure that the coyote had been incapacitated, she dragged her uncooperative body after the traitor until it was clear she would never catch him, not in this chaos. By the time she reached the stairwell, he and his oversized ally were long gone.

Turning with a snarl, she scraped her boot against a bit of metal on the deck. It clattered to the side, drawing her notice. She was shocked when she looked down to see her captain's fine rapier lying useless on the ground.

He must have dropped it when Calum attacked.

Ignoring the objections of damaged tissue, of tendons and muscles that pressed up against the skin in a wince-worthy mass, she knelt to pick up the blade and caught sight of poor Ensign Wexler. He was standing nearby in the midst of the battle, oblivious and slack-jawed as he stared at the mythical raptors above and around the ship, acting his age at the most inopportune time.

She looked down at the sword in her hands and drew a mustering breath.

"Ensign!" she ordered as she came to her feet, jolting him from his stupor. "Come with me!"

Grabbing his arm as she bolted past him, she made for the edge of the ship, stopping occasionally to defend the lad from wayward weapon strikes and aimless fists. When he noted her labored reactions, the way she kept her left arm pressed against her side, his eyes widened in concern.

"You're hurt!" he cried.

"Yep," she answered noncommittally as they reached their destination and she shoved him behind a stack of crates. "Now stay down and don't move until there's a window. When I have their attention, you need to cut the grappling lines. Listen sharp, Ensign!" She slapped him lightly on the chin to catch his wandering attention. "The gryphons will drive them off, but in order for them to do that we have to separate the ships, understand?"

"Yes, Lieutenant." He nodded fervently, eyes still wide, massive ears drooping in distress.

She held his gaze, knowing to her core that he meant to be strong, that he would do as she asked despite the risks, despite the fear.

He was the bravest of them all, she thought with a smile.

Drawing his sword for him, she wrapped his hands around the hilt and held them. "Do you know the Warriors' greeting?" she asked.

Knuckles white, he shook his head and gripped the handle for all he was worth, as if it could keep him from trembling. "I never joined any of the Guilds, sir."

"Nor did I. But I've heard the captain say it a time or two. *Find honor in your purpose*, he says." She tightened her hands around his. "*And purpose in your sword*."

Wexler looked to his weapon then, seeming a little calmer, a little more confident that maybe there was more to this than shock and thunder. "Honor and purpose," he said. "I understand, sir. I can do it."

"Good lad." She nodded approvingly.

Then, Ròs Eibhlin Ryder, mercenary daughter to a gypsy clan, singer, soldier, and first lieutenant under the faith of her captain, turned to the chaos of an embattled ship. Above her, the mizzen mast used her fervor as a cue to surrender. It crackled and snapped, succumbing to the damage done by the carronades and collapsing through rigging and sails. She walked calmly beneath it as it crashed to the deck behind her with only a few feet to spare. Turning along its length, she found the ship's pennant in the rubble and pierced it with the tip of her captain's sword.

Lifting the flag into the wind above her head, she shouted, "Enemies of the *Albatross*! We are soldiers of Secora! Know that we will not fail! We will not fall! And we will rail against the bearer of death until our captain orders otherwise! Stand and fight, if you dare! This is a good place to meet your end!"

The crew joined her then in a long wordless shout that steeled their determination, the nerve of their grit fairly breathing its own life as they rallied to her side, organizing in a way that would have made Marshall proud, were he only there to see it.

The young ensign watched in awe as he leapt to his task, forgetting the magnificent gryphons as they dropped from the sky like heavy lightning, striking, killing, and driving the onslaught into retreat. He forgot the wings and talons and watched instead the unfolding of courage and valor.

The honor and purpose of those who fought.

The glory of those who fell.

Commander Calum

9
FIFTY-SEVEN AND COUNTING

"What was that?!" Lady Sira slammed her hands into the table. "*You* said they would be unprepared! Explain to me how an *unprepared* vessel manages to best three Kathkan warships!"

Her rage was so thick and so palpable it might have asphyxiated an ox, were one so unfortunate as to be present in the wardroom of the *Havoc* where she, Von Ulric, and the former commander Gray Calum stood, eyeing one another from opposing corners.

It was almost like they didn't trust one another.

"My intention was never to bring the *Albatross* down." Von Ulric shrugged in a slow, noncommittal gesture. "I had an objective. I obtained it."

Sira's glare shot to the former commander. "You mean *him*? You put my ship at risk for a single Secoran?!"

He smiled with condescending teeth at her seeming naiveté. "In taking this *single Secoran* we've removed the good captain's every advantage. The map, the medallion, even his ability to rely on the loyalties of his crew."

Her gaze did not move from the silent ringtail in the

corner. She seemed to be willing him to look at her, to prove he could ever be worth the embarrassment of being so soundly bested, of being forced to run away. He did not return her stare. He did, however, seem remarkably well composed for one who reeked so of discomfort and shame.

"Never underestimate the power of betrayal," the Baron continued. "Nothing whittles strength quite so quickly as a loss of faith in those who are meant to support you. The captain will begin to doubt himself. I assure you, his failure will follow."

"*His* failure?" She looked back to him with a smile that was anything but humorous. "*His*? This captain, he calls creatures from lore to tear us to pieces, and you? What do you have? A rodent with a necklace!"

"*I*," Von Ulric said treacherously, leaning to meet her eyes over the table. "Have everything I need to find the scepter. Which was the entire point of our oh-so-quaint alliance, you may recall." A growl crept into his voice. "And while you're in a spot of reminiscence, you might do well to remember your place, little Kathkan. I'm not to be trifled with."

"Trifled?" She laughed, her face turning furious on the instant. "Who's trifling? I'm *yelling*!"

Just like that, Von Ulric was over the table, with her pinned to the wall beneath his claws, monstrous teeth parted in a grinning threat. For a moment, Calum was certain he meant to bite off her face.

"I don't have it," he blurted out, earning surprised glares from Kathkan and Baron alike. "I don't have the medallion."

Von Ulric dropped Sira to the floor. She gasped in relief and came to her feet as the wolf turned in Calum's direction, forgetting her entirely.

"Marshall must have grabbed it when I knocked him down," the ringtail tried to explain. "We were on the *Havoc* and gone before I even realized it was missing."

If Calum expected a violent response, he received none. Instead, the Baron stared at him with black eyes and deliberate breath. Then he lifted his hand to a blank scrap of parchment on the table.

"Draw," the wolf commanded.

Calum took a slow breath and swallowed before speaking.

"No," he said.

The Baron's tentative wall between patience and fury came crashing down. He leaned in and tipped his head to peer at Calum sidelong, seething in disbelief, "*What?*"

"I will not draw the entire map. Not now," Calum said. "I lost the medallion and I know you mean to kill me for it. You made that clear enough in Marshall's cabin. But you can't be done with me until you have the map. So you aren't getting it. Not all at once. I will write what I remember a bit at a time until I know I can safely leave this ship. Only then will you have what you need."

"I *don't* have what I need." The wolf lowered his head and pulled back his lips. "You *lost* what I need."

"And you'll get another chance to rectify that. Marshall's going in the same direction you are, remember. As long as you know where he's going, the medallion isn't lost. But you still need *me* to get you there."

The Baron was horribly silent. Calum could see his terrible mind working behind angry eyes. If he retaliated, as he clearly wished to do, the former commander would be dead. At the very least, he would be impressively crippled, with reason enough to sabotage whatever information he might be willing to provide. If the Baron wanted to avoid a total loss of his efforts, Calum had to believe that his knowledge of the map would be enough to buy his safety.

This traitorous ringtail had him by the scruff of the neck.

Suddenly, the great wolf let out a roar that was somewhere between a snarl of frustration and a howl of warning. It was enough to make Calum's fur stand on end. Wincing, he took a step back. But only one. He could not back down now, not if he wanted to live.

With a furious flick of his cloak, Von Ulric turned to leave, driving his fist into the wall alongside the door as he passed through it, shattering the boards and cracking the adjoining frame. Lady Sira stared at Calum for a long moment before following in the wolf's mountainous shadow.

When they were gone, Calum forced his breathing to slow.

But he couldn't quite stop the shaking of his hands.

≈

Captain Marshall had awoken in the med bay, secluded from the many others he knew to be there. He'd left without being treated. He would not lie idle while his ship struggled to put itself back together. More than that, he'd needed to see. And see he had. The very picture of calm, he had walked through the aftermath, through the blood and tears of his crew, past the dead and those who sang their noble laments. He had seen, and now he stood in his cabin, staring blankly through the aft-facing windows and waiting for the death toll from Ryder.

"Fifty-seven, sir."

She stood at attention as best she could, with her arm in a sling beneath her crippled shoulder. The strain on her back was tremendous but, seeing her captain, she knew better than to complain. Dried blood still clung to his brow and the collar of his coat. Even with his rigid stance, she noted the slight slump to his neck, as though his body was trying to force him into a ball around the pain in his torso, but he willfully refused. A cup of tea was held motionless in his right hand, only inches from his face. Somehow, she knew the tea to have turned cold some time ago.

"Fifty-seven dead. With more than a hundred wounded," she continued in an even voice. "We lost three lieutenants, as well as the carpenter."

He read between the lines easily enough. The reduction in officership would have an impact on morale, and without the carpenter, repairs to the ship would be slow and substandard. Overall, the *Albatross* had been significantly weakened.

"The aft section of the ship took the brunt of the damage from the carronades. The mizzenmast was shorn away entirely. We had to sever the shrouds and stays when it rolled off-deck to prevent it from dragging us down, so we lost the majority of the aft rigging. The crew is working to reinforce what they can, but..." She had the good grace not to mention their limited roster. This was a first-rate ship of the line, a class of vessels usually manned by a crew of over eight-hundred sailors. The *Albatross*, by contrast, had a crew of five-hundred. They were hand-picked. Each of them the best. They performed their duties better and more efficiently than three others in their place. But when the task was to distribute a workload such as this? The loss of so many put an unenviable strain on Ryder's job.

Marshall set the teacup on a nearby table and clasped his hands behind his back. With that simple motion, he forced his emotions into a box at the base of his stomach. A part of him wished he could leave it open, at least for a while. To feel the guilt, to reenact the anger and sadness, to lash out in frustration. But he did none of these things. He held it down until the lid was firmly latched, knowing that he wasn't the only one with a life's obligation. His crew... They'd taken their oaths, same as him. He let them down once. He would not do it again by refusing to respect their decision to follow him, to dedicate their lives to the welfare of the Secoran Kingdom.

If he wanted to honor them, he would best do it with silence.

"They can handle the aftermath, sir," she assured him.

"They can. And, despite having offloaded all non-essential supplies in Secora Tor, we'll find a way around the repairs. But Commander Calum…"

That was another matter entirely.

The box couldn't hold that one.

He looked to her then, his mouth a grim line set beneath eyes of wounded steel, and she knew better than to finish the sentence.

There was a gentle knock at the door and Ensign Wexler stepped inside.

He seemed remarkably unharmed.

"Pardon the interruption, sir." He saluted. "Calum is here to see you."

Marshall came around with a start.

His reaction faded when an elderly ringtail came into the room with her hand on her hip and a medical satchel slung over one shoulder.

"I see. *Doctor* Calum," he said. It sounded not so much a greeting as a way of chiding himself.

Ignoring the tone in his voice, she approached with a disapproving glare and slapped him on the back of the head.

"*That* is for walking out on me without treatment," she scolded.

Ryder put a hand to her mouth while Marshall clenched his jaw to keep from grimacing.

"I was well enough to stand," he said. "There were others not so fortunate. They required your attention more than I."

Calum narrowed her eyes. "Of the people in this room who attended the Health Guilds, only *one* of us remained long enough to be called a doctor. That person isn't you. So *I* will decide what my patients do and do not need, thank you very much. Sit down." She pushed him into a chair with firm, efficient hands, her examination surprisingly gentle for all its briskness. "You have a concussion. And three broken ribs. This gash should be stitched, if you'd sit still long enough, but I know that you won't." She shoved a vial into his hands and turned to Ryder saying, "You. Stay with him and make sure he takes that. If he gets confused or shifty on his feet, you bring him to me. Otherwise, I don't want to see his face until he's ready to apologize."

Ryder's attempt to hide her grin failed as Doc Calum gathered her things, preparing to leave as quickly as she'd arrived. Marshall shook his head. Neither of them mentioned the actions of her nephew. They both knew she'd deny it. Gray was like a son to her.

Still, as she left, they heard her mutter, "You kids. What will you do when you don't have me to worry over you?"

Ryder's smile faded.

She knew the doctor was speaking as much to her absent nephew as she was to anyone else.

"What will you do?" She said again in a quieter voice, her face sad.

Marshall almost stopped her, almost said something. Didn't he owe her that much?

The thought was interrupted by a loud *thump*, followed by two more. The ship lurched with each sound, then rocked back and forth a moment before settling.

When they filed onto the deck, they immediately saw why. Three gryphons stood side by side at the center of the ship, having landed with such force that it shifted the mighty boat in the sea. Despite its enormity, the ship seemed so limited with them in place. Massive creatures, each of them large enough to dwarf even the Baron himself, their lion's bodies were feathered from head to mid-back, where the feathers lengthened and thinned, bleeding over sleek, mammalian pelts taut with predatory muscle. Their ears were tufted like those of a lynx, but pressed back against aerodynamic skulls. Birds of prey with feline instincts. Predators from talon-ed toe to feathered tail.

Understandably, the crew was giving them a wide

berth.

Only one person was foolish enough to think he should do otherwise.

Eadric stood beneath them, at the place where their shadows overlapped. The queen's advisor was falling over himself to earn their attention, but they paid him no mind. Both shadow and beast stood, regal and detached, waiting for something or someone. When Marshall stepped on deck, their fierce eyes shot instantly in his direction.

True to form, the captain was neither reluctant nor timid when he came before them, nudging Eadric aside with his sword. Lifting his fine rapier before his face, he offered no words, only a slight bow of his head.

One by one, the gryphons each extended a foreleg and returned the bow, leaning low over owlish feet in a solemn salute. Then they launched themselves into the air without having uttered a sound. It was an untouchable sight, these three great creatures dropping in succession to swoop the circumference of the ship, their feathers skimming the surface of the water as they angled their wings in farewell and climbed again to atmospheric heights. There, they disappeared beyond the reach of a war that was never their own, leaving the *Albatross* in awe and gratitude.

"Sir?" Ryder watched them through the fog, her voice full of wonderment, "If I may ask, how did they come to be on board? Before last night, I would never have believed they even existed, and somehow you had them hidden here on the *Albatross*, this entire time. How did you ever convince them to fight with us?"

Marshall's gaze was still on their retreat, though they were already far beyond his sight. "They were never with us, Lieutenant. Not truly. They owed something to my..." He caught himself. "To Masguard, and by extension, the House of Prideaux. So when the queen called, they came. I doubt they cared for our cause, if they knew of it at all. It was a matter of honor and reciprocity, of an old debt being repaid."

"It must've been quite a debt," she smiled. "Considering what they left for you in the brig."

Young Wexler, who stood at her hip, made a face. "They didn't…"

"Oh no, Ensign, it's much worse than that," Ryder replied, shaking her head in amusement and saying to Captain Marshall, "You've got to see this, sir."

≈

Six life rafts bobbed on choppy waves, lost in the mist. No words were spoken. Even through the biting cold of a sudden rainfall, the ire burning between the boats was tangible enough to warn away the chill.

Anger was such an effective numbing agent.

McKinley sat at the prow of the foremost vessel, silent, still. Though his eyes were fixed on the emptiness before him, his thoughts were on what lay behind.

His ship swallowed by a dismal sea.

Sodden canvas dragged by unfeeling waters to the gates of Oblivion, alongside his chances of ever finding Mosque Hill.

Unacceptable.

"Why did you do it, Chimmy?" Amelia was saying in a soft voice, as though she genuinely meant to understand. "Why would you do this to anyone at all?"

"Wh-what do you care?" he stuttered glumly. "It was just a ship, anyway. J-just a pile of sticks."

Her eyes narrowed inside of a pained face. "That was our *home*, Chimmy."

"Don' bother." Ormac put a hand on her shoulder.

"He don't care who he's hurt." Lumber agreed.

"Only matter te him is that 'e got caught." Gil stared the possum down.

Chimmy put his head down. "It was just a ship," he repeated in an angry tone, as though using the thought to refuel his resentment. "And you're just pirates."

McKinley clenched his jaw.

Unacceptable!

The hiss of his cutlass was intentionally careless as it came up and around in a lightning swipe, severing Chimmy's bindings and taking plenty of his fur in the process. The possum licked once at the blood on his wrist before nervously shifting his eyes to the surrounding crew. They knew what was coming. He could see the eagerness on their faces.

The Marauder stood over him, his expression dark and unreadable. "Well, you wanted to scurry off, didn't you, boy? Now's your chance. Get on with it."

Chimmy looked up at him in confusion.

Surely the Marauder didn't mean for him to run away now, did he?

"What, are you worried about them?" McKinley pointed with his sword to the six rafts filled to the brim with angry crewmen, then brought the blade back to Chimmy's gullet in an idle gesture. "Never you mind your pale little head. They're only *mostly* looking to tear you limb from limb. How's this? I'll put you in the water ahead of the rafts, where they can't reach you, and you can tow us wherever it is you thought you were going to go. That way, your chances of arriving there in one piece are at least slightly higher than none."

The pale possum turned even paler. "B-but, I can't. It's too far!"

"*What's* too far?" McKinley leaned down, his adamancy forcing its way through his conversational tone.

Chimmy's voice failed as he rubbed his bleeding wrist and desperately tried to plan an escape, understanding at last that this was an interrogation.

And it would not end well.

Grabbing him by the front of his shirt, McKinley hoisted Chimmy in a sudden, one-handed motion, dangling his feet over the edge of the boat. "Perhaps I wasn't clear," he seethed. "My crew wants to kill you. I want to kill you. Hesitate in your answer again and my very slight inclination to keep anyone at all from killing you will disappear altogether. Savvy?" His angry smile carried more menace than Chimmy was certain he'd ever seen. "Now, I'll ask again. After you'd betrayed your crew, stolen from your captain and *BLOWN UP MY SHIP*!" McKinley yelled the last into Chimmy's face, then lowered his voice immediately to its even and sinister tone. "Where. Were you preparing. To go."

"S-south!" Chimmy winced, his legs flailing. "I was going south. To the Sea Bones. The Manus."

"To meet whom? You didn't do this on your own. Someone sent you, and that someone would want to be there when you finished. So who was it?"

Chimmy's mouth opened and closed in a floundering manner until McKinley gave him a threatening shake. "The Baron," he confessed at last. "Von Ulric. He was supposed to send a frigate to pick me up once you were out of the way."

Now it was McKinley's turn to look confused. "The Baron? What interest could he possibly have in me? Why my ship?"

Chimmy didn't answer right away. He was too busy staring at something in the mist.

He swore he saw movement there.

A form where there should be stillness.

"I-I don't know…" he said, sounding distracted. "You just… had something he needed."

Lumber screwed up his face. "That's it? You trashed our ship 'cause the Baron said so, and nothing more?"

"We let you into our home!" Gil pointed angrily.

"Treated you like family and you betrayed us!" Ormac crowded in behind McKinley.

"And so what?!" Chimmy yelled back. "You're pirates! All of you, nothing but pirates! It was the right thing to do! I did the right th—!"

His eyes flew open wide as a dozen disembodied hands

shot from the mist – wispy, ethereal things that clamped over his mouth and arms like ghostly bonds, replacing those the Marauder had sliced away. In an instant, the possum was ripped from the raft into the sea. And just like that, Chimmy the Leech was gone, leaving only a few final bubbles in his wake as the mist closed around McKinley's empty hands.

The Marauder stepped back, panting in disbelief.

That didn't just happen.

It couldn't have.

He stared at the water beneath the fog for a long time before turning to see his crew staring back at him, terrified, desperate for guidance.

"Well, what are you all gawking at, you scurvy tars?" He yelled, his voice shaking only slightly as he jerked his arm to the south. "You heard the dead man! Row for the Manus!"

≈

"LET ME OUT!"

There was a war being waged inside that room. There must have been.

Ryder licked her teeth in an attempt to ward off a smile.

"Near as we can tell, she belongs to the Baron. A message runner or maybe a spy, we don't know. Your legendary friends kept her safe throughout the fight and brought her to us when it was over," she said.

Marshall furrowed his brow. "There must have been a reason that they singled her out for capture."

"Aye sir, but they offered no explanation."

He couldn't help but think of Calum's earlier visit below decks, but mentioned nothing of it.

"Why wasn't she placed in a cell?" he asked instead.

"The bars were spaced too widely to hold her," Ryder answered. "She slipped right through them."

Marshall stared wryly at the door, trying to imagine how one so small could make so much noise. The thumping of tiny hands as they battered on the door went far beyond the point of futility. They bordered on the hysterical. The guards cringed, having been pushed to their mental limits by the unbelievable ruckus.

"She's been at it since we locked her up, sir," Ryder explained.

Marshall took pity on the tired sailors. "Take some idle time, gentlemen."

With a salute, they gratefully complied.

When they were gone, the captain gave a single nod and Ryder turned her key in the lock. Immediately, a tiny ball of gray fur exploded through the door. Ryder caught her by the scruff of her neck.

Held firm in Ryder's easy grip, the raccoon tugged and grunted comically, even going so far as to run in place. The lieutenant yawned. Marshall studied his fingernails. Finally, after several long moments, the raccoon seemed to tire enough to cease her ridiculous display.

"Are you quite finished?" Marshall looked down at her.

She glared up at him impudently before beginning her struggles all over again.

As if for spite.

Eventually, she settled enough for them to sit her down in a chair. Her feet didn't quite reach the edge of the seat, so the pout on her face and the twitch of her fluffy tail looked to be directed at the wood on which she sat. How dare it dwarf her so? She was small enough already.

Marshall tried to remind himself that he was in the aftermath of an unfortunate battle, that she was an enemy combatant, a prisoner of war. But he couldn't help himself. He felt too much like an elementary school principal.

"I recognize you now," he said. "I didn't see it before, in the hold, but you're Careful Steps Kal, orphan of Bryton. The head of Secoran Security has been after you since you were old enough to crawl. Which is when your thieving began, if I'm not mistaken."

"It is." She glared proudly. "And good on you for finally catching me. It only took you ten years."

"A hungry, parentless child stealing only enough to make it through the day?" Marshall raised an eyebrow. "Believe it or not, putting an end to your reign of terror wasn't exactly a priority."

At that, she folded her arms.

"You attempted to steal this from me," he went on, gesturing to his father's medallion. "Why?"

"No," she corrected. "I *did* steal it from you. Because that's what the Baron hired me to do. Well, not directly, but he needed it. And your commander made like he wasn't up to the job on his own. So I snuck onto the ship to help, for all the good it did me." When the captain fell silent, her glare softened. "Didn't see that one coming, did you?" she asked. "If it makes you feel any better, he betrayed me, too."

Seeing the tightness around her captain's eyes, Ryder stepped in. "You're very forthcoming about all of this."

C.S. shrugged. "Not much point in lying now, is there? It isn't like I'll be getting off of this ship anytime soon, and when I do, I'm guessing the Baron won't much be bothered with me anymore. If I'm not being killed and I'm not being paid, I'm not very motivated to keep any of it to myself."

"You don't much care for Von Ulric, do you?" Ryder noted.

"Von Ulric's a monster." The little raccoon's words were matter-of-fact. "*Nobody* cares for him."

"Then why work for him?" Marshall found his voice at last.

"Why not?" C.S. fired back. "It's not like anyone else would hire a kid like me. And a thief, at that. Secoran nobles like you only care about the young and poor when we're underfoot. If you'd had your way, you'd have locked me up long before I ever gave you reason to."

"Don't be so certain." Ryder stopped her.

"Pfft," C.S. scoffed in return. "What do you know about it?"

Kneeling alongside the chair, Ryder pointed to her distinctive earrings and said, "Everything."

It took a moment for their meaning to register on C.S.'s face. The jewelry – slender, wooden hoops with golden accents – marked the lieutenant as a gypsy. Guildless, nomadic groups, once seen as outsiders to be ignored or otherwise dealt with by the high-class citizens of Secora Tor, their culture had been almost completely consumed by the last few decades of societal growth. Those who still existed were scattered and hidden, orphans in their own right, keeping their identities a secret in order to gain acceptance. But Ryder wore her earrings proudly.

"He didn't lock *me* up." She held the raccoon's gaze until her tiny shoulders heaved in a sigh that drained her of defiance. "They call you Careful Steps because that's how you move, am I right? You don't want to be noticed, don't want to be caught by the wrong person in a bad situation. You allied yourself with the Baron because he's strong, and you didn't want to be seen as weak. But you *aren't* weak, Kal. You don't have to put up a front for me to recognize that."

When C.S. finally responded, it was with quiet words, in a much younger tone of voice. "I didn't know they were going to attack. If I'd have known anyone was going to get hurt, I... Well, I have to believe I would have said something, warned someone."

Ryder put a hand on her shoulder. "I believe you. And it isn't your fault. The Baron would have come for us eventually, whether you were here or not. He wanted the medallion, remember? But do you know why?"

"No," C.S. said. "I do know that they must be terribly important, for him to take such a risk in trying to retrieve them."

Marshall stepped forward, exchanging surprised looks

with Ryder as he asked, "Them?"

"Well, yeah." The raccoon gave him an odd look, as though the response should have been apparent. "He wanted both halves, not just yours. What good is a broken necklace?"

"And the other half?" Marshall asked.

"I don't know that, either." She actually looked apologetic. "He gave that job to somebody else. Another theft, another betrayal. He seems to like that sort of thing. I can tell you that we were all supposed to meet at the same location, regardless of whether or not we succeeded. If the other person made good on their task, you might still be able to catch them there."

Ryder looked hopeful and hungry at the same time when she asked, "Where?"

"The only hiding place this ocean seems to have." Again, C.S. seemed to be saying the answer was obvious enough. "The rocks of the Manus."

≈

Scattered, white stones protruded like teeth from an elliptical formation of rocky islands. They were ruins, the foundations of an ancient city with no known history and no name beyond a vague reference to their stark appearance. Some called them the Sea Bones. Others, the Manus. For tonight, at least, they were individual gravesites, and the only sign of life they held was the glinting of several dozen blades from six little boats.

The crew was quiet. McKinley supposed they might each be coming to terms with the idea that they were waiting in the shadows for an unsuspecting but well-armed ship. One that would likely deal them heavy casualties before falling, if it fell at all. Or maybe they were still in shock after seeing what they'd seen with Chimmy.

It hardly mattered.

He welcomed the silence, no matter the reason. It

made it seem normal for him to stare out at the empty bay with a dangerous expression, like a predator in wait. In reality, he was just avoiding Father Faiz. The fox would never dream of gloating. He would never say 'I told you so,' never remind that his warning went ignored, or even hint that it was given at all. McKinley would still feel chided. His conscience would make sure of it.

The Marauder drew a breath and firmed his jaw, thinking to himself that it didn't matter. His ship may be gone, but another was coming.

He would take it.

And he would finish what he started.

Hours passed before the vessel arrived, but arrive it did. It began as a shadow in the distance, a patch of night creeping behind the dense fog at a fearless pace. When the shadow grew into detail, McKinley's back tensed. He sat up, clutching at the sides of the miniscule raft with a grim sense of resignation and felt his crew doing the same. Chimmy had told them to expect a lesser vessel. Something small and fast, capable of putting up a meager fight, at best. But the oceanic fortress rising up before them was no frigate. It was the first in first-rate ships of the line, the largest and most efficient weapon in the queen's arsenal, the one-hundred-and-ten-gun flagship of the Secoran Kingdom.

It was the *Albatross*.

"McKinley the Marauder." A tall figure emerged from the soldiers lining the rails, his voice calm, his gaze both cool and regal. "Captain of the pirate ship *Negvar* and enemy to the crown."

McKinley recognized the accusation for what it was. Gritting his teeth, he locked eyes with his nemesis for the very first time, naming him in return. "Captain Marshall."

The Prodigy of Secora smiled then, the very slight smile of one who had no interest in reveling, but always knew this day would come.

"You and your crew," he said, "are under arrest."

179

10
HOLDING UP MIRRORS

No sooner had the words been spoken than a splash marked McKinley's escape into the water. Several arrows followed him through the surf, skidding past his face and cloak before he heard Captain Marshall calling for a halt from above. The firing ceased immediately.

McKinley dove beneath the keel of the *Albatross*, taking refuge in the shadow of its underbelly. He resisted the urge to scream, to pound his fist into the coppered bottom of the boat in frustration.

It could not end like this.

Not here. Not now.

To the east and west, he could see inclines in the seabed where the ocean met the curve of the shore. He was a strong swimmer. Maybe he could make it without being detected. Maybe he could wait in the rocks for an opportune moment, or a smaller ship, something easier to target. Maybe he could find them again through the fog and still reach Mosque Hill before the third full moon. Maybe his crew would forgive him for leaving them behind.

Maybe.

If only they knew.

If only…

Suddenly, McKinley felt a jolt of physical desperation in his chest. He'd stayed submerged in indecision too long. His lungs were *screaming* for air.

Stay or flee.

Hold the course or save his skin.

It was now or never.

≈

"Hold your fire!" Marshall ordered with a steady hand. "He can't go far, and I doubt he'll abandon his crew. Bring them aboard." As able soldiers organized themselves to carry out his command, he turned to Ryder. "Secure them below decks. As few to a cell as possible. No reason to make their inevitable escape attempts any easier than they need to… Lieutenant?" Marshall waited patiently for his words to register, noting that, for the first time in Ryder's tenure of service, he did not have her full attention. He followed her gaze to one of the rafts below, searching for the source of her distraction, but saw only a fox in cleric garb. "Is something wrong?" he asked.

With difficulty, she pulled her eyes back to his. "Um… no, sir." She recovered. "Nothing's wrong."

"Are you certain?"

She stood to attention, reassuring firmly, "Aye, sir."

He nodded once and she returned to the job of intimidating her subordinates.

But Marshall was too troubled by her actions to smile at the way they jumped to do her bidding. He glanced over his shoulder to the fox with the humble posture and found him staring back, as though searching for someone along the rails.

A certain collie, perhaps?

Priorities, Marshall reminded himself.

Pivoting in his smooth military step, the captain started for his cabin, ordering, "Post guards along the rails and send word to the topmen. I want everyone keeping a weathered eye on the water in case the Maraud—..."

Marshall's foot, like his words, froze in mid-stride. Inches beneath his heel was the sopping-wet toe of someone else's boot. He lifted his gaze to find himself nose to nose with McKinley, darkly clothed and soaked. Where anyone else might have looked bedraggled, the Marauder managed to look sinister and imposing, a harsh figure unperturbed by the elements.

He was every inch the perfect pirate.

"You're right," McKinley said. "I won't abandon my crew. But boarding on someone else's terms? Well, that doesn't sound like me, either."

Marshall withdrew his foot and noted with disapproval that McKinley had made it to the middle of the deck without having been stopped or even seen. In pitting the pirate's skills against those of his crew, that did not bode well.

"So I'll board your little vessel," he went on. "I'll even let you apprehend me, which I know you're just *dying* to do. But, just so we're clear, I have no intention of staying wherever it is you put me. Not for long."

"I suppose you are prodding me to respect your candor," Marshall said flatly, his face unmoved.

"Oh, no, no, not at all," McKinley scoffed, internally annoyed by the way Marshall's crew hung back. Much as he'd have liked to think they did so out of fear, he knew all too well that they were simply waiting for their captain's order. They were showing deference, not hesitance. "If you were to admit to respecting anything about me, then I'd have to find something to respect about you, and I just don't think I'm ready for that sort of thing. Best that we stick with blatant insults. At least until we get to know one another."

182

Marshall stared back at him for a long moment, showing nothing.

When he did speak, his deadpan response caught McKinley by surprise.

"I thought you'd be taller."

Before the Marauder could react, Marshall gestured to his crew. They searched, disarmed, and bound McKinley almost upon the instant. As they dragged him below, destined for the holding cells on the orlop deck, the captured pirate found room to bite childishly over his shoulder, "Funny, I thought *you'd* be shorter!"

≈

McKinley had just finished carving the phrase 'Marshall is a maggot' on the rear wall of his cell when a boot whacked him upside the head. Indignant, he dropped the knife and hurled the unlikely projectile back at its owner with a drawn-out, deliberate, "*OW!*"

Gil ducked just in time.

"Oh! Sorry, Cap'n!" he gushed in a stage whisper. "We was goin' fer the keys!"

With his back to the bars, McKinley glanced over his shoulder to the far wall, where a set of keys dangled temptingly from an iron hook. "And, pray tell my moronic friend, what in blazes is *that* going to accomplish? Is your woefully inaccurate thimble of a boot going to retrieve them for you after it knocks them to the floor? Hmm? Tell you what. When it doesn't, and you realize what an idiot you are, I get to smack you in the head with the other boot. Deal?"

Amelia looked up from the floor of her cell, where she sat on her heels, staring intently at McKinley's back. "Even if you could reach them, Gil, you won't be using them to break out of your cell," she said.

"Oh, aye, that's exa'tly what we's gonna do," Ormac argued.

McKinley leaned his head against the bars, shooting an exasperated sigh to the ceiling. "Honestly, how the three of you ever got to be the masters of the Thieves Guild is a mystery and a travesty. I weep for outlaws everywhere."

"Those are the keys to the supply closet, guys," Amelia said, giving them a sympathetic smile.

They looked from her to the keys in unison, their faces falling.

Then Ormac sighed and moved to sit beside Lumber at the back of the cell.

Gil sunk against the bars. "Drat."

"Told you," Lumber said.

"Shut up."

As their conversation descended into brotherly jibes and questions as to why anyone was bothering to whisper, Amelia again brought her gaze to the Marauder's back. His bitterness spent, he'd turned his venom to off-handedly flinging his dagger into the floor between his feet. Sarcasm was never far from McKinley's mouth, but it wasn't normal for him to condescend like that. Not to his crew. He seemed tense, and she could gauge from his breath that he was angry, even apprehensive. Between Chimmy's betrayal and subsequent, disturbing death, the loss of the *Negvar*, and the now the capture of his entire crew, the Marauder had more than ample reason to step away from his chipper self and brood in a spot of despondency. But somehow, she knew the darkness in his disposition was more than just a hostile turn of Fate.

Something in her captain was breaking.

She only wished she knew why.

At the sound of approaching footsteps, they all fell silent. Gil pulled on his boots. McKinley tucked the knife smoothly into the sleeve of his cloak. Then they turned to see Lieutenant Ryder coming to a stop at the center of the deck.

Guards filed in around her as she eyed the prisoners distantly, like a farmer staring down a crop, calculating harvest and sizing up the ripest fruits. Her sling had been removed, allowing her to stand with her hands clasped behind her back in an appearance of strength. It was too much to hope they wouldn't remember her wearing it. But she couldn't allow herself to show a weakness here.

"Sneaking that past Marshall's men was no small feat," she said, bringing her fierce canine eyes to McKinley's cell. "They are the best the Navy has to offer."

McKinley withdrew the knife and openly resumed his target practice, as if in silent challenge. "That speaks volumes about the Navy, doesn't it?"

Fluidly and without obvious intent, Ryder moved to stand over the Marauder, her tone turning harsh. "I'll have your blade. Now."

As he came to his feet and turned to tower over her, he chuckled, "Madam, you'll have to come in here and take it from me. Or better yet." He leaned in toward the bars, "Let me out of this cell. And I'll give it to you."

With only the flick of her tail to mark recognition of his threat, Ryder smiled an unreadable smile and moved closer to his cell. Then her hands shot through the bars at an alarming speed. Grabbing him by the cloak, she slammed his face forward into the door. There was a harsh *clang!* as flesh met reinforced iron, forcing a surprised grunt from McKinley as he dropped the knife and stumbled back. Wiping the blood from his nose, the Marauder ignored the guard who stooped to retrieve the smuggled blade in favor of glaring at the lieutenant through the bars. She held out an open hand for the knife, seeming unperturbed. The guard placed it in her palm and, just like that, she walked away.

McKinley had half a mind to call her back for another round before she stopped at Father Faiz's cell. The humble fox was kneeling in silent prayer, but bent his head even further as she approached. He drew a deep breath, as though preparing himself.

"Look at me," Ryder said. There was a strain to her

voice that seemed oddly similar to the way McKinley had addressed Chimmy on the raft. Hints of anger and contempt, laced with the hard-to-swallow shock of one who's been deeply wronged and doesn't understand why. When Faiz made no move to comply, the lieutenant put her gloved hands on the bars and seethed her demand a second time. "Look. At. Me."

When at last he lifted his eyes to meet hers, McKinley saw the reason for his hesitance. It wasn't defiance or dismissal. It was shame. Profound and sincere repentance.

"Do you recognize me?" Ryder asked. "Do you know who I am?"

Drawing another deep and steadying breath, the gentle priest nodded once.

When he did, the lieutenant set her mouth, leaning nearer with an icy glare, saying simply, "Good." Then she nodded to the guards and they jumped to obey, unlocking the door without question. Before the fox could exit, she slammed the flat of her hand into the doorframe, blocking his path. "I'm watching," she warned, adjusting her grip on McKinley's dagger.

McKinley leaned curiously against the bars as they passed, watching Faiz for some sign of understanding or explanation, but the quiet priest offered none. His eyes were fixed firmly on the floor beneath his feet, his gait even more subdued than usual.

Salvation, Faiz had said. *A final chance to atone.*

He couldn't have meant *her*? Could he?

When they were gone, the Marauder withdrew a second knife from his sleeve and resumed his pointless target practice. Maybe it was none of his business. It was becoming clearer than ever that they all had their secrets.

Ormac let out slow whistle. "She's a piece o' work, eh?"

"She's definitely *something*," Lumber agreed, derisively.

"I 'ope she's still on duty when they be interrogatin' me." Gil chuckled.

"Don't worry," McKinley chimed in with a roll of his eyes. "I'm sure she'll get to you around lunch time. Hungry work, interrogating."

Leaning through the bars, the raccoon wouldn't be dissuaded. "There be worse ways te go!"

"Don't mind him none." Lumber waved a hand in McKinley's direction.

"He's jus' sore 'cause she drew blood, ain't 'e, Cap'n?" Ormac concluded with a hoot, lifting a palm towards Lumber. He slapped it heartily, and the three Kotas laughed as though congratulating one another on their good humor.

"There be one thing what I don' get, though," Master Tobb said, interrupting their amusement. "Accordin' te Chimmy, this was the pickup point fer the Baron's li'l thief. Don' ye think he moight've mentioned it if he knew that Cap'n Marshall were gonna be the one doin' the pickin'? Seems like big news, that."

At the mention of Marshall's name, McKinley mouthed the word '*maggot.*' Twice.

"Maybe 'e didn't know?" Ormac offered.

"I'd hate to be the one giving Her Majesty that news," said Lumber. "Can you imagine how she'd react if she found out her pet student was really the Baron's lackey?"

Gil scratched the fur beneath his chin. "Oh, aye, but Marshall? The Prodigy of Secora? Seems 'ard te believe."

"The Baron has spies everywhere," Amelia said. "If Chimmy proved anything it was that loyalties aren't always obvious."

McKinley's dagger silenced all debate as it *thunked* loudly into the floor at the middle of the deck, far from his cell. "Are you guys kidding? More appropriately, are you *blind*? Have a look around. Their sheets are in tatters, the mizzen's gone, and their cannons are practically fuming. Does this ship look like it's been rubbing palms on the sly with pals of any sort? For Fate's sake, the decks are so bloody thick with gunpowder I'll be lucky to get the residuals out of my cloak without soaking it in rum – not that I'm altogether opposed to the idea. Much as I'd like to think that Maggot the Navy Boy is the bad guy in all of this, he's not. His ship was just in a battle for her life and I'll wager two to one it was with the Baron. The only difference between us and them is that they managed to limp away."

Amelia caught his gaze from across the deck and shook her head, warning him to tone it down. There was no reason for anyone else to gain an eye into his angst. When he squared his jaw and turned away, she knew he'd caught her meaning, even without words.

"If 'e didn't come fer Chimmy, why's 'e in the Manus?" wondered Tobb.

"The *Albatross* probably had a mole of her own," McKinley replied, a little more calmly.

"They'll be shaken by it," Amelia said. "Likely more than we were."

McKinley nodded. "You're right, but it won't be enough to give us any sort of an advantage. If anything, it'll push their bright-eyed awareness to an even higher standard. They'll be wary, watchful little soldiers, every one."

"Then what can we do?" she asked.

McKinley smiled an *o-ye-of-little-faith* smile as he swung his cell door open and strolled to the center of the deck to retrieve his dagger. Then he returned to his so-called prison, where the bars parted whenever he willed.

Amelia laughed.

When confronting Ryder, he must have stolen the keys just long enough to unlock his door, then replaced them before the guard could notice their absence. But she hadn't seen him do it. No one had.

"You *let* her grab you like that," Amelia grinned knowingly.

"Well," McKinley shrugged. "One must be willing to bleed for their craft and crew every now and again, yes?

So, my comrades in deviant behavior, are we ready for a glorious bit of larceny?"

A chorus of enthusiastic *aye-ayes* flared up in response.

"Then prepare for a takeover of the righteously-repugnant jewel of the Secoran Armada." By now, the Marauder's smile had returned in full. But he didn't look jovial, or even hopeful. Simply determined. "Come tonight, the *Albatross* will be yours!"

≈

Marshall could hear the clanking and clashing of tools overhead. He could smell the oakum and pitch being used to seal the cracks in the deck and mend the splintered wood in the hull. He knew that able seamen were aloft, running new rigging and patching the sails where they could. They were doing their jobs. And he was here. Drumming his fingers on the back of the only chair in the room. Feeling uncharacteristically impatient.

"This is exciting!" Eadric blundered into the room with a quill and too many rolls of parchment. "McKinley the Marauder, on this very ship! This is quite a catch, quite a catch indeed!" He looked about in consternation for a moment before realizing he would have to make do without a desk and plunked himself down in the corner of the room, spilling papers and ink bottles clumsily to the floor.

Sighing, Marshall pinched the bridge of his nose.

Maybe he should let Ryder handle this.

Then she arrived with the prisoner in tow, and he knew that he should not.

She didn't shove him hard – not hard enough to warrant a reprimand, or even to interrupt his stride. Given the size and strength of the cleric fox, Marshall doubted anyone on the whole of the ship was strong enough to affect his movements, even a little. But the look in her eye, the tension in her clasped hands, both spoke volumes as to why she should not be left alone with this one.

Stepping to the back of the room, he waved a finger for her to follow. "For whatever reason, Lieutenant, I was expecting you to bring the Marauder."

"McKinley's very difficult to gauge right now, sir. I didn't want to bring him through the ship without being able to predict what he might do. This one's less likely to make an escape attempt." She tipped her jaw in the father's direction. "And his position will make him more likely to answer whatever questions you may have."

Marshall thought a moment, then nodded his satisfaction with her assessment and returned to stand before the prisoner.

Ryder released a held breath.

What she *hadn't* said was that she needed to hear what this unassuming goliath of a canine had to say for himself.

Long accustomed to being the tallest on his ship, Marshall found it strange being forced to look up in order to meet the other's gaze.

"Please," he gestured to the chair. "Have a seat."

The fox obeyed without hesitating.

"My name is Captain Marshall. This is my ship, the *Albatross*. You and your crew have been detained for obvious reasons. Would you be so kind as to state your name for Advisor Eadric's record?"

There was a long pause, as though the priest were attempting to hold onto his moment of peace as long as he could before shattering it with his reply. "Deagan Faiz."

At that, Eadric's quill froze in flight from the ink jar, blotting the page. An audible gasp came from one of the guards outside the door. Marshall blinked.

"*Sir* Deagan Faiz?" he asked, a note of disbelief in his voice.

"Once, yes," the fox admitted, sounding shamed.

Marshall inhaled as if to speak, then closed his mouth and furrowed his brow. "Lieutenant," he said benignly, gesturing again for her to follow, this time to the outside of the room. "You knew about this?" he asked when she joined him, closing the door. There was nothing accusatory in his voice, but he was clearly not pleased.

Ryder nodded apologetically. "Yes, sir."

"And you said nothing?"

She tried to respond, to make her defense or ask forgiveness for her dereliction, but it was several moments before words found their way from her mouth. "What could I say, sir?"

It took little time for Marshall to put two and two together. Given her background, there was only one place where a gypsy might have crossed paths with an elite member of the Warriors Guild. He understood now the reason for her anger.

"Is there anything else I should know, Lieutenant?"

Yes, she wanted to say. *He is not the knight they speak of in fireside tales. No hero. No valiant soul. He is a monster. And I cannot abide his presence on your ship, nor even the knowledge that any of his like should ever be permitted to breathe free.* Silently, the words raged, just behind her tongue. But she did not say them. She would not say them.

She was a better soldier than that.

"No, sir," she said aloud in a strong voice.

He held her gaze for a long moment. Then, with a nod, he turned to hold open the door, gesturing for her to enter ahead of him.

Though Eadric had not moved from his corner, he looked shocked that they had ever left him unattended. Faiz hadn't moved either, except to wrap his rosary around his hand. Marshall studied him, surprised in hindsight that he hadn't recognized this fixture from his childhood. Though Masguard himself had never joined the Warriors Guild – or any guild at all, for that matter – he'd often rubbed shoulders with the Secoran Knights when they were still in commission. Faiz had been younger then, by far. Younger than the captain was now. Still, it had not been uncommon for Marshall to see the promising weapons master in sword practice with his father, or silencing a tavern simply by walking through it. He recalled the two of them sitting across from one another, swapping tales and smiling indulgently at the child who pulled himself up at his father's knee – just as he'd pulled himself up at the cottage window – to watch a legend unfold from the other side of a transparent barrier.

"My father spoke of you," he said at last.

Faiz smiled in response. "Of you as well."

His meaning was clear.

Yes, he remembered Marshall.

No, he would not divulge the captain's identity to those in the room.

Swallowing, Marshall tipped his head ever so slightly in appreciation. The gesture would have been imperceptible to anyone who wasn't watching him carefully.

"My ship and my crew are in dire need of my attention, so I will be as brief as possible," Marshall began. "Where is the *Negvar*? Why is she unmanned?"

"The ship was destroyed," replied Faiz.

"Why and by whom?"

"As to *why*, Baron Von Ulric is the only one who can offer a worthwhile answer," the father told him. "It was done on his orders. *Who* is no longer of consequence. He was a traitor. He is dead."

"Is justice always so swift on pirate vessels?" Ryder asked from the back of the room.

"It was not our doing." He spoke without turning to look at her.

She folded her arms. "You'll forgive me if I find that difficult to believe."

He bowed his head without complaint. "Of course."

Marshall watched their exchange without interrupting. "Then you are not, I take it, working for the Baron?"

"We are not."

"What was your vessel doing out here? The Manus is a poor place to hide and there are few merchant routes worth pursuing in these waters."

Faiz met his eyes then, seeming somewhat amused in his response. "We were following you."

Marshall raised his brows. "Another duckling," he said to Ryder, referring to the Baron's identical pursuit. "It seems our mission has sparked something of a trend in the Secoran underground."

"McKinley wants the Mosque Hill Fortune," she concluded. "Seems fitting that his greed should ultimately get the best of him."

At that, Faiz turned somewhat in his seat. "Greed is more the virtue of monsters than thieves. Captain McKinley may be a thief, but he is far from monstrous."

And you'd know all about that, wouldn't you, her eyes bored into his back.

Marshall sighed. As much as he should have taken a measure of pride in the capture of his nemesis, he had come to the Manus in search of answers regarding the Baron. He recognized now the reason for his impatience. This was unfortunate timing, to say the least. A distraction he couldn't easily afford.

"That will be all, Father," the captain said, earning a groan of disappointment from Eadric, who seemed to be enjoying his work for the first time.

"Alternate arrangements should be made for Sir Faiz's detainment, Captain," Eadric said. "Knighthood does allow for certain privileges under Article Thirty-Two."

"That is kind, but unnecessary," the knight-priest objected.

"The advisor is correct," said the captain. "It may be unorthodox, given the company you've chosen to keep. But I would be inclined to honor those privileges. After all, your title was never revoked."

Faiz stood from his seat and turned to face him. Before allowing himself to be escorted to the door, he responded honestly, "It should have been."

When the father was led away, it was amid awed

glances and whispered identifications of *Sir Deagan Faiz, Warrior*, and *Last of the Secoran Knights*. But were his senses not so mastered, were his hearing just a little less acute, he would not have heard them call him *Murderer*.

≈

"That is enough, Grogoch." Lady Sira sighed from the other side of the deck, where she leaned nonchalantly against the hull. She'd been there for hours, watching the brutish albino lay into their prisoner in every way imaginable, to no avail. Abner would not talk. "I do not wish the old fool dead. He's tougher than he looks." She came to stand over the battered old badger, saying, "You've earned your silence, for whatever it's worth."

"You'll understand," he panted through bloodied teeth, "if I don't go out of my way to express my gratitude. I'm still not desperate enough to fall for the kindness act."

"Don't be so dramatic." She rolled her eyes. "I do not do this as a kindness. In the Kathkan Empire, trials by pain are practically mandatory. This was nothing. But you weathered it well enough, so I will do you the honor of obtaining my information elsewhere. It is that simple. I will never understand why you Secorans must complicate things with motives and ploys. Take the compliment for what it is and sit in peace until the wolf decides what he will do with you. Come, Grogoch."

They were turning to leave when the wolverine decided to take one final swipe at his victim and found his path blocked. Gray Calum caught him by the arm, knocking his fist aside just before it could come in contact with Abner's bruised face. "She said that was enough!" the former commander growled.

The albino stared back at him a moment, confused.

Then he grabbed Calum by the front of his uniform and threw him into the hull.

Gray grunted in surprise as the wind was knocked from

his lungs. He crumpled to the floor like a ragdoll, gasping for breath. Before he could recover, the wolverine was on him, pinning him to the wall and snarling into his face. "You dare stop Grogoch?! Stupid soldier! Maybe Grogoch tear smug uniform from shoulders! Maybe soldier not so brave without it!"

Calum forced his arm from under the wolverine's grip. With a grunt of effort, he grabbed for his sword and managed to lift it just enough to slice across the inside of Gavroch's leg, forcing him back. "You are not touching my uniform." He planted his feet and pointed his sword, a determined look in his eye.

Howling with rage, the wolverine coiled himself for a lunge but whirled about yelping in surprise when Lady Sira grabbed him by the tail, saying, "Enough, Grogoch. Leave the brave little soldier be." Brushing Calum's sword aside, she came to stand between them in a relaxed manner. "You like to interfere, don't you, Secoran?"

"I wasn't aware I'd made a habit of it."

"No?" She arched an eyebrow. "But again, here you are, sticking your nose into someone else's violence. Just as you did in the wardroom."

Reluctantly, he sheathed his sword. "I don't know what you're talking about."

The coyote placed her hands on her hips. "Games, games, always games with you people. Do not bother with the pretending, it makes me nauseous. The wolf meant me harm. You stopped him with your," she waved a hand, searching for the right word, "*blunder* about the necklace."

"Oh, that. That was just... accidental chivalry."

"*Accidental,*" she said, mocking his accent. "This, I do not believe. Do I look like I need your protection, Secoran?"

"Certainly not," he answered quickly.

"Good." She put a claw beneath his chin. "Perhaps you will remember this the next time you challenge someone greater than yourself. *Accidents* like that will only get you killed. Come, Grogoch. Let us see if we can find the little soldier something less offensive to wear."

Calum stopped them. "I'd prefer it if you didn't."

Sira eyed him curiously. "You do not wish your uniform damaged. And you do not wish to change. Why the sentiment? Dress as the ship demands."

"What would that prove?" he asked. "Everyone on this ship knows who and what I am. I *was* a soldier. And I was Marshall's friend. I could put away the uniform and dress like everybody else, yes. But that would just be," he threw her word back at her, "*pretending*. And Fate knows we wouldn't want to make you nauseous, now, would we?"

At that, the coyote laughed heartily, looking at former commander with something akin to approval. "You say you betrayed your captain? This Marshall?"

"Yes," he said.

Arching her brow yet again, she shrugged and turned away.

"What?" Calum called after her.

"Nothing." She paused to glance back at him over her shoulder, concluding, "You just... do not seem the type."

When they were gone, Calum knelt alongside Abner and tried to place a hand on his shoulder. The badger recoiled, growling, "Don't touch me!"

Calum obliged, lifting his hands away in a calming gesture. "Are you alright?"

Abner glowered up at him while attempting to straighten his glasses. They were bent in absurd directions and one lens was almost completely shattered. Still, he left them in place, as though defiantly determined to remain as much himself as possible. "I'll be considerably better when I don't have to share the deck with the fiend who stabbed my Marshall in the back. So off with you, you blackguard!"

With a confusing grin, Calum stood, deciding that the Elder was in far better shape than he seemed. "Captain Marshall wasn't exaggerating. Curmudgeonly to the bone, aren't you?"

"Only when reason is given," he scowled. "I'd say betrayal is about as good a reason as any."

Nodding in understanding, Calum filled a tin with water from a barrel on the far side of the deck, and offered it to Abner with a sincere look, "Please believe me when I say I never would have done what I did without reason, either. I did it because I had to. Because I was the only one who could."

Abner snatched the tin from his hands, sloshing water on his feet as he brought it to his lips. The exertion made him tremble, an impulse he did his best to hide. "There is nothing more compelling to a small person's ego than the idea that they're doing what no one else can. Making the hard decisions, carrying the burden of being the bad guy because others haven't the mettle. The truth is, son, you had other choices. You just haven't the guts to step up and say you made the wrong one."

Calum bit the inside of his cheek and glanced over his shoulder, to the stairwell. He looked as though he wanted to say something.

"I followed his career, after he left," Abner went on. "Kept tabs on him as best I could. Marshall traveled the whole of Secora. Did everything worth doing. Do you know that in all that time, he never had a close relationship? Not one. People were too busy treating him like a resource. A rival or an ally. Yet you claim to have been his friend."

"That's right." The ringtail pulled himself upright, as though standing at attention, or showing pride.

"Then I hope it was worth it, son," Abner shook his head. "I really do. Because that may have been your one and only chance to really and honestly be what no one else could: the kind of person a hero could rely on."

Calum was quiet through several breaths.

Long enough that Abner was forced to wonder what he might be thinking.

At length, the former commander swallowed, smiled,

and came to his feet. "I'll bring you some food when I can," he said, fetching Abner another tin of water. "If the wolverine gives you any more trouble, pound your cup on the chains over your head. The sound should carry, and I won't be far."

"Is that supposed to be a comfort?" Abner sneered.

"Not really." Calum shrugged as he made for the stairwell. "But take it as you will."

"Wait," Abner called, bringing him to a stop. "They have a point, you know. Wearing that uniform on this ship is asking for trouble of the worst sort. You can't hide your past, I get that. But you're smarter than to brandish a constant reminder of it. So what's the real reason you won't change your attire?"

Again, that strange silence.

"Like I said," Calum eventually found his voice. "I know who I am.".

11
SHOWDOWN

The *Albatross* had been well designed.

Locks were not the problem. With the right tools, McKinley could pick each and every one of them in a matter of moments and make for the wheel with a full crew at his back. But it would serve them little to rush above decks when they were so thoroughly outmatched. For them to have any chance at all, McKinley had to take Marshall out of the picture. And before he could put his mind to accomplishing that, he first had to solve his current problem.

Location.

The orlop, where the prisoner cells were housed, was positioned near the bottommost section of the ship, just above the hold. It was topped by both the middle and lower gun decks, which were thoroughly active by day and populated by sleeping crewmen at night. Assuming he could slip through those two levels without notice, he still would have to bypass the night watch and cross the main deck under the noses of the 'round-the-clock repair details. So, by design, the whole of the ship – and its crew – stood between him and his target.

The Marauder smiled in the hours before dawn.

He did so enjoy a challenge.

He waited as long as his patience would allow, carving crude figures in the wall and listening to his fellow prisoners tire and cease their brigand conversations. Then, when he was certain that most of the crew might be lost in slumber, McKinley removed his boots, parked his hat in the cleanest corner of his cell, and opened the door.

For several breaths, he paused, listening for signs of movement from above. When none came, he stepped from behind the bars and paused again over the slight rustle from a nearby cell. It was Father Faiz, kneeling in penance.

McKinley swallowed. He remembered the slowness in Faiz's step, the hang of his head as he returned from the interrogation earlier that evening. There in the quiet, where his thoughts could be as loud as they wished, the Marauder felt a keen sense of regret for the way he'd distanced himself from the clairvoyant creature.

Whatever else he may have been, the warrior-priest was still his friend.

It seemed so horrendously wrong that he'd ever treated him as anything less.

"Father?" he interrupted quietly.

An ear pivoted gently in his direction, though the fox kept his eyes closed. "Yes, Captain?"

"Are you alright?"

He waited through the stillness for the reply that eventually came.

"Yes, Captain."

After a moment, the Marauder looked away. Then he nodded and continued on his course, hoping the priest could sense the subtle gesture, even if he couldn't see it. He hugged the wall on his way up the stairs like a mobile shadow, disturbing nothing in his path. Not the boards beneath his feet, not the breathing of the soldiers who tossed and turned occasionally in the night, and certainly not the illusion of security voiced by the thirty-minute whistle overhead.

No matter his skill in stealth, wandering openly onto the quarterdeck would have been suicidal. The gun ports would each be buttoned down, and trying to open them over the sleeping heads of Marshall's sailors would have been equally foolish. His only option sat at the rear of the middle gun deck, past the surgeon and lieutenants' quarters, where the stern windows of the wardroom opened directly beneath the captain's cabin. Once there, he could climb to Marshall's room – hopefully, without waking him – and remove him in whatever way became necessary.

At the sound of approaching footsteps, he ducked into the darkness and pressed his back into the hull, trying to keep his mind off that last part.

Removing Marshall would be no mean feat, and the likelihood that it would demand violent measures raised a difficult question.

Just how far was he willing to go?

He held his breath as the figure responsible for the disturbance passed nearby and stopped in the doorway of one of the cabins. There, she put a gloved hand on the doorframe and sighed.

Lieutenant Ryder.

Of *course* it was her.

McKinley kept his own breathing shallow, hoping the densely-populated deck would be enough to mask his scent from her keen, canine senses. He nearly stopped breathing altogether when a second set of footsteps approached, smaller and less assured than hers.

"Sir?" The voice was tentative, youthful. An ensign, no doubt.

"Yes, Mr. Wexler?" She responded from within.

"I'm sorry to disturb you, sir. I just thought I heard something untoward." McKinley heard the young lad shuffle his feet. "Shouldn't you be resting now, sir?"

He could hear the smile in her voice as she responded, "Yes, I should, Ensign. As should you."

The Marauder imagined him shrugging. "Couldn't sleep, sir."

"Hmph." She half-laughed, a sound that held no amusement. "It probably doesn't help to know you're not the only one suffering from that affliction tonight, does it?"

"After what Commander Calum did... I'd be surprised to hear that *anyone* was sleeping well, sir."

So McKinley had been right. The *Albatross* had nearly fallen to the same form of blindsiding as the *Negvar*.

The officers were quiet for a moment, as though they each were looking for something in the dark corners of the deck that might soothe their thoughts.

"It wasn't anyone's fault, Ensign. He betrayed us all, and none of us saw it coming. Not his aunt. Not me. Not even the captain."

"He seems to be taking it in stride, sir."

"He's our captain," the lieutenant replied. "He takes *everything* in stride."

"Do you think we'll ever see him again, sir? The commander, I mean?"

"Of course. No one can outrun the *Albatross* forever."

"That's right." He sounded hopeful. "We caught the Marauder, after all."

So you think, lad, McKinley smiled in the dark.

"True enough." He imagined her giving the boy a similar grin. "Now, off to your hammock with you. Neither of us will be much good to our captain if we don't get some shut eye."

"Aye, sir." He paused in the hallway a moment before leaving. "I suppose... Well, at least we still have the map. At least the Commander wasn't able to take anything with him when he left."

McKinley heard her sigh once the boy was out of

earshot. "Only our trust, Ensign. Only our trust."

He waited as she lingered alone for a moment, her breath steady in the center of the room. "Why did you do it, Commander?" her voice echoed sadly. "You had family and crew here. A home. A cause. What could he have ever offered that was greater than that?"

Then she left the room and closed the door.

As she made her way through the sleeping sailors, McKinley moved behind her through the hallway, realizing with annoyance that a part of him actually felt sorry for the mutt who'd nearly broken his nose.

Midway across the deck, the lieutenant stopped, her canine senses catching a hint of something unfamiliar in the night air. By the time she turned around, McKinley was already gone.

≈

Amelia sat awake in her cell, listening for McKinley's footsteps overhead. She wasn't surprised when she heard nothing at all.

The Marauder hadn't built a successful career on being easy to detect.

"Father?" she asked when she saw Faiz come to his feet and stare at the planks over his head. "What is it?"

He turned to her, his answer barely audible, even in the quiet. "A fly in the serum."

≈

The window ledge creaked softly beneath McKinley's grip, giving him a moment's anxiety as he pulled himself up to the sill and peered inside. Marshall's cabin was dark, lit only by the few moonbeams penetrating the fog. It was a practical room. No frills or pointless finery. Though that fit Marshall's oh-so-upright attitude to a T, the realization that his nemesis stored little to none of his considerable wealth on his ship brought a frown of disapproval to McKinley's face. Should he succeed in taking the ship, valuable contents would have been an excellent bonus. Maybe he could keep Marshall alive, ransom him back to the navy for a goodly sum. But even as he lowered himself over the sill and dropped to the floor, McKinley knew better. Marshall would be contained no easier than the Marauder had been, maybe less, for this was after all *his* ship. He would know its weaknesses better than anyone.

If McKinley wanted the magic of Mosque Hill and its Fortune… he had no illusions about what had to happen here.

Crouching in the shadows beneath the window, McKinley closed his eyes, allowing his animal senses to roam until his sight adjusted to the dark. Marshall's heartbeat was easy and rhythmic, the pulse of someone in peaceful slumber. From the nearby desk, he could smell a hint of oil; hear it sloshing in its lamp with the rocking of the ship. He moved between these sounds until he reached opposite side of the room, where Marshall slept.

Well, here he is, McKinley thought, wrapping his hand around the hilt of his dagger. *Helpless. Unsuspecting. Just one flick of my hand, that's all it would take. One. Small. Flick.*

Steeling himself, he raised his hand in the darkness and caught his own shadow from the corner of his eye.

That isn't me… It can't be.

Then he was shocked to see that shadow illuminated, cast in a delicate blue light.

A trick of the conscience, no doubt.

"I love you… my darling…"

He whirled at the sound, both shocked and confused that anyone other than his target might be in the room. He didn't want a witness.

Or another victim.

It surprised him further to realize there was nothing

204

there beyond a residual bit of light over Marshall's desk.

That's when he saw the painting.

He stared in disbelief, his eyes straining to make out the details he knew so well. The distant sails. The lonely beach. The female otter that stood in the corner with a hopeful smile, waving to the departing ship as though it weren't departing at all, but returning.

"It can't be…"

McKinley said it aloud before he could stop himself.

"I've found that the things least likely to occur are the ones that often do." Marshall's voice came from behind, punctuated by the clear cocking of a pistol hammer. "Your presence in my cabin, for example. I might be surprised had experience not taught me the futility of such things."

McKinley didn't bother to turn around. "Speaking of surprising things, you didn't strike me as a gun-wielder. Rather ignoble for such a proper skipper, don't you think?"

"It is," agreed Marshall. "Consider it a compliment that I find you formidable enough to warrant the added precaution."

Groaning, the Marauder rolled his eyes. "That sounds suspiciously *unlike* a blatant insult. What is wrong with you? I thought we had an understanding." He waved his hand, exasperated. "Putting aside your apparent inability to play into this whole *nemesis* thing, if you're looking to actually use that, you may want to point it a little lower. The bullet comes out of the end with the barrel, you see. No brave captain ever killed the evil pirate by shooting a hole in his ceiling."

"Point taken. But I'm not about to shoot the evil pirate in the back, either."

At that, a violent smile tugged at the corners of the Marauder's mouth.

Then he shrugged.

"Your mistake," he said.

It wasn't that Marshall had underestimated his foe, per

se. The captain of the *Albatross* was not given to such mistakes. He had expected McKinley to move, to run, to attack. He just hadn't expected him to do them all at once, or so quickly.

A flea could scarcely have blinked in the time it took for the Marauder to hurl himself to the side as he spun, flinging a dagger Marshall heard but did not see. He pulled back his hand just in time to avoid contact with the blade, which glanced off of his pistol, sending both weapons skittering away into the darkness. By the time they hit the floor, McKinley was in mid-flight to the open window.

Marshall came to his feet.

He couldn't let the Marauder off the ship.

He knew the pirate wouldn't return, not this time.

Narrowing his eyes, he ripped a sword off the wall and threw it. End over end, it flew until the hilt struck against the pane, knocking the window shut. The point then drove down, into the wood of the windowsill, barring McKinley's path.

The Marauder turned on him in bewilderment. "You would give up your weapon with *me* in the room? Are you mad?"

Marshall drew his fine rapier from the scabbard alongside his cot. "No more than you."

With a look of realization and an approving grin, McKinley pulled yet another knife from the folds of his cloak. "Touché." He looked overhead, toward what would normally be the trumpeter's cabin. In its place was a hatch that served as a skylight. "Back to catching me, then. A bit difficult to do when your net has a gaping hole in it, don't you think?"

In a flash, McKinley mounted the desk and leapt to the skylight, whipping his feet through the opening by gripping the frame with hooked claws. Twisting in the air, he landed in a crouch on the upper deck and grinned over his shoulder, needling the less-agile captain below.

Marshall allowed himself a moment's admiration before

darting through his cabin door and onto the quarter deck while McKinley made for the railing. The escapee was fast approaching the stern when Ryder dropped from the rigging to the deck in front of him, sword drawn. The Marauder fell to his knees and arched his head away from the blade, sliding just beneath it as she thrust forward. Pivoting on one leg, he rolled back the way he had come, deciding against taking anyone with him in his flight over the rail.

It was the wrong decision.

Marshall burst onto the deck in time to see McKinley barreling towards him. He ducked and turned with the Marauder as the pirate captain somersaulted over his head. When he landed, McKinley looked down at the point of Marshall's rapier, mere inches from his chest.

As Marshall held his eyes with a cool aura of composure, McKinley whirled in all directions like a spider caught in a jar, only to find himself blocked at every turn. He was surrounded by a sea of hostile faces.

"Oh come on!" he groaned. "I don't want to have to kill *all* of you. Do you have any idea how much blood that would leave lying around? Who's going to clean that up, huh? My crew? They're pirates, not manservants. Honestly, the lot of you are so very thoughtless."

Even at that, Marshall did not smile.

No one did.

"As a matter of courtesy," said the naval captain, "I will give you one final chance to end this peaceably. Surrender your arms and return to your cell."

And there it was.

His only option was to give in. To let go. To accept defeat.

Forget it.

McKinley firmed his jaw, along with his stance. Locking eyes with his executioner, the pirate forced every ounce of steel and defiance into the gravel of his voice as he said, "That isn't going to happen."

In another unexpected display of wit, Marshall shrugged. "Your mistake."

≈

"They aren't moving," whispered Amelia.

She and Faiz stood apprehensively in their cells below, each of them gripping the bars and staring at the ceiling as if they might burn a hole in it.

"No, they're not," the father affirmed.

Pulling her eyes away from the ceiling, she looked at him, a beseeching sort of calm on her features. "All of the *Albatross* is up there by now. What hope does he possibly have of escape?"

He shook his head. "None."

She leaned into the bars, a grim look on her face. "He's going to fight them anyway, isn't he?"

"He will fight, yes." Faiz nodded. "But Marshall is an honorable captain. He will not pit the whole of his ship against one prisoner. Such a thing would be grievously unfair. No, he will prove his right to capture first, swordsman to swordsman, facing him squarely. He'll deal defeat without dealing shame. And whether in victory or loss, he will know he came by it justly."

She didn't ask him how he could be sure of that.

A knight would know.

Better than anyone.

Tightening her grip on the door of her cell, Amelia closed her eyes. Their captain was an incredibly skilled fighter, one of the best. But he was no weapons-master, no trained member of the Warriors Guild. Against someone like Marshall… one misstep…

In a struggle to keep the fear from entering her voice, she swallowed. "Surely Marshall won't *kill* him, will he?"

No response.

Turning to see Faiz stepping back and away from the bars, she could fight the fear no longer. "Father? Tell me the captain isn't going to die!"

Dipping his head, the father seemed to fall back into himself, as though he did not wish to answer.

As though she wouldn't like the response.

"Unless a miracle intervenes."

≈

Marshall touched the back of his hand to his cheek and looked down at his own blood as though it were a thing he had no cause to recognize. Though many had tried, no one had come so close with a blade as to strike him in a fight, not in years. Certainly not to the point of drawing blood.

He looked up at the Marauder without expression. Passive. Unperturbed. Then he advanced. In a single fluid motion, Marshall lunged, swiped, and reversed his rapier in a sideways stab. He found each move anticipated and acted upon even as it was executed. The crew watched on in breathless silence as pirate and captain crossed blades again and again.

At no point was McKinley able to gain ground.

But he wasn't losing any, either.

Bringing his sword down, Marshall was surprised when its motion was halted by not one, but *two* blades.

Like the twin daggers now in his hands, the Marauder's eyes glittered with amusement as he slid the crossed weapons forward and up, tossing Marshall's rapier into the air and leaning back to kick the captain in the sternum. Marshall suppressed a gasp, numbing himself to the sharp pain bursting through broken ribs and punching McKinley in the jaw as if for spite. Into the air, he leapt, catching his sword with ease and pinning McKinley's daggers to the rail beneath the blade. Then he kicked McKinley in the face. Hard. The Marauder felt his teeth cutting along the inside of his cheek as he stumbled... and lost his grip on his weapons. McKinley could only watch as Marshall swept them into the sea with a flick of his sword. Baring his teeth in a humorless smile, the Marauder flipped backwards, springing off his hands until he reached the far side of the deck.

When he stood, both of them were bleeding, both of them breathing heavily.

It wasn't exactly going as planned, for either of them.

Then, with his cloak flapping in a contrasting gentility, the pirate's arms snapped to his side, fingers outstretched to grasp the two daggers that shot violently from his sleeves. Marshall barely had time to wince in annoyance before both blades came flying at him.

How many knives could he have?

The captain steeled himself. There was a placid sense of his hand on the hilt and a small motion of his arm, his wrist, then time and reality slowed as he deflected first one, then two daggers from their deadly path. By the time he returned his focus to his adversary, McKinley was gone – having catapulted himself into the rigging. The single topman who moved to intercept him took two feet to the gut and fell breathless to the deck, many yards below. From a higher yardarm, two others grinned to one another before wrapping themselves in a line and dropping one end of the heavy rope through the rigging, just out of Marshall's reach. He glanced to Ryder, who needed no instruction. Instantly, she laced her gloved fingers together in front of her. Marshall took three running steps. The fourth landed his foot in her cupped hands, which she propelled upward, springing the captain into the air. He grabbed the end of the rope just as the two eager sailors threw themselves over the yardarm, using their combined mass as a counterweight to propel the captain aloft at breakneck speed.

McKinley looked down and groaned. Tossing yet another dagger into the air above his head, he jumped, catching the blade with his teeth while changing ropes between his hands. As he swung past Marshall's spontaneously-rigged pulley, he swiped and split the rope.

At the crest of his swing, he released the line and leapt onto the topgallant yard of the main mast – the highest horizontal point on the ship. Again, he looked down, this time to see the topmen tumbling to the deck, their counterweight gone.

But Marshall was nowhere to be seen.

"Are you looking for me?"

Through the flapping of the ship's banner, McKinley turned to see Marshall standing calmly and unharmed on the opposite end of the yardarm. Confused, his eyes shot from the rigging to the yardarm and back again. "Did I miss a shortcut between there and here? That's so very unlike me…"

"Far be it for my knowledge of my own ship to leave you feeling inept." Marshall held his sword easily at his side. "I just didn't want to disappoint you by ending things too quickly."

"Actually, a quick ending was precisely what I was going for." The Marauder gestured to his surroundings before lunging across the yardarm. "Not to be rude, but if you hadn't noticed I'm in a bit of a hurry, making my escape and all."

Marshall brought his sword up in a cross motion that was too fast to be seen, scoring the Marauder's right hand and forcing him to drop his dagger. "And how is that going for you?" he asked placidly.

McKinley growled in frustration, clamping his hand over the wound and watching as his weapon disappeared into the waning night. When he looked up, his eyes made it clear that his seemingly-endless armament had finally been spent. "To be honest?" He grimaced. "It could be going better."

Without warning, the Marauder latched onto the banner and threw himself into the open air. Hefting his weight in an outward arc, he swung behind his opponent, wrapping the banner about his head and blinding him.

The captain responded on instinct. Dropping to a

211

crouch, he drove his claws into the wood beneath his feet for stability and swiped at the ties securing the banner to the mast. McKinley waited for him to finish. When the banner was no longer attached, he stepped down on the inside of Marshall's elbow, stripping him of his weapon.

Then he kicked Marshall from the yardarm.

Marshall felt his feet come off the wood with a shocking jolt of vertigo and panic. But even without sight, Marshall knew his ship. He knew when to reach out, when to close his hand to grip a passing line and halt his descent. He even knew the distance between the masts well enough to flip himself onto a forward yardarm. His landing was less than smooth, but it was enough to save him. Pressing his back against the forward mast, he pulled the banner from around his head and looked over to see McKinley resting in a crouch on the lower yardarm, directly opposite, with the captain's rapier lying flat across his bent knees.

He was waiting, patiently.

As though he hadn't expected this fall to kill Marshall any more than the last.

The captain was beginning to understand why this guildless pirate had given him such trouble in the past. McKinley was untrained, certainly, but he was fast, adaptable. He used his surroundings in a way that wouldn't even occur to most fighters, and his self-assurance would be unnerving to anyone without a tremendous amount of experience. For Marshall, Warriors training had been a discipline. He imagined for McKinley, it would have been an amusement.

In besting a pirate, perhaps he should apply a little creativity of his own.

The captain climbed down, locking gazes on his opponent, who followed him onto the deck with deliberate grace.

McKinley smiled when Marshall's crew parted before him. This time, their hesitation was clearly that – hesitation. Not deference or duty, but the plain and simple reluctance of those who knew they were no match for the person before them. His smile widened when Marshall removed his belt and scabbard. The belt, he wrapped three quarters of the way around his right hand. When he closed his fingers around it, the polished buckle dangled several inches from the captain's fist, while the leather formed a solid guard for his knuckles. The scabbard, he held in his left like any sword.

"You can't be serious." The Marauder gave a derisive laugh.

But he was. The buckle that slammed its imprint into McKinley's forearm was ample proof of that.

As they closed for the final time, Marshall kept the rapier at bay with his scabbard using precise movements, somehow striking only the flat of the blade, never its edge. Time and again, McKinley was forced to dodge the buckle that flew toward his face and recoiled like a deadly spring. Through it all, Marshall never bared his teeth, never tensed, never gave in to the savage heat that must be coursing through his veins as it did through McKinley's. He was cool, calm, and in complete control at every turn.

It was maddening.

And McKinley knew, even before the captain cast away his belt and scabbard as playthings he no longer needed, even before the impossible turn of expert simplicity that ended with the sword back in Marshall's hands, McKinley knew.

He was going to lose.

At long last, the Marauder fell back against the wall around the cockpit. His chest heaving with weariness and angry defeat, McKinley closed his eyes and prepared himself for the final blow.

I tried, Maya, my dear. I tried…

He felt a moment's pressure in his chest, but nothing more.

It took several seconds for McKinley to realize the moment had passed, that he was not dead, and that the blade had stopped when it pinned something up against his flesh. He looked up to see the gold of his broken medallion reflected from the sword to Marshall's eyes. But he saw no emotion there, no reason for this unexpected act of mercy.

The Marauder could only stare blankly in confusion when Marshall asked, "Is there a carpenter in your crew?"

12
DON'T TELL THE PIRATE

"**P**ermission to speak freely, sir!" Ryder fought the urge to slam the door behind her.

"Permission granted," Marshall responded impassively, pulling a vial of rare mineral oil from his desk. He seated himself and began the delicate task of wiping his sword, not bothering to look up as his first lieutenant continued, her voice thick with bewilderment.

"Have you lost your mind?"

He raised an eyebrow, but kept his focus on the oil and cloth. "Not that I'm aware, Lieutenant."

"Captain," she breathed in exasperation. "They're pirates."

"Yes, they are. And I have granted them temporary amnesty, pending their assistance with our repairs."

"Forgive my thickness, sir. But…" She pressed her gloved hands together and spoke as though explaining algebra to a mollusk. "They're *pirates*."

"Duly noted. Will there be anything further?"

"Captain!" They were interrupted as Eadric burst through the door. "I simply must protest this… this horrendously unorthodox maneuver!"

Ryder grabbed him by the collar as he passed her.

"*You*," she said sharply, dragging him back the way he had come. "Will wait your turn!"

She shoved him back onto the deck and closed the door in his face.

"Sir." The lieutenant turned to him with folded arms. "I understand that time is of the essence here. Their help could buy us a day, maybe more. I see the logic. I just… can't help but think there's more to it than that. Don't think that I am in any way questioning your orders, but…"

"Are you refusing them?" He returned the vial to its place in the drawer and sheathed his sword.

Ryder's arms fell to her sides. The look of shock that crossed her face at his words said plainly that the thought had not – nor would it *ever* – occur to her. "You are *my captain*. Even after Commander Calum's betrayal, you *must* know what that means to me."

"I do not doubt your loyalties, Lieutenant. No more than I doubt your strength." He moved around to the front of his desk and sat down on its edge, meeting her gaze on a level plane. "Which is why I know, however difficult it may seem, that I can ask you to work side by side with an enemy and trust you to handle it. – Are you alright, Lieutenant?" He said the last abruptly when he realized she was standing in an odd manner, as though her wounded shoulder were pulling her to one side.

"I'm fine. And this isn't about the Knight, sir." She shook her head, dismissing his concern and reading his meaning clearly. "You know what he did and what he's capable of. I know you will prepare accordingly."

"I see. Then your unease is over the unknown quantity," deduced the captain. "McKinley."

"McKinley," she concurred.

"It is a risk, but a measured one. You said it yourself, Lieutenant, that the Marauder is motivated by his greed. He wants the Fortune. He can have it. And we will deal with him again when our mission is over. For now, our priority is the scepter."

Ryder nodded. They both knew gold might buy some measure of loyalty from McKinley and his crew, but it would not buy their lives. If things got dangerous, they would flee. And they would take the ship to do it if they could.

This was not going to be easy.

"I understand, sir," she said.

Just then, McKinley threw open the door to the cabin and strode vigorously inside, towing Eadric alongside him. "Found this outside, looking out of place. Nearly broke my heart."

"Unhand me you vile cretin!" Eadric shouted as he struggled to free himself, then glared at the pirate, who held up his hand in a benevolent gesture.

"No need to thank me, my feathered friend. I'm sure they'd have let you in eventually." He glanced to the two officers, then pulled himself upright with a sheepish grin. "Oh, I'm sorry. Was I interrupting?"

"Yes," chorused Marshall and Ryder without missing a beat.

"Well, don't mind me. I'll just wait here until you're done." McKinley seated himself in a chair near Marshall's desk, leaned back, and planted his heels on the desktop with a reverberating *thunk*. "Or, for the sake of expediency, I could sum up this morning's interactions so that we can get on with the loathsome business of sharing the same space. *You*," he pointed to Ryder, "Think this is a bloody mad idea because pirates are dangerous. *You*," his finger moved to Eadric, "Think this is a bloody mad idea because pirates are icky. And *you*," he gestured at last to Marshall, "Just want your ship in order for honor and duty, the greater good and all of that nonsense." Then he repeated the cycle in quick succession, proclaiming, "You're right. You're right. And you're completely barking bonkers, but you're the captain and that's all there is to it, so there.

Now, if we're all caught up, why don't the two of you scuttle along and leave the sussing of the details to the scary folk, aye?"

Ryder gave him a glare that said she was restraining herself.

Eadric sputtered indignantly.

At a nod from Marshall, the lieutenant ushered Eadric from the room, only to have him pull from her grip and storm to McKinley's side, where he jabbed an angry wingtip into the Marauder's face.

"You! Are a foul and repugnant ruffian and I'll be drowned if I will spend one *second* in your presence without protest! I was thrilled with your monumental capture – *thrilled*! But this idea, this, this... *pretense* of being on the same level of civility, I cannot accept! I won't do it, I tell you!"

McKinley stared at him blankly for a moment. "I'm sorry," he said at last. "I stopped paying attention after you said something about being drowned. Were you asking for help with that? Because I'd be more than happy to oblige." He bared his teeth in a malicious smile. "That's the accommodating sort of repugnant ruffian I am."

Eadric made a strangled sound and pulled his wingtip away from the Marauder's mouth, as though he might bite it off.

"Come on, Advisor." Ryder put a gloved hand on the bird's back. "No one's going to let the big, bad pirate hurt you. Let's go see about breakfast while they decide how and when to unleash the rest of his ilk into the populace."

McKinley watched them leave, then turned to Marshall with gratification on his face. "Am I mistaken, or did he just call my capture '*monumental*?' Not that I disagree, I'm just surprised he was able to recognize it."

"To the matter at hand..."

"Indeed!" The Marauder sat studiously forward and clapped his hands. "Before we begin, I'd like to say out of conscience that I don't like you. And, well, being a pirate and all, I've grown into the habit of dispatching those I don't like. But, as I'm sure you pointed out to your faithful lieutenant, this can-do ship of yours has something very special to offer. Namely, the Fortune. Perhaps even better, the chance to spit in the Baron's enormous, muscle-bound eye and maybe sack his ship in the process. Thanks to him, I am in the market for a new one. Seems only fitting. So, seeing as your glorious leadership skills are set and prepped to spearhead their way to my revenge and prosperity, I'm more than willing to put aside our differences and, at least moderately, swear fealty to you and yours."

"Hm," Marshall said, strapping on his sword. "Well, then you and I might be in a bit of a pickle from the outset, Mad Dog, because if all goes according to plan, we'll not be crossing paths with the Baron again. Not on this voyage."

McKinley looked confused. "Whyever not? The dastardly devil is doing his evil best to stand in your way, isn't he? How is confronting him not in the plan?"

"Because our mission is not to pursue a distraction for the sake of vengeance."

"So, let me get this straight," said McKinley. "You're just going to set a direct course for Mosque Hill, no bones, no waylaying, is that correct?"

"Correct enough," Marshall allowed.

"That's a terrible plan."

"Is it now?"

McKinley sighed in dramatic fashion. "Take it from someone who knows a thing or two about the fine art of acquisition. First you take out the competition. *Then* you go for the prize. Much simpler as a general rule. Besides, I've seen the float he's riding. She's lighter and faster than the *Albatross* by far. If you turn this into a race, he could be there and back before we ever caught sight of our destination. He could fund his every evil inclination, steal the throne, sign dozens of anti-do-gooder laws into effect, banish every beast with a positive bone. Imagine it, Marshall. He could make your stoicism illegal."

"You're right," Marshall replied stoically. "He could. If he had any idea where to find the island."

"But the Baron has your traitorous commander. Won't he offer up the directions from that map you have hidden away in here somewhere?" Then, when Marshall looked unhappy with his apparent knowledge, he said, "What? I have ears. I use them."

"It won't play out that way, I assure you," answered Marshall. "The map alone isn't quite the advantage Von Ulric believes it to be. It is only one of two elements required to find Mosque Hill. Without the second, he's as good as lost."

"What *is* the second?" He waited a moment for Marshall to respond, then held up his hands in surrender. "Right, right. Don't tell the pirate."

"Moreover," Marshall continued, "taking the time to find and confront him would be riskier than you realize. The Baron has allied himself with the Kathkan Empire. We have no way of knowing how many ships he has at his disposal, or what their interests in this endeavor may be. There are too many players in too many positions, and I'll not fight them blindly. Or do you think it wise to tackle the Empire with a single ship?"

McKinley answered with a roll of his eyes. "Fine, I get it, you aren't one for the long shots. We'll do it your way. And remind me to never play chess with you."

"As to the terms of your release…"

"Yes!" Coming to his feet, McKinley placed his palms on the desk and leaned forward. "Firstly, if you want to hold onto any delusions about me not sneaking into your cabin and slitting your throat in the middle of the night, you'll never, and I mean *never*, call me 'Mad Dog' again, savvy?"

"Conceded," Marshall stood to match him. "Your carpenter, along with any of your crewmen knowledgeable in ship design, will be assigned immediately to the repair crews, where they will work without complaint and *without sabotage*. I can't make it clearer that, by assuring me of their full cooperation, you are putting your life on the line. Should any of them do anything at all to jeopardize the safety of my crew or the success of our mission, I will end you without ceremony."

"Conceded," agreed McKinley.

"Very well then," Marshall pushed off the desk and turned for the door.

"I wasn't finished!" The Marauder stopped him, his features hardening to a seriousness, an anger, that Marshall wouldn't have thought him to own. "When we get there, the Fortune is mine and mine alone. No debates, and *no one* stands in my way."

Marshall held his eyes for a long moment.

"Conceded," he said at last.

"And…" McKinley stepped forward to meet him. "Don't think for one second that I owe you anything for sparing my life."

Moving to open the door, the captain gestured for his pseudo-prisoner to exit ahead of him, assuring, "The thought had never occurred."

≈

It was a strange scene on the deck of the *Albatross*. Pirates and soldiers standing eye to eye without strategy or malicious intent. Amidst the uncertainty, one individual turned quietly to another.

"I'm curious, Father," Amelia whispered. "Is this what you might consider a miracle?"

The muscular fox smiled his answer. "Could it be considered anything less?"

Amelia Ling

13
OFFICER DOWN

The next few hours were the most difficult. Age-long tensions weighted the thoughts of everyone aboard as repairs were laid out and tasks assigned. Every glance was given by a wary eye, and every word was short. By day's end, only the captains seemed immune to the psychological wear of the situation. When Amelia found McKinley leaning over the ship's railing, he seemed far more interested in watching the fog than watching his back.

"It's like dust kicked up by an unseen war, isn't it?" she said.

"Are you talking about the mist? Or about the tension on the deck?" He smiled wryly in return.

"Both." She joined in his amusement. "It's an oddity, in either case."

McKinley shrugged. "Well, no one's killed anyone yet. Suppose we should be grateful of that."

"They follow your lead, whether or not they understand it."

Though his sidelong glance proved that he recognized

the bizarre nature of his arrangement with Marshall, the Marauder did not offer to shed any light on it.

"Sir," she went on. "I didn't want to say anything in front of the others. But are you alright?"

He turned along the rail, leaning on one arm and giving her a disarming grin. "Madame Ling, I couldn't be finer."

Amelia gave him a look that said she wasn't buying it. "It's been clear for some time that you've had something gnawing at you. You're distant. Unreadable."

"Mysterious," he corrected. "The word you're looking for is *mysterious.*"

She cocked her head and said no more.

McKinley sighed.

"What do you see when you look out there?" He gestured to what little could be seen through the mist.

"Don't change the subject," she said.

"I'm not. Truly. Just tell me what you see."

She exhaled, playing along. "Terror and silence. A deadly loss of control."

In the seconds before he realized she was serious, McKinley started to laugh. Then he drew his brows together in confusion. "Wait a minute. You're afraid of the water?"

Her expression did not change, but she gave a single, placid nod.

"You do realize, my dear, that you willfully put yourself on a *boat*, right? Sits on the water. Crosses the water. Nothing but water for months at a time. Any of this ringing a bell?"

She smiled, perfectly willing to tolerate his jibes, even enjoying them.

He shook his head in amusement and disbelief. The revelation certainly put her near-drowning experience in perspective. "Are all the members of your species as *sensible* as you?"

"If one wishes to earn strength," she explained, "One has to face their fears."

"I guess no one can accuse you of coming by your strength the easy way." He bumped his shoulder into hers. "The point is that we pirates and hooligans, even these soldiers at our backs, we're all out here looking for something. For you, it's strength. For Faiz, it's salvation. If I'm preoccupied, it's because my search has a time table. And if I don't soon find what I'm looking for... Well, you voiced the alternative rather well. Terror and silence."

She nodded, knowing that this was as sincere as her captain was likely to get.

Before she could speak further, McKinley pushed away from the rail and called out to his idle carpenter. "Master Tobb! Your captain tires of the doldrums – liven up this deck, won't you?"

At that, the beaver cracked a broad smile. Ignoring the sudden tension in weapon arms all around him, he hopped atop a nearby crate and produced a pipe flute from his pocket. As he began to play, a few joined in, clapping along to the pirate's cheery tune.

"Oh, gather 'round, ye flaggin' hounds,
I've words te share wi' ye,
'Bout a cap'n's bonny fortune gained,
'Pon the blue o' boisterous seas.

Our tale begins where oceans end,
It were a younger year,
When first 'e bent a poirate's sail,
An' dark clouds did appear.

Ahoy, me Cap'n,
Aye and aye,
Me arm be wi' ye true.
This storm'll pass us,
By and by,
I 'opes we see it through.

'E lassoed 'im a whale what swam,
A hundred thousand miles.
'E drew us on te distant shores
An' left that gale behind.

A battle, it were ragin' there,
In yonder, nameless town.
An' caught us in th' cannon fire
When that whale set us down.

Ahoy, me Cap'n,
Aye and aye,
Me sword be wi' ye true.
This war'll pass us,
By and by,
I 'opes we see it through.

'E led us on te pillage the lot,
Til none had coin at all.
Then slipped off through their lines, 'e did,
And left the battle stalled.

So, me hero, 'e's a villain,
In someone else's tale.
But I'd follow 'im te Oblivion
On the back o' any whale!

Ahoy, me Cap'n,
Aye and aye,
Me soul be wi' ye true.
This life'll pass us,
By and by,
I 'opes we see it through.

This life'll pass us,
By and by,
I know we'll see it through."

He finished to a thundering round of applause and thumping feet.

Amid the whoops of appreciation, McKinley nudged Amelia, pointed to Ryder, and said, "Don't look now, Madame Ling, but I believe our terrifying lieutenant is actually smiling."

"Don't read too much into it," Ryder cautioned. "I'm just enjoying the music."

"The lieutenant is from a gypsy clan, if I'm not mistaken," explained Amelia. "Music is a very intricate part of her cultural background."

"That's right," Ryder confirmed, sounding impressed.

"It is something I wish we had in common." Amelia smiled. "My countrymen seemed morally opposed to the idea of song."

Ryder turned to her, intrigued. "You're from the Hathe Peninsula? You're a long way from home, aren't you? That's practically the other side of the world."

"I like to travel," Amelia shrugged her explanation. "How did you know? Most Secorans haven't even heard of Hathe."

Ryder seemed to dismiss the idea. "I've been in the service long enough to know basic geography."

"But not long enough," the feline chided, "to know better than to remove a sling so soon after an injury?"

The lieutenant stiffened.

Amelia lifted her hands. "Please don't take it as anything but concern. You just aren't as good at hiding your pain as you think." Her attempt at peace turned to sudden scrutiny. "In fact, you're not looking well at all."

Ryder had just opened her mouth to admonish the presumptuous pirate when she stumbled.

"Lieutenant?" McKinley asked, then stepped back as she fell into him. He caught her just before she hit the deck, unconscious.

Amelia knelt at his side. "She's breathing, but she's

burning up." She looked over her shoulder to the backs of Marshall's crew. They were too caught up in Tobb's musical display to take any notice. "What should we do?"

McKinley glanced to Ryder, then to the water beyond the rail. "Throw her over?"

Amelia gave him a withering look.

He sighed and rolled his eyes. "Fine, fine. You there!" He called to the two nearest crewmen. "I think your lieutenant may be in need of medical assistance!"

The squirrel and marten each took one look at Ryder before whirling on McKinley.

"What did you do?!"

"Get your hands off of her!"

"Take it easy," McKinley argued as several more crewmen turned an angry eye his way. "I didn't do anything. She just collapsed."

"Bollocks!" said the squirrel.

"Maybe it was the cat!" argued a third crewman, forcing McKinley to step between them before things could escalate.

"Alright, I admit it!" the Marauder falsely proclaimed, drawing their attention. "It was me. Amelia had nothing to do with it."

They jumped him, and he remembered nothing after that.

≈

"It wasn't him," Doc Calum glared. "Not unless pirates have suddenly been granted the power to dole out major infections."

"Exonerated! Thank you!" McKinley glanced around the med bay through a blackened eye. "Now if you wouldn't mind untying me?"

"Have you been using the poultice I gave you?" the old ringtail said to Ryder, ignoring the Marauder completely.

"I'd never risk defying you, Doc." Ryder gave a weak

smile and pulled a small green jar from her pocket.

"Good of you to behave." The doctor took the jar and assessed the used amount as proper and suitable. "But this should have kept you on your feet."

McKinley cocked his head and eyed the label from a distance.

The squirrel from the deck, a lesser lieutenant named Bowers, pointed angrily at the doctor. "So it was *you*? You're the one who did this?"

"Easy, Bowers." The marten, an officer of superior standing, intervened with a raise of her hand.

"I'm just sayin' what you oughtta be thinking, Trimble. If one Calum could betray us so easily, why not another?" His voice was angry, hurt. "How do we know she's not workin' for the Baron, too? Keepin' it in the family and all?"

"Keep your place and hold your tongue, Lieutenant!" Ryder commanded in the strongest voice she could muster, attempting to sit upright.

Even as the doctor moved to push Ryder back into her cot, the situation seemed to diffuse, almost without reason.

They turned to see Captain Marshall eyeing them coolly from the doorway. His calm, authoritative stare forced Bowers to take a step back.

"Use your head, sailor," the captain said. "If the good doctor were a spy, she wouldn't be here. Remember that the Baron attacked us with extreme malice. Only a fool would have chosen to remain on a doomed vessel and only the most inept of infiltrators would attack us by exacerbating one, unforeseeable injury on a single crewman. Since the doctor is neither inept nor foolish, we can safely assume that your rage is misplaced." Marshall paused until the squirrel lowered his gaze. "I'll not have suspicions or theories of conspiracy on my ship. Not without evidence. Is that clear?"

"Aye sir," squirrel and marten replied in unison.

"Now, Doctor." Marshall turned to Calum. "If you

229

would be so kind as to explain the situation."

"I wish I could, Captain," she said, at a loss. "I've been prescribing this mixture for years. It's never failed to prevent an infection. Not once."

"Pardon me." McKinley gave the impression that he would have risen his hand, were they not bound behind his back. "You didn't buy that recently, did you?"

The doctor looked offended. "Of course I did. With the help of my Apothecary contact, I replaced my entire inventory when last we visited the capitol. Keeping my supply current is a responsibility that I take very seriously."

"Yes, my capable madam, I imagine you take *everything* very seriously," nodded McKinley. "But if you'll release me, I may be able to shed some light on your little problem, all the same."

Seeming much more likely to listen now that Marshall was present as a counter to the Marauder's strength, Trimble and Bowers looked to their captain for approval. At his nod, they moved to sever McKinley's bindings, only to find them already cut.

"I got impatient," McKinley shrugged.

"Save the showboating." Marshall narrowed his eyes. "What do you know about my lieutenant's condition?"

The Marauder took the green jar and popped open the lid. "I know that the shopkeeper who uses this particular label is named Barlos. And I know that, courtesy of your frighteningly-burly friend, Von Ulric, Barlos closed his shop. Months ago. So, unless I miss my guess, I also know that your doctor has been had. Her contact is brewing up his own concoctions and passing them off as the real deal in order to maintain his income."

"That's absurd." The doctor glared at him.

"Is it?" McKinley waved the open jar beneath her nose. "Have a whiff. Does that smell right to you?"

She held his eyes for a moment, then sighed. "Blast. No, no it doesn't. I'm sorry, Lieutenant. I've had you coating yourself with snake oil. No wonder you're in poor shape."

"How do you know any of this?" Marshall narrowed his eyes.

The Marauder placed his hand over his heart and said dramatically, "Because. Unlike *some* people, I truly and deeply care about the state of Secora's most important service providers."

"Oh yes," the doctor said sarcastically, pushing past him. "You're the picture of benevolence."

"You can rectify this?" Marshall said to Calum.

She waved a hand and looked over the bottles on a nearby shelf. "They don't call me the doctor for nothing, Captain. I can formulate my own balm. I'll just need…" Her hand paused over a vacant spot.

"Is something wrong, Doctor?" asked Marshall.

Seeming both confused and annoyed, she turned to him. "The boswellia extract is gone, sir. The devil's claw, too. I can give her some white willow bark for the pain, but without something to curb the inflammation, she'll only get worse."

The captain drew a disapproving breath. "You have nothing else?"

"Nothing strong enough." She threw her satchel over her shoulder. "I'll head out on the rocks. The Manus is bare near the shoreline, but if I climb high enough, I may be able to find…"

"No," Marshall halted her. "I'll go. You stay here and keep her comfortable. McKinley?"

The Marauder sighed and folded his arms across his chest. "Yeah, yeah. 'Go to your cell,' right?"

"Wrong. You're coming with me."

At that, McKinley raised an eyebrow. "You're joking."

≈

"I think your Lieutenant Bowers has some trust issues," McKinley said, putting his hand on a bruised cheek. "You may want to keep an eye on that one."

Marshall scanned the brush as they climbed the slope. "Bowers needed no more than a reminder of his oath. He will be fine. My eye is precisely where it should be."

"On *me*, you mean." The Marauder smiled, clearly taking it as a compliment. "And here I thought you brought me along for my dazzlingly abundant knowledge of all things 'medicine.'"

Marshall glanced over his shoulder, giving him an odd and scrutinizing look. "That was a factor, yes."

McKinley paused, uncomfortable with the implication. "You know, the trouble with you being so serious all the time is that I can never tell when you're joking. Have a mood once in a while. If not for me, do it for the *Albatross*. 'Stark' was never a happy word."

"I'll keep it in mind," Marshall said flatly.

McKinley scoffed, then shook his head. "You're amazing. Truly. Like a wooden board with a face. Do you ever give yourself splinters?"

"Do you ever stop talking?"

Rolling his eyes, McKinley plucked a pebble from the ground and tossed it at the back of Marshall's head.

It was too small to cause any permanent damage.

And any repercussions would be worth the chance to see Marshall flinch. Just once.

Rather than cracking against Marshall's skull, the projectile thumped lightly in the captain's palm as he turned and snatched it from the air. Without a word, he bounced it once in his hand, then threw it back in McKinley's direction. The Marauder just scowled as it flew past him.

"This is getting absurd. Don't you know who I am? I'm McKinley the Marauder, the most infamous pirate in the world! I've spent years staying one step ahead of you. Years. And now that I'm on your ship, my edge falters. What gives?"

Marshall stopped in the shadow of the mountain's

peak, turning to survey the landscape. "You've already answered your own question. It's *my* ship."

Curling his lip, McKinley repeated the words in silent mocking, then said, "Yeah, well, when it's *my* ship, I'm making you walk the plank for catching my rock."

≈

Amelia regretted the lack of a door. She would have liked to knock, rather than barge around the screen uninvited, which seemed rude. Luckily, Ryder was too busy being chastised by her doctor to notice.

"It isn't enough to listen to me, girl," Calum was saying. "You have to keep me informed, too. For the love of Fate, how hard is it to come to me when you're in pain?"

"Forgive me, Doc." Ryder sounded as though she were fighting a sigh. "I thought pain was to be expected when someone crushes your shoulder with a mace."

"Don't get cute. And drop the tough soldier act – you're as bad as the captain."

Ryder seemed to derive some satisfaction from that, though she did her best to hide it.

"Now, I have other patients to deal with. If I come back to find you off this cot, I'll have you removed from active duty for the rest of the month, am I clear?"

"Crystal," Ryder said.

"Good," nodded Calum.

Amelia was shocked when the elderly ringtail came around the screen and grabbed her by the arm.

"You." The doctor stuffed a cold compress into her hand and shoved her into a chair alongside Ryder's cot. "Take this. Sit here and swap it out when it gets warm. Go on. Put it on her forehead, dear. You aren't helping anyone by cooling the air around your hand. And see to it that she stays put. She's impossible, this one."

Overcoming her surprise, Amelia gave Calum a gentle

nod. "I will do my best, doctor." When the ringtail was gone, she turned the smile to Ryder. "I came by to see how you were doing. If you're uncomfortable with me here…"

Ryder cut her off with a wave of her hand. "It's fine. If I can handle Calum's berating, I can handle a little awkwardness with a new shipmate."

Even as she said the words, Amelia noticed her shooting a glance to the sword propped against the wall. With an understanding smile, the cat sat forward and placed the compress on Ryder's forehead, as ordered. She frowned to realize the lieutenant was even warmer than she'd been on deck. It was no wonder the doctor was in such a tizzy.

"Strange to see such concern on the face of a pirate."

Amelia's frown deepened. "Does being a pirate mean I must also be devoid of compassion?"

Ryder held her gaze for a moment, then shook her head. "No, you're right, it doesn't. Forgive me, that was out of line."

"It's alright," Amelia said. "You have no reason to trust me. At least not yet. I do hope to change that, given time."

"It's Amelia, isn't it?"

The cat nodded.

"Well, Amelia, you seem like a calm and competent person," said Ryder. "You're considerate, even quiet, but you're sure of yourself and I get the sense that you're a better fighter than many would take you for. You carry yourself like a soldier and I'm not afraid to say that I'd be proud to serve with you, if you were one. So it isn't so much you that I don't trust," she concluded. "It's the company that you keep."

"You mean Father Faiz, don't you?" Amelia deduced. "I've seen the way you look at him. As though he were a ghost or a demon."

Ryder fought to keep her breath even. "Maybe he's both."

"Do you hate him?"

"Hate is a strong word, Amelia." The lieutenant closed her eyes. "But you'd hate him, too, if you knew what he did."

"I can't presume to stand in your shoes, Lieutenant. Or to know how you see him. It may be that he deserves all that you feel. I do know that things change. We evolve, we overcome. I know that he saved my life by convincing me to be true to myself when my culture dictated otherwise. I know that he dedicates himself tirelessly, day after day, to the welfare of his crew. I know that, less than a day ago, you and I were enemies. Now look at us. Did you ever imagine that you'd be receiving bedside care from a pirate?"

"No, I didn't," Ryder said, with the briefest hint of a smile. Then the smile faded. "But you're right. Things change. And we'll be enemies again, when this is over."

≈

"So, what's the skinny on this scepter?" McKinley kicked through the rocks as they climbed. Marshall knew he was only doing it to annoy him. "Between your willingness to put up with me, and the Baron's eagerness to blow up my ship, the blasted thing's got some influence. Seems like an awful lot of fuss over a lousy stick."

"A stick, you say?" echoed Marshall, as though trying on the phrase. "Strangely, I am inclined to agree with you. The scepter itself is nothing more than an historical relic. Article of Fate or no, it belongs in a museum, not in the political arena. But this isn't about the scepter, not really. It's about old laws and power struggles. The Baron wants control of Secora and he's abusing the code and the superstitions of the populace in order to obtain it."

"What do you mean, an 'article of Fate?' Are we talking magic, here?"

"Eadric would likely say yes, but I might doubt his expertise in the matter," Marshall said. "Our ancestors believed that, for anyone to hold it, they must also hold the destiny of those around them. It was a matter of chance. A pure roll of the dice. Each generation, the scepter would be hidden, and the one to find it would have been chosen by Fate to rule. For millennia, it chose the kings and queens of Secora from the humblest of places. Sailors, tradesmen, mothers and widowers. Then, it disappeared. It was decided that the scepter had made its final selection of a single family, and thus was needed no more. Secora was given a ruling House, a single royal bloodline."

"The House of Prideaux," McKinley followed.

"Indeed."

"And I'd guess that the laws surrounding it were never changed. That explains the Baron's play." McKinley furrowed his brow. "But if the scepter disappeared so long ago, what makes Von Ulric think that finding Mosque Hill is going to help him obtain it?"

Marshall paused. "Because that is where Masguard the Explorer believed it to be. If ever there was an authority on obtaining lost relics..."

"Right, right. Masguard disappeared while he was looking for it."

"He did." Marshall nodded, emotionless.

"Do you think he found it?" McKinley asked.

"It's possible."

"Huh," the Marauder said, sounding distant, almost bored. "I guess it's a shame that Masguard never had a House of his own, then."

"A shame." Marshall glanced over his shoulder, but betrayed nothing. "I suppose it is."

The two walked in silence for quite some time until McKinley said, "So, what does a bos-whatchya tree look like anyway?"

At that, Marshall stopped dead in his tracks. "You tell me."

"How would I know?"

"The same way that you knew about the Apothecary's shop having closed." Marshall turned to face him. "The same way you knew which vials to take from Calum's shelf."

McKinley held his gaze, smiled, and pulled the missing vials from his cloak. First the devil's claw. Then the boswellia extract. "And here I thought I'd gone unnoticed by the lot of you. Still, I suppose fooling four out of five isn't bad. But why bother with the charade? You could have confronted me the moment I stole them."

"Why steal them at all? What's to be gained by targeting one of my lieutenants?"

"I asked you first." McKinley folded his arms.

Marshall sighed. "My crew has been asked to set aside their mistrust and accept the assistance of those they've known only as a threat. It is no small request. Had I drawn attention to your misdeed right then and there, all chance of honest compliance would have been removed. I can't afford that, and neither can you. If we're going to reach Mosque Hill in time to do any good – "

"Alright, stop," McKinley interrupted with a raise of his hand and a look of annoyance. "Spare me the 'we have to work together' speech. I get it. I'm also no fool. My crew and I are a temporary utility. When you're done with us, you'll throw us to the wolves. Metaphorically, I hope. You can't blame me for trying to avoid that rather unpleasant outcome." He tossed the vials to Marshall. "Noble captain that you are, I knew you'd want to gather the materials yourself. Taking the vials was a final, desperate attempt to get you off the ship. But then you took the smart route in bringing me with you. Then you caught my rock. See, I had this irrational hope of rendering you unconscious and skipping away with your vessel before you could wax obnoxious, but you've been a party pooper on every end of this plan of mine."

Marshall did not respond. From the mountain's crest, he was staring over McKinley's shoulder to a shadow on the open water.

McKinley turned to follow his gaze through the mist. "What in the world are you looking at?"

"I recognize that ship," Marshall replied.

"You can barely see that ship."

"It's the *Vendetta*. One of the Kathkan warships that attacked us."

Marshall proceeded down the hill, pausing when he realized that McKinley wasn't following. He turned to see the Marauder looking a little too thoughtful.

"No." The naval captain sighed. "You can't steal that ship, either."

"What?" McKinley feigned innocence. "I wasn't thinking anything of the sort."

With a shake of his head, Marshall continued making his way back toward the *Albatross*, muttering, "Pirates."

≈

"We have to pull out, sir," Lieutenant Trimble said, walking alongside her captain as Marshall made for the rear of the ship. With Ryder temporarily out of commission, the marten was now the senior-most officer. "We can take them, but we're not ready for another fight. They'll set our repairs back by hours, if not days."

"No good." Marshall lifted his scope to eye the approaching vessel. "If they haven't detected us already, they will soon. They'll only pursue us if we run, and repairs will still be stymied. Assemble your gun crews. Our best chance at avoiding direct damage is to hide in the rocks ahead and take them by surprise when they enter the bay."

He turned to oversee the preparations, but pulled up short when he noticed the expression on McKinley's face. Though the Marauder said nothing, it was clear that something had occurred to him. Something devious.

"Unless, of course, you have something to add?" said Marshall.

"What, me?" McKinley responded, surprised. With some effort, he folded his arms and pursed his lips. "Um… no. Nope."

Marshall didn't even have the decency to look annoyed. "Very well, then," he said, pivoting for the fore of the ship. McKinley watched his back for several paces before shooting an exasperated sigh to the mist.

"Ugh, alright!" The Marauder groaned, bringing Marshall back to his side. "I suppose it does me no good to let you throw yourself at the bad guys like an idiot."

Marshall arched an eyebrow.

"You have a lot of guns," McKinley went on, grudgingly. "That means you must have a lot of gunpowder. Probably… *barrels* of the stuff."

A slow smile of understanding spread over the captain's face.

Marshall nodded. "That we do."

14
THE TRAP

"It's too far out, sir." Trimble tested the bow in her hand. "There's no way I can make the shot from this distance."Marshall eyed the single barrel floating in the center of the bay, a marker for those that bobbed out of sight, just beneath the surface. Strong swimmers, he and McKinley had made quick work of the trap, binding half a dozen powder casks in a net, secured to the bottom of the bay with a release line. When the enemy ship entered the bay, they would pull the line, releasing the casks, and Trimble would fire a flaming arrow into the dry tinder of the marker barrel, igniting it. The resulting blast would cripple the Kathkan warship without the *Albatross* ever even having to engage.

At least, that was the plan.

"Well, you're going to have to try," the Marauder insisted from the cover of the rocks.

Trimble shook her head, "Maybe from the shoreline…"

McKinley interrupted with a scoff. "They're Kathkan. Don't you think they'll see the potential for an ambush in a place like this? Even if they don't, their weapons will still be primed and ready. They always are. They'll open fire the second you show your face. If you want to take your chances against a bevy of canons, knock yourself out. But I think I'll stay hidden, thank you very much."

The marten sighed, exasperated. "It's your call, sir," she said to Captain Marshall. "The *Vendetta* will be rounding the corner any minute."

Marshall stepped nearer to the shore, judging the distance and the openness of the coast. They were both right. Trimble couldn't make the shot, not from cover. And she'd likely not survive an attempt to do it from the shore. He turned back to those assembled in the rocks. When his eyes settled on Father Faiz, the cleric fox came obediently to his side, without needing to be asked.

"Father," Marshall kept his tone low. "Ryder is the only member of my crew accurate enough to light the fuse from this range. We could use your help."

"I wish I could help you, Captain." Faiz inhaled his honest regret. "But I swore an oath against violence. Using any instrument of death is strictly forbidden."

"You were a warrior, once," Marshall reminded.

Faiz nodded, then met the captain's eyes meaningfully. "As were you," he said before returning to his place in the rocks.

The captain watched him leave, issuing a tight-lipped sigh and shifting his gaze to McKinley. The reason Marshall hadn't wanted to take the shot himself was standing right there, shaking his head at Trimble's willingness to put herself in danger for the sake of the mission. The line would not be easy to pull. Even with Faiz's assistance, it would require the strength of everyone present to release the barrels from the net. If Marshall stepped away to light the fuse, his place could only be filled by McKinley.

And if the Marauder didn't pull his weight, the *Albatross* would be forced into a fight.

Without its captain.

"McKinley," Marshall said decisively. "Fill in while I take the shot."

The Marauder turned from Trimble with a surprised smirk. "Honestly? Me?"

"Yes, you. Can I trust you to do the job?"

"I don't know," McKinley smiled, clearly enjoying his position as a potential liability. "*Can* you?"

Marshall frowned as a shadow emerged from the mist and entered the bay. They didn't have time to argue. "On the line, Marauder."

To his amazement, McKinley complied, albeit with a roll of his eyes.

Marshall took the bow from Trimble and gestured for her to fall in behind the rest.

They were fully under cover when the ship approached the barrel.

Marshall lit the arrow, signaling Trimble, Faiz, and McKinley to tug against the rope, straining with the effort of towing through hundreds of cubic yards of water. Pulling taut his bowstring, Marshall sighted along the shaft of the flaming arrow and waited for the trap to be sprung.

Any moment now…

When nothing happened, he glanced to those on the release line.

"Sir!" Trimble called between grunting breaths. "The line must've caught!"

"Blast!" Marshall cursed, blowing out his arrow and leaping behind Trimble. Taking the rope in a firm grip, he commanded, "Together. One. Two. *Three!*"

In the same breath, they leaned back, pulling with all their might.

The rope quivered.

Then, suddenly, it gave, and they all tumbled to the ground.

Marshall sprung to his feet just in time to see an explosion of water as the barrels burst into the air around the ship and came down with a threatening splash that brought the enemy crew to life. They scrambled, shouting as the captain took up the bow from his hidden position, lighting the arrow and drawing the string as quickly as he could. To his dismay, the dry marker barrel was nowhere to be seen. The *Vendetta* was moving fast and, in trying to clear the explosives, they'd pushed the barrel around the ship's stern, safe from the path of any arrow.

Marshall didn't hesitate.

He catapulted himself from behind the rocks and darted along the shoreline.

In plain view of the cannons.

He scarcely had the chance to hear McKinley shouting in frustration "Ugh! *Idiot*!" before the *Vendetta* opened fire with reckless abandon. The first few shots fell short, or skimmed along the surface of the water before disappearing beneath it, until they found their range. The fourth shot blasted into the rocks just behind his feet as he ran, missing him by mere inches. He stumbled, but kept on until the barrel came into his line of fire.

Then he came to a dead halt in the center of the beach where he steadied his breath, drew the string, and took the shot with the only arrow he had.

But he missed.

His heart sank as the arrow plunged into the water near the barrel with a disappointing fizzle. Then a cannonball exploded nearby, pelting him with shards that tore his uniform and cut through the flesh of his cheek, reminding him of his place. He had to get off this beach.

Turning for the *Albatross*, he was shocked to find Father Faiz blocking his path, a lit arrow in his hands.

"Maybe I can't use it myself," he explained. "But I can carry it for you."

Marshall smiled and gave him a warrior's nod. Holding firm on the open shore, the captain pivoted through the cannon fire, ignoring the din, ignoring the blood on his face and hands.

This was it.

An unnatural stillness settled in his frame as he took the final shot.

They watched the arrow arc through the mist, descending on its target, dim and distant as a falling star. When it struck, a small flame marked its end, burning only for an instant before dying to an ember. Then a spark.

And it ignited.

The cataclysm began with a single explosion that led to another, and another, and another. By the time it was over, what was left of the enemy vessel was listing so far to port that its remaining mast was practically parallel to the water's surface. There was one last explosion. Not of a barrel or resulting blast in the hull, but of a final cannon, set off by accident or desperate crewman.

Marshall felt himself thrown to one side, crushed harshly into the sharp terrain by none other than McKinley.

He sat up to find a cannonball-sized hole in the beach.

Precisely where he'd been standing.

Mouth open, he looked to the Marauder in disbelief.

"What can I say?" McKinley shrugged, as though dismissing the silly notion that he'd just saved his rival's life. "I'm a sucker for rewarding stupidity. Nice shot, by the way. You couldn't have done it that way the first time?"

"Ranged combat was never my forte," Marshall said as Trimble helped him to his feet. "Perhaps next time I can leave the shot to you as to avoid any untimely delays."

McKinley paid him no mind. He was too busy watching Faiz, whose ears had perked forward, held suddenly rigid in that knightly awareness Marshall remembered from his youth.

"Captain, look," Faiz said. Urgency then crept into his voice as he lifted his arm, pointing to the sky where something had taken to flight. "The blackbird! You must stop the blackbird!"

Marshall did not question. Taking an arrow from Trimble, he drew a bead on the bird, now a speck in the distant sky, scarcely within his range. He fired, only to see the projectile stick in the space between him and his target.

Though they couldn't be sure, it looked for all the world as though a hand had come from the mist and snatched the arrow from the air, mid-flight.

But they knew that such a thing was impossible.

McKinley thought of Chimmy's demise and cringed at the similarity.

"He's gone to warn the Baron," said Trimble.

Faiz nodded in response, looking somber.

"Why the concern?" Marshall asked. "Learning of the ship's destruction doesn't give them any advantage that we don't already have."

"What's the worst that could happen?" Trimble added.

"Don't." McKinley held up his hand, chiding, "Don't ask that, blast it."

"Why not?" she asked.

Faiz drew his mouth into a grim line, one full of regret and no small amount of fear. Then he bowed his head and walked away, without a word.

"Because," McKinley sighed, watching his friend move along the shore with a familiar sense of unease. "If the look on his face was anything to go by… you don't want to know the answer."

≈

Many miles away, in a small-village harbor, a white wolverine crouched on the shore, pounding his club impatiently in the sand. Dim lantern light floated out from the scattered huts and simple homes behind him, carrying whispers. The villagers were afraid.

It was well after nightfall before the blackbird landed near his feet. Nervous, the bird fumbled on the rocky shore, twitching every time the wolverine tightened his grip on the club… knowing he didn't need it. Grogoch's red eyes narrowed at the news it carried.

The bird only just managed to skitter out of the way before the albino's enormous club came crashing into the ground with a roar of rage.

He knew not how the Baron would respond.

He didn't care.

All he knew was that his Lady would not be pleased.

≈

Abner woke to a *clink*! as the chains fell away from his wrists.

"Come on." He felt a hand shaking his shoulder. "We haven't much time. The *Havoc* is docked, but I don't know for how long. We have to move quickly if we're going to get you out of here before anyone notices."

Abner blinked up at the face of Gray Calum, the traitor.

"I… I understand…" he said, taking Calum's hand and staggering to his feet. Giving a discreet glance to his surroundings, he hoped the ringtail didn't notice when his eyes settled on a nearby candlestick. "Let's go, then."

Calum nodded and turned toward the stairs.

As they passed the table where the candlestick sat, Abner lunged for it, striking Calum on the back of the shoulders before he knew what was happening.

"Ack!" Calum cried out as he stumbled away. "What are you doing, you old badger?!"

Abner took a threatening step forward, raising the candlestick again. "Do you take me for a fool? I know you only want off this ship because you're afraid of your employer. I'll be drowned if I'm going to help you get away from him."

The ringtail pulled himself from the ground with a look of astonishment. "Help *me*? Abner, I'm here to help *you*! You're the only reason I came aboard."

He lowered the candlestick, but only slightly. "What are you talking about?"

"Abner, we don't have time for this."

"Wrong." The old badger brandished his impromptu weapon tauntingly. "I have all the time in the world. Talk, or I'm leaving you here to deal with that brute on your own."

Calum groaned. "Dash it all, you impossible creature. I saw the look on Marshall's face when they told him you'd been taken. He was terrified. For you. And with good reason, for all that I've seen." He gestured to Abner's wounds. "I'd been posing as an informant, feeding the Baron false information for weeks. It was our hope that I'd be able to meet with him and extract his plans before he could make any major move, but you can see how that turned out. When they boarded the *Albatross*, as far as they were concerned, I was still on their side. That meant I could come aboard and find you. I alone. Marshall knew what I was doing when he saw me with Von Ulric. He asked me not to come. But I had to. Because Marshall is my friend, and I was the only one who could help him in this. He would have done it for me."

Abner held his eyes for a long moment, then lowered the candlestick and shook his head. "No. Marshall would have done it for *anyone*."

"Yeah, that too." Calum agreed, pointing to the stairs. "Can we go now?"

"Well, get on with it, then! We haven't got all day, you know!" Abner pushed past him.

Calum sighed, shrugged, and followed.

≈

Lady Sira plunked her boots on the table and peered around the near-empty tavern with amusement. Though it was little more than an exchange point on the route given to them by the former commander Calum, the townsfolk had not taken kindly to their arrival. None had come to greet them, not even out of fear – choosing instead to hide in their hovels once the Baron had made his presence known. Apparently, his reputation preceded him.

She'd chosen her allies well.

At least, in strength, her eyes narrowed as she stared at the Baron's colossal back.

"This spirit, the one that talks to you," she said. "How do you know that it means you well?"

The Baron growled, earning a jump of surprise from the timid barkeep, a droopy-eared hare. "Having second thoughts, milady? A bit late to be getting cold feet."

She scoffed. "Please. These feet haven't felt a chill since I was a child, bathing in the ice-cold rivers of the Eruche. You use my ship and my countrymen. If this spirit points you wrong and you die, what do we gain? We Kathkans do not like having our time wasted, least of all by Secoran superstition."

With a smile that did nothing to cover the furious glint in his eyes, Von Ulric stood and circled Sira's chair. "*Superstition,* you say? Why, that implies that I am a fool, does it not? That I lean on my own lack of understanding to fill the gaps in my reality. But you have seen the Voice with your own eyes, felt the misty chill of its presence. So it cannot be that you doubt its guidance. Only my wisdom in following it. Either way, you should know better than to question my intelligence." He put his enormous hands on the back of her chair and leaned over her shoulder. "It isn't healthy."

Swallowing, the barkeep took to polishing an already-clean glass while Sira returned the Baron's smile with a hearty showing of teeth. "In my language, *healthy* and *tiresome* are the same word. I care nothing for your threats. The Empire helps you because they know you to be ambitious. Ambition is… simple. Predictable. But now I fight alongside you, and I see something else. Something complicated. It disturbs me."

Just then, Grogoch burst through the door, and the hare dropped the glass. It shattered in disturbing time with the Baron's rise to his full height.

"Bird comes to Grogoch," the big albino seethed. "Says puny otters smash *Vendetta*."

Sira came to her feet with a snarl. "*Otters*? Both of them?"

"They work together," Grogoch confirmed.

"And the other half of the medallion?" asked the Baron.

The wolverine shook his fearsome head. "No necklace. No possum. Only otters."

Sira leaned on the table and levied an accusing gaze in the Baron's direction. "We did not take these Secorans separately. Now they fight as one. How do you expect to obtain your trinket now?"

The Baron's breath was heavy, angry. Visibly, he forced himself to calm.

"Their destination is the same as ours," he said. "They will pursue, and I *will* have what I need."

"That is your plan?" she said through a curled lip. "To let them follow us?"

He turned to her with a scheming glare.

"No," he said. "You aren't the only one who needs assurances, Kathkan. Follow me to the shore. You will see my *ambition* in action."

≈

Marshall leaned back in his chair and closed his eyes, listening to the waves that crashed into the hull like a conversational greeting. It was good to feel the ship moving again. Not only had they completed repairs in record time, they'd eliminated a threat with no casualties and no setbacks.

He opened his eyes and stared at the ceiling, knowing he had McKinley to thank for both of those small miracles. To say nothing of the fact that the pirate had likely saved his life.

Seated side by side in his thoughts, the events of the day were not sitting comfortably with Marshall.

His discomfort only increased when he realized his breath was fogging before his face.

"*Son of Masguard…*"

Marshall came to his feet.

"You again," he said to the blue haze that rose up in his cabin, this time forming a distinct female face. She was beautiful.

"*Son of Masguard, I feel a mother's fear. Blood comes. So much blood. Save the innocent, make the choice. Help me…*"

"It's alright." He stepped forward, raising his hands, feeling compelled to ease her distress. "I will help you in any way that I can. Just tell me what it is that you need."

"*A word,*" she said. "*An answer. The one who left your ship — the traitor with the kind eyes — can he be trusted?*"

Marshall was taken aback. "Gray? He's alive?"

"*Can he be trusted?*" she repeated without confirmation.

Again, he felt that pang of guilt, the one that had so profoundly struck him after the attack, the one that left him unable to explain the truth to his crew. How could he tell them that Calum had left because of him? Put himself in the most dangerous and impossible of circumstances, unasked, to appease a sense of duty? Drawing a deep breath, the captain fought through his guilt to nod with certainty, placing weight in his words. "Commander Calum is one of the finest officers I've ever had the pleasure of knowing. His actions are not those of a traitor. They are those of someone whose loyalty far exceeds military demand. Yes, he can be trusted. With any task or secret that is yours to give."

"*Thank you…*" the face in the haze said, reaching an insubstantial hand toward his.

Then, as suddenly as she had come, the wispy blue visitor was gone.

≈

The Baron stood silent and unmoving on the shore, staring at the sea as though willing something to happen. Having seen this song and dance before, Lady Sira knew it would not be long before *something* did.

Mist swirled and shifted.

The ocean moaned.

Then a form rose up from the water and lunged for the Baron's throat.

To Von Ulric's credit, he did not flinch.

"*Yoou faaail meee!*" seethed the harbinger. "*We told you to snuff out the Son! Yet still he draws breath!*"

He stretched his neck ever so slightly, but showed no further signs of discomfort. "The keepers of the medallion are proving pesky indeed," he said in a calculated tone. "They work together, and so the Son is protected. Which means that you and I must alter the terms of our arrangement."

"Do you know what it is that you ask?" the harbinger replied. "Even as our strength grows, you would drain it!"

"If you want us to succeed…" The Baron let his sentence hang unfinished.

The harbinger was silent for a moment, as though weighing its options.

"*Blood for blood, mortal,*" it said. "*It is the way of the Ancients. My assistance will come at a cost.*"

Von Ulric gave a slow shrug. "Rest assured, your demands will be met. Ours is an expendable world, after all."

His nonchalance over what seemed to be a dire request caused Lady Sira's eyes to narrow. She knew a lop-sided deal when she saw one.

Noting her disapproval, the Baron reminded, "We adapt as we must, Kathkan. Like it or not, our road has taken an unexpected turn."

A hollow sound that might have been laughter poured from the mist around them. "*More than you know…*"

Von Ulric felt his lips pulling away from his teeth. "What do you mean?"

The harbinger moved its nebulous head nearer, hissing low into his face, "*You're going the wrooong waaaay.*"

Realization was instantaneous as the Baron whirled from the harbinger's icy grip, forcing the mist to dissipate with a snarl of ravenous fury.

"CALUM!"

≈

They tore through the underbrush with the wildfire sounds of pursuit roaring close behind.

"For the record, dashing through the dark with the enemy on our tail is a *terrible rescue plan*!" Abner shouted, his run more of a carefully directed stumble, where his legs struggled to catch him at every turn.

"This wasn't the plan, Elder!" Calum shouted back, grabbing him beneath the shoulders before he could fall headlong into a tree. "I don't understand, no one saw us leave! How could they have found us out so quickly?"

"Hardly matters, my boy. The best we can do is to keep on and hope that we don't get caught in any sort of…" his voice trailed off as they rounded a corner only to be confronted with an enormous cliff face. "Dead end."

Calum groaned. In the dark, he hadn't seen the mountain range. Now they were trapped.

"Look, we can still salvage this," he said, drawing his sword. "Start climbing. I'll hold them off as long as I can."

Abner laughed humorlessly. "Start climbing? Who exactly do you think you're talking to? These old bones have barely made it this far."

"Then we fight our way through," he planted his feet resolutely.

Sighing, the Elder leaned wearily against a tree and

lowered his voice to a somber honesty. "Look, my boy. That you came for me at all is a testament to your decency. But it's time to face facts. Only one of us has any chance at getting out of this. And you need to take it, do you understand me? Someone has to tell Marshall..." again, his voice trailed off, this time as a faint blue light grew up behind Calum.

"Tell him what?" the commander asked, having not noticed the figure in the mist.

Renewed, Abner came to his feet and moved to face Calum squarely. Looking him in the eye, he placed an old hand on the ringtail's shoulder. "Tell Marshall that, when the time comes, he *must* choose his words carefully."

"I don't understand," said Calum.

"You don't have to, my boy. Marshall will remember it, and that's all that matters. Now go."

The commander shook his head, "I'm not leaving without you."

"I'm not giving you a choice." Abner smiled. Then he shoved Calum with all of his feeble might, forcing him back into the strange blue mist. It swallowed him whole and, just like that, mist and commander both were gone.

When the Baron reached the base of the cliff with a multitude of angry Kathkans, Abner was alone.

"Where is he?!" Von Ulric snatched the old badger up by the front of his robe and snarled into his face with a surprising lack of composure.

"He's gone," the Elder gasped, forcing his defiance through strained breath. "You'll never find him. Don't bother trying."

The Baron's snarl built to a thunderous growl that burst from his chest as he threw Abner aside like a ragdoll. "Spread out!" he commanded. "Find him!"

Lady Sira watched several of them make off in random directions. The rest cast fruitlessly about for a footprint or any other indicator that the commander had fled, to no avail.

"So," she said. "The rodent disappears, having given us neither necklace nor direction. Things are not yet looking up. What now? Your meeting with the spirit must have given us *something*, no?"

"The Voice wants blood." He glared down at the lights of the village, a fearsome glint coming off his teeth. "And blood it shall have. Take the old one back to the ship, then meet me in the center of this quaint little town. Bring your torches," he said to the crew surrounding him. "Bring your blades."

Sira came to stand alongside him and followed his gaze to the sleepy houses below. Simple homesteads. Farmers and fishermen with little to their names and nothing to mark them as a threat.

He meant to rout the place, she realized.

Such a waste of perfectly good slaves.

"You were right. I see it now," she said at last.

"See what?" he growled, still eyeing the village with a vengeful hunger.

"Betrayal." She walked past him into the night. "It really does weaken a leader. Doesn't it?"

15
THE TRUTH

It had become a game. In the eighteen hours since the ship had gotten underway, McKinley had made five separate attempts to hurl something into the back of Marshall's head, always with whatever was handy (an apple, a can... a hammer), and always without success. Each time, the projectile was caught with ease by Marshall's uncanny awareness. And each time left McKinley a little more baffled than the last.

He'd come to the conclusion that Marshall was, quite simply, a freak.

On one unfortunate occasion, the Kota brothers had tried to join in on the fun only to find themselves knocked to the ground by Ryder, whose condition had significantly improved since the application of Doc Calum's new brew.

"Just because you can, doesn't mean you should," she warned them. "Ever."

Following a brief, stunned silence, the three had laughed jovially and agreed to leave the shenanigans to their incorrigible leader who, they happily admitted, brought far more flare to the stunt than they ever could.

"As long as we get to watch!" Lumber joked.

"Ain't no nevermind,"grinned Ormac.

"Mind helpin' a lad up wi' that lovely gloved hand o' yers?" Gil winked.

Between Ryder's temporary friendship with Amelia and Gil's shameless adoration of her, the strong-willed collie was gaining an odd favor with the pirate band. She found their tolerance astonishing, especially considering her clear and intense loathing of their most-revered member, Father Faiz. They argued little when she moved her hammock from the middle to the lower gun deck, nearer to the *Negvar* crew. Some of them fancied her reason for doing so as a growing fondness for them. Amelia knew better, noting that Ryder hung her hammock between the crews.

She was acting as a shield.

Her suspicion came with good reason, of course. Not even Amelia could be certain whether the Marauder was genuinely amenable to this alliance, or if he was just biding his time. That uncertainty dominated her meditation until she was interrupted by someone sitting bolt upright from the neighboring floorboards.

"Father?" concern creased her features as she came to Faiz's side.

He was drenched in sweat and his fur bristled with a primal tension that made him look far more frightening than a priest ever should.

"What is it?" She put a hand on his shoulder, trying to calm him. "Was it that same dream?"

He stared at her for the longest time, as though trying to remember her face through a fog. "No," he finally said. "It wasn't something from my past. But it easily could have been, for it was just as bad."

She waited patiently, knowing he might not continue at all.

"It's this mist." He leaned forward, bowing his humble head and staring at the space between his splayed hands. "Something dark lurks within it, something evil. It was…

gloating, as though about a terrible crime. As if it had strangled, gored, and killed, and still wasn't satisfied." Hesitantly, he met her eyes. "For all the evil it has done… it isn't finished yet. Not by a long shot."

Amelia drew a deep breath, reading the true meaning behind his words. "You're saying that it is coming for us?"

He did not respond, not right away.

"It's alright," she reassured him. "You can tell me."

He relented, a visible heaviness in his shoulders. "For one of us, yes."

"I see." She nodded. After several very long minutes, she simply grasped his hand and said, "Whatever is to come is what must happen. We will find reason in it, or we will make our own. Either way, life will go on."

Then she returned to her bedroll and rested her head, seeming utterly at peace.

Ryder, who had been watching the exchange with a growing sense of loss, pretended to be asleep when Faiz looked her way.

He pretended not to notice.

≈

Marshall had not slept. Unable to free his thoughts from the blue aura and the beautiful face in the apparition, he was still staring through the aft windows when Wexler knocked at his cabin door.

"I'm sorry for disturbing you, sir," the young fennec said. "But the topmen have spotted something through the mist. It looks like smoke coming from the shore. A lot of it. Should we move to investigate?"

"Are we near any villages?"

"Bryton, sir," Wexler confirmed.

Marshall frowned in disapproval. Bryton was a fishing town with no military presence. If they were in trouble, there would be no one to help them.

"Take us in, then, Ensign," he turned, donning his

black captain's coat with sharp movements. "Rouse the next shift and have Ryder assemble an investigation party. I'll need a full boat on that shore if we're to be of any real assistance. And Ensign?"

Wexler stopped en route to the door.

"See to it that McKinley joins us."

"Aye, sir." The dutiful youth did not hesitate in his response, but his voice wavered ever so slightly. Enough for Marshall to notice.

"Have you ever played chess, Ensign?"

"Aye, sir," nodded the fennec.

"And when you play, where do you always want the opposing king to be?"

Wexler paused thoughtfully, then smiled. "Within striking distance?"

Marshall nodded. "Very good, Ensign. Quickly to your duties, now."

Once outside, Marshall strode purposefully for the middle deck, where he rapped once on the door of Calum's abandoned room, unlocked it, then entered.

C.S. glared up at him from beneath a mountain of blankets.

"If you're here to ask about the Baron, you're wasting your time," she yawned. "I already told you everything I know."

"Actually…" He looked around her impromptu cell. "I'm here to ask whether you'd like to go home."

≈

"That's Bryton?" C.S. put her face between the rails and stared at the smoking village with sad eyes.

The captain looked down at her, his features calm and subdued. "It is."

"It… it looks so different."

"The fire may have something to do with that," McKinley interrupted as he came from below deck. "You know, Captain, that better not be the reason you woke me from a dead sleep in the middle of the night. If so, I gotta tell ya, rescues aren't really my thi—" He broke off abruptly when they turned around to face him. He recognized Maya's thieving friend immediately.

She averted her gaze.

Marshall looked from one to the other. "Is something wrong?"

"I, uh…" McKinley recovered as quickly as he could. "I just didn't know you let kids on this ship. Apart from Wexler, that is." His expression morphed into one of disapproval. "You're in a dangerous line of work, Captain. Maybe let the little ones play 'officer-on-deck' in a safer venue? A butcher's shop, perhaps?"

"The Ensign is no child, Marauder," said Marshall. "And C.S. came to us as a fugitive and an orphan. This port is her home. I was hoping to find her a relative when we put ashore. Preferably, one that will keep her out of trouble."

But the nearer they drew to the coast, the more hopeless that idea became.

Both captains, lieutenants Ryder and Trimble, Doctor Calum, Father Faiz, Master Tobb, and even Eadric, mounted the shore to find the village in ruins. Smoke and fire and ash filled the streets, but nothing moved, not one living thing. They were forced to cover their faces as they strode through vacant alleys, calling into what remained of the devastated homes, only to be met with silence until they found themselves standing before the enormous double doors of a town hall – the only portion of the building left standing. Across them, darkly scrawled in soot or something altogether worse, was the phrase: "*Reap what you have sown.*"

Marshall gritted his teeth as he read the Baron's words, knowing full well that they were intended for him; a pointed finger blaming him for the fall of this sleepy little village.

"Fate keep these people," said Eadric, having for once put his ego out of the way. "Horrible. Just horrible."

"What happened here?" C.S. shivered, seeming so small beneath the wreckage.

"Von Ulric happened here," said McKinley as he turned to survey the devastation. He had always thought that one ruler would be the same as the next. Corrupt. Untouchable. Looking now at the ruins of Bryton, it was hard to take that notion seriously.

For the first time, the Marauder realized what the Baron would make of his daughter's home.

And it angered him.

"I... I had no idea. I knew he was bad, but this? The entire town..." A tear crept into her voice. "They were helpless and he killed them. *Everyone.*"

"Not everyone." Father Faiz walked up behind them, his eyes fixed on the trees behind the broken houses. He turned to Marshall. "Captain, we should search the woods."

≈

"Over here!" Ryder was the first to spot the hidden cellar. Even before Faiz, who had led them almost directly to it through the thickness of fog and forest.

Dozens of tiny feet scrambled away from the door as it opened.

"It's alright," the lieutenant coaxed, her voice gentle. "We're with the Navy. We're here to help."

Seeing the fear and reluctance in the cellar's many pairs of eyes, C.S. moved forward and held out her hand. "No one's going to hurt you," she said. "You're safe now, I promise."

There was a shuffling and an uncertain whimper. Then, one by one, the children were moved by her encouragement to file from the safety of the cellar. They seemed confused, but otherwise unharmed.

"Is the bad wolf gone?" the youngest one, a knee-high hare, asked. "Can we go home now?"

Officers and pirates looked one to the other, sharing a sense of pity for these innocent youngsters.

They'd been orphaned by a madman.

Father Faiz lowered his head and took a step back, into the darkness. "I will tend to their families," he said in a low voice, so the children would not overhear.

Marshall drew himself upright. "Lieutenant Trimble and Master Tobb, please join the Father in his task, but make use of Eadric's flight to continue your search for survivors. Lieutenant Ryder?"

For an instant, Ryder seemed too lost in her empathy to reply, but her soldier's verve returned quickly enough. "Aye, sir?"

"Kindly escort our young friends to a fortified area where Doctor Calum can safely see to their well-being. We will scour the village in shifts until dawn while they recover from their ordeal."

"Sir," Trimble hesitated, torn between dutiful obedience and dutifully noting that they were still strapped for time. "Dawn is several hours out."

Marshall nodded. "We knew that when we came ashore, Lieutenant. We came anyway, because these are our people." He looked back at the rubble, grimly knowing what lay beneath it. "We aren't leaving them like this."

≈

The children slept without difficulty, even with the doctor hovering over each of them, checking for injury. Ryder had explained the situation to the youngsters as gently as she could. Now, between exhaustion and grief, their tiny frames hadn't the strength to muster anything beyond sleep.

As they nodded off, McKinley had made a show of entertaining them with jokes, sleight of hand, and acrobatic tricks. He even earned a smile or two in return. But when his shift came around, he joined the search with the same somber glint in his often-merry eye that everyone else had. Marshall had on his captain's face. So strong. So together. But the appearance had a touch of stone to it; one that might reveal to a keen observer just how deeply he was grieving in silence for each of the young Secorans now in his charge, should they care to look.

And through it all, C.S., a child too old for her age, sat awake and to one side, thinking thoughts that no one could hear and questioning all the choices that had led her to this end.

She was still like this when McKinley and Ryder returned in a rush, a wounded, soot-covered hare held up between them.

"Marshall!" McKinley called as they entered the clearing. "This poor bloke could use some help!"

The captain turned, pausing only a moment with an odd look on his face before rushing to their aid.

"I found him!" Eadric hopped alongside them in an ecstatic manner. Apparently, he'd never been useful before. "That was me, Captain!"

"Yeah, you did your job well enough. Now calm yourself, Featherface." McKinley frowned down at him. "There'll be plenty of time for gloating later."

"My son…" the hare managed, weakly. "Where is my son?"

"Easy, citizen," Marshall addressed him as the doctor took charge, ushering the bloodied hare to the fireside, where she could examine his wounds in full. "The children are with us, safe and well. I believe your son is there among them." He pointed to a bedroll on the far side of the camp. The hare relaxed at the sight of his boy as Marshall continued, "Can you explain to us what happened?"

Struggling to hold himself upright, it was something of a miracle that the droopy-eared barkeep was able to stave off unconsciousness long enough to tell his tale. He recounted the scene in the tavern, Grogoch's entry, and the curious pursuit through the woods. "We thought maybe they were gone for good, but then the strangest thing happened. A Navy lad just appeared in the center of town, out of nowhere. Like magic..."

"Magic, you say?" McKinley perked up.

"Sounds crazy, I know. But there was this blue mist..."

Now it was Marshall's turn to seem intrigued. "A blue mist, you say?"

The hare looked back and forth at the two otters. "Um, yes. The Navy lad, he said his name was Calum and that the Baron was not far behind. He offered to take the children to safety. We let him, because we knew that what was coming might be bad."

"Why did none of you go with him?" asked Ryder.

The hare looked at her and gave an odd smile, as though hoping she might be proud of him for his response. "We stayed to fight. This is our home, isn't it? We couldn't let that monster storm in with no one to resist him. Not to mention that, if we'd run, he might have followed. Staying behind was the only way to ensure he didn't go after the kids. We did the right thing, didn't we?" He looked over his shoulder to the devastated town. "Tell me we did the right thing."

Ryder seemed at a loss for words. She looked to McKinley, then to her captain.

Marshall caught the hare's eyes with his poise and held his gaze for the longest time. Finally, he said, "I can't speak to the proper choices regarding family and home, for I have neither. I *do* know warfare, however. I know that one can often tell at a glance how low their odds of success may be. And I know that it is rare and brave for one to stand against an unbeatable enemy, despite those odds. So I can say without hesitance that you, sir, are a rare and brave individual. And these children are alive because of you."

The hare relaxed then, his smile sincere and grateful. "That officer? Calum? Is he with you? I'd like to thank him, if I may."

Marshall lost some of his poise.

"I'm sorry, but no." He swallowed. "We've not yet seen the Commander."

"Oh," frowned the hare. "Well. I do hope the lad turns up." He looked to where his son lay sleeping with the other youngsters, concluding, "I owe him everything."

Doctor Calum interrupted by loudly unfurling a bedroll at their backs. "Alright. You've questioned him enough. He needs rest. Captain, if I may speak to you in private?"

When they were out of earshot, she turned to him and folded her arms in a very cross manner. "You knew about this, didn't you?"

Marshall hesitated. "Doctor…"

She held up a hand. "*Don't* lie to me, Captain. I want the truth."

The captain sighed and clasped his hands behind his back. "I knew that he hadn't betrayed us, yes."

"And all that time, you let me think…?" Shaking her head, the doctor struggled to keep her scolding in check. "Never mind. I can guess why you did it. Just know that, from now on, you can be ashamed of what your status engenders in your followers when my heart *isn't* in the middle of it, understand?"

With that, the doctor stormed off to tend to her patients – directly past Lieutenant Ryder, who had been waiting patiently aside as they spoke.

"I should have known what he was doing," she said, stepping forward and coming to attention. "If I had, I might have gone in his place."

"Your sentiment is a noble one, Lieutenant."

She seemed to read something in his words that he did not say. "Our loyalty to you, sir," she assured him. "It isn't a vice. For better or worse, we are at your back. Always."

Marshall firmed his jaw, then tipped his head. "As I am

at yours. Thank you, Lieutenant."

McKinley watched each of these exchanges from the shadows, never saying a word, never calling attention to himself. When they were finished, he returned unbidden to the task of searching the village and helping the Father lay its inhabitants to rest.

All the while doing his best to ignore the sinking feeling in the pit of his stomach.

≈

Careful Steps Kal stared into the fire, brooding in a way that reminded Ryder of herself not so long ago.

"Are you alright?" Ryder seated herself next to the young raccoon.

"Sure," C.S. shrugged. "I mean, as well as can be, I suppose. But the Baron won't be. Not when I'm finished with him."

The Lieutenant tried not to smile at the image of the tiny youngster squaring off against the mountainous Baron. "Is that what you're doing over here by yourself? Planning Von Ulric's demise?"

"Just look at this place. Look at these kids!" C.S. bit back, not meaning to direct any hostility toward Ryder, but not knowing where else to point it. "What else am I going to do?"

Ryder looked down at the cap in her gloved hands. After a moment, she returned a soft but determined gaze to the angry child and said, "I'll tell you what you're going to do. You're going to give it to us. All of that anger and all of that need for revenge. It's our burden now, understand? The *Albatross* will hunt him down. We'll make certain that he can't hurt anyone ever again. And you, young lady, will get on with your life without hate. You're too good for that."

C.S. was quiet a moment, mulling over her words with deflated shoulders. "I'm a thief, Lieutenant. *And* I worked for the Baron. I took his money for horrible tasks that I now know had horrible consequences for real people. Knowing that, how can you possibly say that I'm good?"

Ryder smiled. "Call it an intuition. Had you been raised in different circumstances, who knows? You might have grown up to be an honest courier, or a storyteller, or maybe a soldier, like me. You can still be any of those things, if you want."

"Really?" The young thief looked hopeful. "You think so?"

"Of course," said Ryder. "After what happened to my clan, I did a lot of things I wasn't proud of. When I met Captain Marshall, I was working for the Mercenary Guilds."

C.S. winced. "They're not a nice bunch."

"No," Ryder agreed. "They're not. But the time came when I was able to make a different choice, and I took it. You can do the same."

The thought seemed to lighten C.S.'s mood, if only a little. Then she realized what Ryder had said a moment earlier. "What *did* happen to your clan?"

Ryder leaned back, unconsciously drawing her gloved hands away from the fire. "That's... that's not important right now," she said.

C.S. knew well when she should let a matter drop. "So, you're saying that you can see around my past?"

"Yes, I suppose I can."

The raccoon nodded, pointing to the rubble, where McKinley and Faiz still labored under Trimble's watch. "Then why can't you see around theirs?"

Ryder followed C.S.'s finger with her eyes, and fell quiet as she watched the shadows in the darkness. Eventually, she placed her cap on the youngster's head and patted her arm. "Get some sleep, C.S."

The raccoon smiled up at her from beneath the hat. "There's something I have to do first. But... thank you for everything. All of you. I really mean that."

Smiling in return, Ryder tapped the brim of her hat in a friendly gesture and left the fire to its crackling. When she was gone, C.S. made for the village.

≈

The Marauder was knee-deep in mortar and broken beams when he heard his name coming from the shadows.

"Mr. McKinley?"

He looked up to see C.S. standing alongside the remains of the home he was searching, a shaky look on her tiny face.

"Kid, what are you doing out here?" he scolded. "You should be back at camp."

"I know." She kicked at the dirt beneath her feet. "Can I talk to you for a minute, though? I swear it won't take long."

The otter sighed and brushed off his hands. "Alright, but let's get you out of this ash first." When they were back among the trees, he pointed to Ryder's cap, which still adorned the little one's head. "Becoming a soldier now, are we?"

"Maybe," she shrugged with a grin. "Someday."

"What did you want to talk to me about?"

"I... I know it probably doesn't matter to you," she said hesitantly. "But I think I should tell you that I know who you are."

Unabashed, the Marauder stroked his chin, "Well, I should hope so. My beautiful mug is plastered on many a Wanted poster."

C.S. shook her head. "That isn't what I meant. I saw you that night, in Maya's room. I was outside the window, while you were talking to her. I know that she's your daughter."

McKinley's self-worship vanished upon the instant.

"Is that so?"

"Like I said, I know it doesn't matter. Not to you,

anyway. But this is one of the only things that I feel like I've gotten right. So I… I just wanted to let you know that I didn't tell the Baron. I won't tell anyone else, either." She fumbled in the pocket of her tattered vest and pulled out the stolen trinket. It wasn't much. Just a beaded bracelet with a brass star dangling from the center. McKinley couldn't even recall where he'd gotten it. Maya had loved it, of course, but she professed to loving *everything* he brought her. C.S. looked at it like it was the only thing she'd ever loved. "They said they're taking us to a priory in Port Sundry, so I don't know how long it will be before I see Maya again. Would you… would you give this back to her for me? Tell her I'm sorry for stealing it. I shouldn't have done that." She looked over her shoulder to the smoking village. "I shouldn't have done a lot of things."

McKinley followed her gaze and sighed.

"You aren't alone in that," he said quietly, reaching down to take the bracelet and holding it in his palm. "Why did you steal it? There were other things on that table that were far more valuable than this."

She held up her arm to show the series of strings on her wrist. Dingy bits of yarn in different colors. "I like bracelets. I just never owned a real one before. And… I don't know, I guess a part of me thought that, even if Maya's parents were using presents to bribe her into seclusion, it was still more than my parents ever loved me."

McKinley swallowed, the skin around his eyes softening.

"I was wrong about you, though," C.S. went on with a smile. "I knew it as soon as I saw you hug her. You're a good dad. She's right to believe in you."

The Marauder was quiet as he looked down at the bracelet. After a moment's thought, he unclasped it and knelt to the ground, placing it gently around the little raccoon's wrist. "Tell you what. How about you keep it safe for her?"

Her eyes lit up. "Do you mean it?"

"Of course," he stood, brushing her excitement aside. "Look at me, in this mess. She'd make a fuss if I got it dirty. And can you imagine if I lost it altogether? The girl would have my tail. No, better you take it with you. She'd be happy knowing it was with someone who cared about it."

Her smile beamed down on the simple piece of jewelry with the warmth of a thousand suns.

McKinley almost teared up when she turned that glee and gratitude in his direction.

"Thank you," she said. "Thank you so much! I will think of her every time I look at it."

"Well," he cleared his throat. "I can think of no better way for someone to remember my little girl than with a smile like that. Now get back to camp. Ryder's probably looking for her hat as we speak."

The little raccoon turned to do as he bade, paused, turned around, and threw her arms around him with a quick hug. Then she bolted out of sight, presumably, back toward the fire for a few spare moments of sleep before they moved out.

Squinting in annoyance, McKinley pressed his fingers firmly into his eyes, as though berating them for so nearly letting a bit of liquid past their lids.

"Keep it together, Marauder," he told himself, trying to pretend that it would be easy for him to do precisely that.

≈

Hours passed. Dawn came. And the camp on the outskirts of the village had not moved.

Marshall, for the first time in his career, was hesitating.

"Look at that sunrise!" McKinley proclaimed with false enthusiasm. "Gotta hand it to this pesky mist, it may be a hindrance to travel, but it makes for a beautiful daybreak, don't you think, Marshall?"

Paying him no mind, the captain continued his stoic watch over the rescue efforts still being carried out by Trimble, Tobb, and the seemingly-tireless Faiz.

"What's wrong, McKinley?" Ryder said as she snuffed out the fire. "Are you in a hurry to be somewhere?"

"Why, yes, Lieutenant. As a matter of fact, I am. Just as *you* are, if I'm not mistaken."

"We aren't leaving," she countered. "Not while we can still do some good."

"Fat lot of good we're doing sitting here."

Ryder looked as if she meant to silence him.

Marshall stopped her. "The Marauder is right. If the Baron reaches his goal, this won't be the only village in ruins." His voice carried a clear sense of disappointment as he gave the order, "Rouse the children and call off the search. Prepare for our return to the *Albatross.*"

"Did you hear that, Lieutenant?" McKinley grinned. "I'm right, he says. Now let's blow this place. I've had all the 'depressing' I can handle for one night."

She shook her head. "Is there *anything* you take seriously?"

"Death," he quipped. "Well, depending on who's doing the dying, that is."

"One would think," Marshall turned to him with a hardened tone. "Considering the circumstances, that even you might avoid making light of mortality."

McKinley laughed, a laugh that held no humor. "Yes, I suppose one would. But then it appears *one* would be very much mistaken, as *one* so often is."

Marshall leveled a steely gaze at him. "If you've a point to make, Marauder, then make it. I've no patience for pretenses, and this is hardly the time for jest."

"No patience for pretenses? Really? Well, let's see. Do I have a point to make?" Folding his arms, McKinley planted his feet and met Marshall's stare with irritation. "Maybe I do. But then, the noble bureaucrat, the high-and-mighty Marshall, probably wouldn't be able to grasp a whiff of it. He's too steeped in an absurd sense of duty to see any of this for what it really is. You think these people were brave, do you? That they threw their lives away for a cause, and therefore deserve to infringe on the greater picture? Forcing us to take time away from a vital task in order to honor their supposed decency? They were fools, Captain. Plain and simple. It was a pointless tragedy. One that we cannot mend by dragging our heels while Von Ulric goes along on his merry way."

"That's a lot of emotion for someone who's only after wealth," said Ryder.

"You don't know the slightest thing about what I'm after, Lieutenant," he bit at her. "Just as you don't know the slightest thing about your good captain's intentions."

"What are you talking about?" she demanded.

"You didn't see your benevolent leader's face when we found the barkeep, did you?" he looked accusingly to the quiet captain. "He wasn't relieved, or even concerned. He was disappointed. Because he was hoping it would be someone else. Admit it, Marshall, all of this wasted time hasn't been for the sake of those poor people buried in the rubble. It's been nothing more than a stalling tactic. You've been waiting for one thing and one thing alone. For your lost commander to come flitting out of the forest, so you wouldn't have to feel guilty for his loss. How very honorable for one with no patience for pretenses, don't you think?"

Marshall tightened his jaw and lowered his head. "*Do not* presume to know my mind, pirate. Yes, I was hoping to find Commander Calum in our search. But don't think for an instant that it clouded my concern for these people."

As their voices rose, so too did the children in the camp behind them.

It wasn't long before the brewing argument drew the attention of those in the village, either, who returned from their searches of their own accord to find out what the fuss was about.

"Maybe the two of you should keep it down?" offered Eadric, indicating the children's concerned faces.

"Hope is a fool's virtue, Marshall," McKinley went on, too angry even to notice the advisor's interruption. "Odds are, your commander is already dead."

"Dead or alive," Marshall came toe to toe with him. "We do not leave our own behind."

"You already left your own behind!" McKinley yelled with the verve of someone who was speaking to himself on a very personal level. He looked at Marshall as though looking in a mirror. "You left him to fend for himself, just like these villagers did to their kids! What kind of person does that, huh?! What kind of selfish fool ditches those he loves and then pretends it was the only option?!"

"Captain…" Father Faiz put a calming hand on McKinley's shoulder. "Perhaps you should let it be."

McKinley knocked his hand away, breaking loose with a harsh shove to Marshall's chest. "Perhaps *he* should own up to his failure as a father!"

"A father? You're truly mad, aren't you, *thief*?!" Captain Marshall shoved him in return.

McKinley balked, having realized what he just said. "Maybe," he deflected, furiously. "But I'm not the only thief here, am I, *Captain*?!"

Then, in perfectly mirrored movements, the two drew blades – McKinley producing yet another knife from nowhere. They grabbed one another by the lapels, jerking the other forward until they were nose to nose, each blade pressing into the other's throat. Their angry shouts came simultaneously, their voices indistinguishable.

"*What are you doing with my mother's painting*?!"

"*What are you doing with my father's medallion*?!"

The meaning of their words hardly had time to strike anyone at all before Eadric interrupted in a feverish burst of tension, "This is no way for the son of Masguard to behave!"

Immediately, he clamped his wings over his beak.

272

"What?!" McKinley flew at him, his rage now carrying a stunned edge of uncertainty. "How did you know that?! How could you *possibly* know?!"

Marshall took a step back, lowering his blade. "No…"

Eadric looked in terror and confusion from McKinley's knife, to Marshall, and back again.

"You…" McKinley loosened his grip, realization spreading over his face. "You weren't talking about me, were you? You were talking about…" He followed Eadric's gaze to where Marshall stood, staring at him as though rejecting a truth. "No…"

"Fate alive…" Ryder looked at the two. For the first time noting their exact same build, the way they carried themselves, their eyes. "They're brothers."

All hostile intent forgotten, Marshall and McKinley looked at each other in equal parts disdain and reluctance. Pirate and soldier. Captain and thief. Both of them now on a footing they had no desire to share.

As if to punctuate their new reality, Marshall pulled a chain from beneath his vest, revealing the other half of the medallion worn by McKinley.

The Marauder could only bury his face in his hands and groan, "You have *got* to be kidding!"

16
SHIP UNDER SIEGE

Within the hour, the children of Bryton, along with its surviving adult, had been ferried to the *Albatross* by a quiet crew. None of them quite knowing what to make of the recent revelation, they'd opted for silence over investigation. And the newly-outed sons of Masguard had, for the most part, done a successful job of avoiding one another.

Now that they were seated side by side on the final raft, however, it was difficult for each to pretend the other didn't exist. A brief instant of accidental eye-contact and McKinley could contain himself no longer.

"Alright, that's it. If no one else is going to say it, then I will," he folded his arms impudently. "I don't buy it. How can I believe that if I'd grown up in the same household as Captain Maggot that I'd be some salt-of-the-earth, nose-in-the-sky noble? Does that make *any* sense to *any* of you? Honestly?"

Ryder chuckled between rows, "Something tells me you still wouldn't have been the wholesome type. But you're a noble, alright. No denying that one anymore."

"Ugh, don't remind me. At least I had the good sense to reject my station, unlike stuffed-shirt here who practically bathed in it. With his uniform and his education and his... Wait a minute." He pointed at Marshall, accusing and ecstatic all at the same time. "You're rich, aren't you? With copious amounts of *family money*! Ha! Half of that is mine!"

"Quiet," Marshall held up his hand. He sat alert and rigid, staring through empty skies to his too-visible ship, seated on waters that shimmered with unusual clarity. "What happened to the mist?"

Having not noticed the sudden change in their surroundings, everyone aboard fell silent.

Ryder stopped rowing.

Even McKinley looked uneasy.

From the rear of the raft, Father Faiz lifted his head, his fur bristling as he looked to something on the horizon that only he could see. "It's beginning in earnest now," he whispered in a somber tone, as if to gird himself. "They're coming."

Marshall stared at him, wondering why the Baron's darkly-scrawled message was forcing itself to the forefront of his mind, wondering why the stillness taunted him like an enemy with a superior weapon.

Then Ryder pointed to the sea, just beyond the bow of the *Albatross*. "Captain."

It began as an odd ripple. Then a pulse from somewhere deep within the ocean. Ominous. Slow. Sounding out a warning like the beat of a war drum. The ripples swelled, becoming breakers, becoming waves. In seconds, the tide had risen to a tsunami that exceeded the waters themselves, looming over the ship. A predator poised to strike. Only then did those in the raft realize the awful truth. That the wave rising from the ocean and bearing down on their ship wasn't a wave at all.

It was the mist.

"ROW!" Marshall shouted, hoisting an oar as everyone

onboard rushed to follow suit.

As fast as they moved, they were still some distance away when the mist struck.

Violently, it slammed into the *Albatross*, jarring masts and pushing the ship sideways in the water. In the frightening moments before the fog bled away over the hull, it was impossible to know whether any of the crew had been thrown from the safety of the deck, into angry waters. The only certainty was that, by the time the ephemeral wave had passed, those remaining on the ship were not alone. An army stood among them, wispy and seething.

Marshall and McKinley both stood to a crouch, gripping the sides of the raft.

"Captain!" Ryder shouted, incredulous. "What are my eyes seeing?!"

He looked over his shoulder to McKinley and found the Marauder looking back.

"They need their captain," he said, seeming to know Marshall's thoughts before he could give them voice.

Marshall gave an abrupt nod.

Then, without another word, the two dove into the icy waters with a grace few animals could match, cutting through the ocean toward the ship, where the impossible army had already begun their assault.

≈

"Move the children below decks, now!" Amelia cried as she pulled a spare sword from the scabbard of a passing crewman. Unfortunate that Marshall had heeded his crewmen's fears by denying the pirates their own weaponry.

Gil jumped to assist, ushering the youngsters away from the intruders, who came at them with household items, antiques, and the occasional rusty sword.

So *that's* where the items from Secora's rash of petty

robberies had gone.

Brandishing a mop in defense of the children's retreat, Lumber and Ormac looked in perfect conformity with their enemy as they leapt behind the children, jeering at the army as if at schoolyard bully.

"Of wi' ye, pesky brutes!"

"Pick on someone your own size!"

True to form, Marshall's crew joined them in their task, Ensign Wexler and Lieutenant Bowers taking point, looking frightened but determined as the first of the attackers came their way. But when the enemy's strange weapon fell, Wexler froze.

Amelia stepped between them, blocking the wrench with speed and grace. In an instant, she was behind him, her blade passing through her opponent's midsection like a horizontal guillotine. She lunged back, horrified, when he simply parted and drew himself together again, completely unharmed.

"Mist!" she cried. "They're nothing but mist!"

"Fate alive!" Bowers called in return. "How do we fight them?!"

Amelia shook her head.

The answer was simple.

They couldn't.

They could only retreat as the army advanced yet again. This time, when the wrench fell, Amelia's confusion left her watching in slow time as the garish attacker smiled its certain victory.

That smile vanished on the instant when his weapon was halted by a strong hand.

He looked up to see Marshall, captain of the *Albatross*, standing before him, dripping from head to toe in stoic fury.

The grim set of his mouth said it all.

*How **dare** you attack my people?*

With a deft movement of his blade, the captain disarmed the misty figure and brought the wrench around in a lightning strike across the ghastly being's face. The blow landed with a wet *thud*! that sent the creature flying across the deck through the wispy forms of his fellow attackers. They dispersed and reassembled, staring back at this hostile otter with a new respect, and a hesitance.

"Their weapons are real enough," Marshall called back to his crew.

"Take their weapons!" The order echoed across the deck.

But as they rushed forward to do precisely that, both sides were halted by the very out-of-place sound of boisterous laughter.

They turned to see McKinley standing off to one side, every bit as drenched as the captain, with a mountain of the bizarre weapons already at his feet. "Pirates," he explained with a smile. "We're *very* good at taking things."

Ormac's face split into a similar grin. "Ye heard 'im, lads! Let's relieve these 'ere stowaways o' their belongin's!"

"Oiy!" hollered Gil.

Lumber agreed with a hearty, "Booya!"

With that, the pirates set about acting like pirates.

And Marshall's crew stuck to what they were good at.

As one, they pressed forward, dodging and attacking with well-trained precision. The intruders were surreal and frightening, but they weren't soldiers. It wasn't long before they were cornered and disarmed, seemingly without hope of recourse.

But if there was one thing Marshall had learned in his years of dedicated service, it was that appearances were nothing if not deceitful.

"*McKinley…*"

The voice echoed from the center of the misty mob like an accusation.

"*McKinley.*"

The Marauder searched the crowd in confusion, but the source of the voice could not be seen.

"Show yourself," he said.

At length, the mob parted to reveal a familiar face.

McKinley's jaw dropped.

His mouth felt dry as he said the dead possum's name aloud, hardly believing what he was saying as the word passed his whiskers, "Chimmy?"

"*I did the right thing, Captain,*" the pale spirit repeated his dying words. "*I did the right thing, and they still took me. It's your fault, you know. All of it.*"

"You made your choices, Leech," McKinley said, a hard look in his eyes. "Don't lay them at my feet."

"*Not at your feet, no,*" Chimmy laughed a misty laugh of insanity. "*On your head!*"

No sooner had he said the words than the mob dissipated in an angry burst of light, spewing a giant, writhing form out onto the deck that tore through pirates and soldiers with tooth and claw and brutal club. Impossibly, it was Lady Sira's foremost henchman, the very solid, very alive Grogoch.

McKinley was the first to fall.

The albino's club found his chest with a horrific blow that spun him around, sending a fountain of blood spewing from his mouth as he tumbled over the deck. He tried to rise, and was thrown again to the deck by an explosion of pain that weakened his limbs and dizzied his senses.

On some level, through the pain and the frustration with his own body – the one that would not heed his calls to fight for breath – he was aware of a sound. Faint and far away. It grew to a mocking height, closer and closer, until he realized what it was.

Laughter.

"*Die, you filthy pirate,*" the possum whispered in his ear. "*Diiieee…*"

McKinley gasped and writhed.

Then he heard Marshall calling his name, saw the heroic figure shouting orders to his crew and pirates alike as he rushed to defend him from the misty figures that reached to recover their weapons, and McKinley found strength enough to respond.

"How does it feel, Leech?" he pushed the words through bloodied teeth, spitting into the mist with all the vigor he could conjure. "To be dead, with nothing more to fear? And to know that you're still a coward?"

"*You'll find out soon enough. You're done now.*" The possum's voice became an echo that McKinley could scarcely hear. "*You should join us, now that you're done…*"

"No." McKinley struggled to shake his head. He wasn't finished. Not yet. Not while his little girl still needed him.

His little Maya…

Who would save her now?

"No…"

But, even as he gave voice to his objection, he knew its futility. His desperate body screamed up at him like a shattered vase, now broken and useless, unable even to contain air.

The light of the breaking dawn was dimming in his eyes.

And the air was cold.

≈

Grogoch was a monster, an unstoppable force rivaled only by the Baron himself. Backed by an army that felt no pain, would not tire, and could not fall, he swept across the *Albatross* wreaking devastation.

And there were no gryphons to save them. Not this time.

When the raft arrived, Ryder pulled herself on deck to a horrifying scene. Her crew was scattered, their usual conformity torn asunder by a white wrecking ball with teeth. Her captain was standing over the fallen form of McKinley.

He was angrier than she'd ever seen him.

"Tobb and Trimble!" Marshall ordered between

engagements with the enemy. "Escort McKinley and Doctor Calum below decks on the instant!"

"Captain, what's happening?!" Trimble fought her way across the deck.

Marshall whirled on the marten. "GET MY BROTHER TO THE INFIRMARY NOW!"

The doctor pushed Tobb immediately to the Marauder's unresponsive side and together they lifted him as Trimble defended their escape to the stairwell, a confused expression on her face.

"On my back, Lieutenant!" Marshall barked in Ryder's direction.

She whirled around an attacker, ducking and sliding into place at Marshall's tail, weapon at the ready. She was shocked when she realized that Father Faiz was at her side, having just defended her from an attack to her blind spot. No longer were his ears pressed humbly against his head.

"I thought you weren't allowed to fight, priest," she said to him, over an angry shoulder.

He winced, a distraught expression on his face as he replied, "I'm not."

She ignored him as she pulled her sword away from what should have been a fatal stab to her foe. "Tactics, Captain?"

He responded by stripping a candlestick from a nearby apparition and tossing it into the air over his head.

Ryder caught it without instruction as Faiz grabbed the hilt of one apparition's weapon mid-blow. The misty figure looked up at the muscular fox with a growing expression of fear, released his sword, and dove off deck into the water, of his own volition.

"Use their weapons against them," Ryder nodded approvingly. "Got it."

"It isn't enough," growled Marshall, noting that their adversaries just kept coming, with no regard to repeated failures. For those in physical form, the fight was already taking a toll. The mist was bound to overwhelm them, given time. "We must contain the wolverine, but we can't do that with these wretched wraiths hounding us from every direction. They *must* have a more substantial weakness."

"Eadric," Faiz replied, as if without thinking.

Ryder laughed aloud. Also, without thinking.

"The advisor?" Marshall called over his shoulder in disbelief as he fought.

"You're kidding, right?" scoffed Ryder. "Eadric couldn't fight his way to the other side of a wet tissue! He isn't even *here*! The coward's flying in circles over the ship, out of reach!"

"Then you must bring him to the deck," Faiz replied, catching a torch as it flew for the captain's head. Though he would not fight directly, he was doing a phenomenal job of intercepting blows without harming anything or anyone. "Please believe me, he is the only way!"

Reluctantly, Marshall nodded.

Ryder peered through the mist to find a shadow hanging in the air.

"I'll need a bow," she said.

Tossing the torch to the captain, Faiz flew across the deck in a flash, weaving with a strength of precision and grace that Ryder had only seen in one other person: Captain Marshall. It wasn't long before he found a bow and quiver wedged out of sight behind the vacant wheel. Snatching it up, he turned to see the white wolverine bearing down on the young Ensign Wexler, just a few yards away.

Without a second thought, he leapt between them, catching Grogoch's club in the curvature of the bow, spinning in a deft move that carried the club up and around until the wolverine could hold it no more. Into the sea it went, soliciting a snarl of rage from the beast who turned his red eyes to the Father. There, for the first time, Grogoch found himself toe to toe with an equal, someone who faced him without fear or hesitance.

"Brave fox," the wolverine snarled, unsheathing his claws and bearing brutal teeth. "Think Grogoch need weapon to kill? Grogoch crush you with his bare hands!"

He pounced, but Faiz was already gone.

As quickly and gracefully as he had reached that end of the deck, he returned to where Marshall and Ryder still held their ground, the furious albino hot on his tail, desperate to catch him through the chaos.

Faiz threw the bow and quiver in Ryder's direction as he passed without slowing. "I will keep him busy! Find Eadric!"

≈

In a literal and mental fog, the queen's advisor flitted about the *Albatross*, bobbing though the air as though trying to dodge the clashes and shouts that shot up at him like physical things. He could hardly contain his surprise, squawking in clumsy protest when something physical did indeed shoot up at him, streaking through his tail feathers and separating him from a tuft of down.

"That was a warning shot, Eadric!" came a call from below. "The next one finds your foot! Get down here!"

With a groan and a desperate look to the horizon that left him wondering whether he couldn't escape the next arrow in time to make a run for it, the kookaburra dropped timidly from the sky. Things were even worse than they'd seemed from his prior vantage point.

"Do something, Eadric!" Ryder commanded as he landed at her feet.

"What?!" The bird shrank and shied as the battle raged over his head, wincing with every movement. "What in the name of all the old gods am *I* supposed to do?!"

Marshall and Ryder exchanged a look as Ryder gritted her teeth.

So much for trusting Faiz's input.

Just then, an attacker sprung toward them, levying his

weapon at the queen's advisor.

Shrieking in pitiful fear, Eadric raised his wings to shield his face.

And caught the light from the torch behind his feathers.

The fire backlit the symbol dyed on his wings, the ancient symbol for knowledge, the mark of his Order. Its shadow fell across the apparition's face with a sizzle. Then, in a rush that sounded like the dousing of a flame, the misty attacker evaporated.

The three stood in silence for a moment, half-expecting the spirit to return.

It didn't.

Marshall looked over the deck and said, "Right, then. I think we're going to need a bigger torch."

≈

Amelia watched the Father lead Grogoch around the deck, over and over again, until the wolverine was practically spitting with fury. However strong and fit Faiz may have been, he'd spent the last many hours digging graves and carrying bodies on far too little sleep. He couldn't keep it up forever, not without fighting in earnest, which she knew he would never do. He would tire eventually. And when he did…

The mist is coming for one of us, he'd warned.

"No," she said. "Not for you."

When the two came around for another pass, with the wolverine gaining ground at a substantial pace, she leapt between them with her sword drawn. Grogoch ducked, narrowly avoiding the blade that was destined for his throat, which he instead caught across the face, scoring his cheek and taking his left eye in the process.

He whipped around, slamming into the mainmast as he howled an angry howl of pain.

The cry drew Faiz's attention, who had not yet noticed

Amelia's intervention and was already at the rear of the ship. She scarcely had time to see the distress on his face before the wolverine caught her in his sights.

Enraged, the beast launched himself at the unprepared cat, who flew across the deck and into the rail with a spine-splitting *thud*! She grunted in pain and looked up to see the beast leaping at her with his claws spread, his mouth frothing like the waves she so feared.

She closed her eyes, waiting for the inevitable.

≈

"Now, Eadric!"

The kookaburra was shaking as he obeyed Marshall's order, stepping to the exposed edge of the rear deck and raising his wings. Attackers flew at him from all sides, but the captain did nothing to defend him. When they were nearly upon the horrified bird, Ryder smashed an oil lantern over the stack of broken barrels as Marshall dropped his torch onto the same. Instantly, it ignited. The resulting burst of light cast a massive shadow over every apparition within fifty feet, snuffing them from reality with a single whoosh of wind.

Eadric laughed aloud in relief.

With half of the deck now cleared, Ryder could see the wolverine bearing down on an incapacitated Amelia. Immediately, she reached for her bow only to find the quiver gone, having been abandoned as useless at the center of the deck once Eadric landed. A horrible feeling washed over her as she remembered the exchange between Amelia and Faiz the night before.

But she was too far away.

There was nothing she could do.

≈

When Amelia opened her eyes, she was being lifted in

firm but gentle arms and thrown out of the way.

It all happened so quickly.

She looked back to see Grogoch standing where she had been, his claws firmly embedded in the stomach of her savior, the one who had taken her place just in time. She recognized the uniform, but not the ringtail himself.

"Gray!" The cry seemed ripped from Captain Marshall's throat as he catapulted himself from his place at the rear of the ship.

"Ha!" Grogoch exclaimed in gleeful recognition as the ringtail bled out over his wrists. "Stupid soldier! Looks like Grogoch gets to touch smug uniform after all!"

Gray gasped and dropped to his knees as the wolverine wrenched his claws from his gut.

The spirits still were dispersing, one by one, at Eadric's continued efforts.

Grogoch looked to his waning army in concern, then grinned sadistically and relieved the commander of his sword.

He had time for one more kill.

Seeing his intent, Ryder threw her weapon to the only person near enough to intervene, Father Faiz, who caught it with a strange look of bereavement. He looked to the sword in longing, as though he were still a fox unarmed.

"I don't understand," Amelia whispered, still staring at the fading Commander Calum with a horrified sense of confusion and guilt. "It was supposed to be me."

Faiz looked from her to the albino and took a hesitant step forward.

"But it was supposed to be me!" she cried again in genuine distress, as though she had dealt the fatal blow to Calum herself.

The red dawn seemed to intensify around them as Grogoch turned to her and lifted Calum's sword.

Faiz tightened his grip on his own blade, but still did not move.

"Stop him!" Ryder pleaded as she ran from the rear of

the ship, bow in hand.

In slow time, the Father's shoulders slumped in surrender, then the blade fell from his hand, clattering to the deck just as Grogoch let his weapon fly.

"It still is you," the guilty fox whispered.

Ryder reached her quiver just as the sword sunk its way into Amelia's chest.

"NO!" she cried, shaking in fury as she drew the bow and loosed an arrow into the albino's shoulder.

Again, the white wolverine howled, then he turned and leapt into the mist off the bow, which swallowed him, along with the few spirits still remaining on the deck of the *Albatross*.

Then, in a flash of light, he was gone.

Ryder continued firing into the mist until her quiver had been emptied, then she stared hollowly over the sea, her breath ragged.

The crew had closed on Gray, with Marshall at his side, covering his wound, desperate to stop the bleeding.

"The medallions." The ringtail clutched at Marshall's vest. "Did the mistwalkers get the medallions?"

With a look of realization, Marshall thrust his hand beneath his jacket.

The medallion was gone.

"Blast," he said. "That's what this was all about? That was their goal?"

With effort, Calum nodded. "They were to take the pendants and do as much damage as possible. I should have gotten here sooner. Time is so strange in the mist."

"It's alright, soldier." Marshall's voice caught as he increased the pressure on Gray's stomach, to no avail. The bleeding was too much. "We'll get them back. Just stay quiet now."

"No I have to tell you everything…" He sputtered. "Everything before I go. It's important. They know where they're going now, sir. They don't need the map, not anymore. The mist is guiding them, it wants them to succeed. But you still have an advantage. Their communication is scattered. They don't see things as we do. You have to recover the scepter ahead of them, Captain. If not, regardless of whether the Baron succeeds, he will attack Secora with the full might of the Kathkan Empire."

"I swear to you, Gray. They will not succeed," Marshall said.

He relaxed then, though Marshall could not tell if it was relief over his captain's promise or the dreadful weakening of his limbs.

"I'm so sorry, sir," the commander said.

"For what?"

"Abner. I couldn't save him. I tried. The mist had other plans for me, it seems."

"We have the children," Marshall smiled down at him. "They are safe below decks. We'll see to it that they find a new home. You did well."

"That is a comfort, at least." Calum smiled in return. "As for the Elder, they didn't take him for information, but they need him for something, so he's alive." Calum laughed then, unexpectedly, as his eyes started to close. "He worries over you so much, the old blighter. Wanted me to tell you something..."

Marshall shook him as his voice began to fade, forcing Calum to open his eyes once more.

"Wanted me to tell you... when the time comes... choose your words carefully..."

Though Marshall did not know what he might mean by that, he chose not to question.

They didn't have time for idle words.

"Thank you, Gray," the captain spoke around the lump forming in his throat. "You are the single most courageous person I've ever known."

"Not courageous," Calum whispered, his eyes closing for the final time. "Just hopeful."

Marshall looked down at his pointless hands, so coated in blood. With effort, he pulled them away from Calum's stomach.

"Sometimes hope and courage are one and the same," he said.

Calum smiled his gratitude. "It has been an honor, sir."

"The honor was mine," Marshall whispered down to the still form that did not respond as it expelled one final breath. "Sleep well, soldier."

17
NOTHING TO FEAR

Tears fell.
The mist roiled.

McKinley fell in and out of consciousness in his screened-off portion of the middle deck. It was quiet and private.

The type of place where one is sent to die.

It seemed the entire pirate crew had taken turns in standing outside the infirmary, one after another. Marshall had entered under the pretense of finding out whether or not the mistwalkers had stolen the Marauder's half of the medallion as well, which of course they had. Afterward, he'd refused to leave McKinley's side.

"There's nothing more I can do." Doc Calum, devastated over the loss of her nephew, was clearly having difficulty concentrating. "The blow shattered his chest. I have no way to know the full extent of the damage to his organs but, judging by the swelling, I'd say it's severe."

"What are his chances, Doctor?" Marshall asked without expression.

"He has none." In an uncommonly kind gesture, she

put a hand on his shoulder saying, "I'm sorry, Captain. He won't last the morning."

Marshall drew a stiff breath. "You should tend to your other patients."

She nodded. "I'll have someone bring you a chair."

After she'd gone, he stood rigidly for as long as he could, hands clasped behind his back, as though they alone were holding him up. Then he wilted.

He could not think. For a moment, he couldn't seem to breathe. Sheer emotion stripped him of the ability to do anything – anything at all – other than acknowledge his pain, his anger, his guilt. He shook, resisting the urge to drive his fists into the cot alongside his brother's too-still form. It took every ounce of his will not to fall to his knees and weep.

Then he looked up to realize that McKinley was already weeping for him.

"I have a daughter." The Marauder's mouth scarcely moved as the tear slid over his cheek. "She's so young, your niece. Her name is Maya. Such a warm heart... like her mother. I left her... left her in the children's hospital in Secora Tor. She's sick. Don't..." he choked, then recovered. "Don't let her die, Marshall. There's magic in Mosque Hill, I know there is. Use it to save her, please. Promise me."

"That's enough, now." Marshall swallowed and shook his head. "You will save her yourself. You just... need to recover your strength."

McKinley's broken chest shook with something that may have been a laugh. "Don't be clever, Marshall. It doesn't suit you. I just wish... wish I could have remembered the song... she wanted me to sing... I love you, my darling..." His voice fell to a whisper, as though he were speaking only to himself. In reality, he was listening to the ocean that danced back and forth outside the window, hoping that Maya was listening to her shell. Hoping they could at least share that in his final moments.

291

"Love you, my girl… "

"Would you like me to sing it for you?"

Marshall turned to see Ryder standing near the screen with a chair in her gloved hand. She came to his side, a sympathetic smile on her face as she waited for his response.

Her offer lit something behind McKinley's eyes, something that neither of them could name as he gave a very slight nod.

At his unspoken instruction, Ryder opened her mouth and sang in quiet confidence, like a mother to her child.

"I love you, my darling,
I love you, my girl,
I love you, my sunshine,
My starlight, my world.
And though you must go,
How I wish you could stay.
But rest your eyes knowing,
I'm one dream away.
And while you are sleeping,
My darling, I'm here.
I promise, there's nothing,
Nothing to fear.

How long, my darling,
Have I been away?
You growing older,
While I stay the same?
Please let me go now,
This is how it should be.
We'll be together,
One day, dear, you'll see.
And while I am sleeping,
I'll miss you, my dear.
Be good while I'm gone, love.
You've nothing to fear."

By the time the song was finished, McKinley was unconscious once again. This time, with little hope of waking.

Ryder and Marshall stood over him, the chair forgotten.

"What do we do now, sir?" Ryder said, her voice carrying the weight of one who knew the full extent of their failure. They had suffered heavy losses. The Baron had every advantage. And hope was all but lost.

Whatever their mission had been when they began, the scope of their objective had widened to swallow them all into a darkness they could not fight.

"We keep moving forward, Lieutenant," replied Marshall, placing a weary hand on his brother's brow.

Perhaps because it is the only direction left to go.

≈

Grogoch fell from the mist like a stone, landing on the deck of the *Havoc* in a flash of blood and laughter.

Von Ulric and Lady Sira were there waiting for him.

Sira looked over his wounds as though approving of the damage. "Report, my pet," she said.

"Did you succeed?" Von Ulric demanded.

His laughter echoing weirdly over the ship, Grogoch held up the medallions in either hand. "Grogoch maybe lost eye, but got necklaces! Smash otter and stupid Secoran soldier, too!"

"Calum?" the Baron deduced with a smile. "He's dead?"

The wolverine extended his bloodied claws in response, earning a slight frown from Sira, though he did not notice. "Make him pay for crossing Lady, pay for crossing wolf! Secorans fill the waters with their blood, and never come to challenge *Havoc* again!"

Von Ulric smiled the slow, confident smile of victory. Pressing the two halves of the medallion together, he held them up to the meager light poking through the ever-present mist like a champion hoisting his pennant. A hunter who has taken his prey and now wishes to savor the feast.

"So you see, Kathkan," he said. "Ambition reigns over the poor illusions of duty and honor. Secora will be mine. Your Empire will have its ally. And there is *no one* to stand in our way."

The Adventure Continues in:

GUARDIAN'S RISE

Written and Illustrated by

VIVIENNE MATHEWS

ABOUT THE AUTHOR

Vivienne Mathews is a nerdy ice queen who talks with her hands and owns far too many hats. A beekeeper with a bee allergy, no one would ever accuse her of being sensible. She spends most of her days in Hermitville, just past Nowhere, with her loving husband, three dogs, and a child who won't stop growing, no matter how desperately she tries to keep him young. More than anything, she hopes you enjoy these books as much as she enjoys writing them.

Stay apprised of new releases and special promotions by joining the mailing list:

https://tinyletter.com/VivienneMathews

OTHER TITLES BY VIVIENNE MATHEWS

THIS SERIES
Guardian's Rise (The Sons of Masguard, Book Two)
The Sons of Masguard Companion Guide
Race to Mosque Hill (Printable Board Game)
The Sons of Masguard Coloring and Activity Book

PICTURE BOOKS
Jax and Mack
Chugga Train
Owner, Dearest Friend
The Dangerous Life of the Honey Bee

COMING SOON
The Rook of Corin (The Sons of Masguard, Book Three)
Ogg and Zogg